HOW CAN YOU ORGANIZE A STAR TREK CONVENTION OF YOUR OWN?

WHAT IS THE SECRET BEHIND THE SPOCK/McCOY PERSONALITY TRANSFERENCE?

WHAT WAS THE TITLE OF THE FIRST STAR TREK NOVEL, AND WHO WROTE IT?

From Star Trek trivia to in-depth studies of the most popular as well as the lesser known characters, you'll find all the information and speculation, all the insights achieved and oversights exposed, as you become a total participant in the Trek experience with—

THE BEST OF TREK #12

THE BEST OF
TREK® # 12

FROM THE MAGAZINE
FOR STAR TREK FANS

EDITED BY WALTER IRWIN & G.B. LOVE

A SIGNET BOOK

NEW AMERICAN LIBRARY

ACKNOWLEDGMENTS

Grateful thanks are due, as always, to the many, many people who have helped to make this twelfth collection possible:

John Silbersack of NAL, our friendly and helpful editor. Leslie Thompson, Christine Myers, and Sue Keenan for invaluable assistance. Kudos to our contributors, too numerous to mention, but not forgotten.

Special thanks to Adam Malin of Creation Conventions and Kerry O'Quinn, publisher of *Starlog*, for including Walter among the anniversary convention guests. Special thanks to Marine Fourrier, Carol DeWitt, and all of the staff of SwampCon V in Baton Rouge, Louisiana, for including Walter among their guests. Thanks also to all of the fans at both cons who stopped by to say hello and tell Walter how much they enjoy these *Best of Trek* volumes. We promise to keep 'em coming!

Finally, our most heartfelt thanks to all of you readers. It's your support and appreciation that keeps us going. Without you, there would be no *Trek*.

CONTENTS

INTRODUCTION

We'd like to thank all of you for purchasing this latest collection of articles and features from *Trek, the Magazine for Star Trek Fans* and our related publications. As ever, we think we have a variety of topics that will interest and entertain you: a short course on the ins and outs of putting on a Star Trek convention; a controversial critical look at Captain Kirk; an examination of literary allusions in Star Trek; the long-requested "complete" listing of Star Trek books and novels; and much more. We're also including—at the last minute—a short review of the Twentieth Anniversary Star Trek convention held in Los Angeles this past June. (A much longer review, hopefully including photos, will be in our next volume.)

If you enjoy the articles in this collection and would like to see more, please turn to the full-page ad elsewhere in this volume for information on how you can order issues of *Trek* and our other Star Trek publications. (And, please, if you have borrowed a copy of this volume from a library, copy the information in the ad, and leave the ad intact in the book for others to use. Thanks!)

If you've been motivated to write an article or two yourself, please send it along to us. We would be most happy to see it, as we are always on the lookout for fresh and exciting new contributions. Once again, *all* of the contributors featured in this volume sent us articles after buying and reading one of our previous collections. If you feel your skills are not up to writing a *Trek* article, but you have a good idea for one, please let us know about it. If we like it, we'll assign it to one of our regular contributors and give you credit when it's published. We're also happy to see contributions of research and opinion that can be expanded into articles. In this very volume is an article made possible by the research and insights of a young man named John Wicklund.

9

(If you're unsure of the proper method of submitting a manuscript, we will be happy to send you a copy of our writer's guides if you send us a self-addressed, and stamped envelope.)

We want to hear from you. We carefully read every piece of mail we receive; we welcome (and heed!) your comments, suggestions, and ideas. Let us know what you're thinking about Star Trek, the films, science fiction, even the world in general. (Please remember, however, that we cannot give you the addresses of Star Trek actors, nor can we forward mail to them. We also can't help anyone get a Star Trek novel published; nor do *we* publish Star Trek fiction. If you send us a story or novel, it's just a waste of time and postage. We will *not* publish it.) We really look forward to hearing from you, however. Mail from our readers is the only way we have of knowing if we're doing a good job presenting the kind of Star Trek articles and features you want to see.

A few final thoughts for those of you who have wondered why some of our articles seem a little "dated": Most people don't realize that it takes about one year to gather up the articles, prepare and submit a manuscript, edit it, print it, and, finally, distribute it as a *Best of Trek* volume. So, as you read this introduction, you are literally a year in our future. You've seen *Star Trek IV: The Voyage Home*, and you know the rumors of a new Star Trek television series are true. We cannot know these things. Sure, we and our writers can make educated guesses, and we're sometimes privy to inside information denied to the average fan, but usually we have to suffer the pain and pleasure of "waiting to see," just as you do. We don't feel handicapped by the unavoidable time lag, but we do ask that you understand it. As much as we'd like to, it is impossible for us to include up-to-the-minute news, reviews, and gossip.

If you'd like to submit an article, obtain information about back issues, or just write to say hello, our address is:

TREK
2405 Dewberry
Pasadena, TX 77502

Again, many thanks, and we hope you'll enjoy reading *Best of Trek #12!*

WALTER IRWIN
G. B. LOVE

THE STAR TREK TWENTIETH ANNIVERSARY CONVENTION: A SHORT REVIEW

by Jay Jengo

New Jersey Star Trek fan Jay Jengo was one of the hundreds who traveled cross-country to attend the "convention of the decade"—the Creation Starlog *Salute to Star Trek's Twentieth Anniversary. Jay wrote and mailed this review of the convention to us as soon as he got home, knowing of the tight deadline we were facing. We would like to thank Jay for his fast and conscientious work. We think you'll agree, even with this brief overview of the convention's events, that it truly was the event of a lifetime.*

On June 21 and 22, 1986, the Twentieth Anniversary Star Trek convention was held at the Disneyland Hotel Convention Center in Anaheim, California. The convention was held under the auspices of Creation Conventions and *Starlog* magazine.

My friends and I expected this to be one totally fantastic event, and so the five of us were waiting at the admissions door at 1:00 a.m. on Saturday. Being in line so early turned out to be well worth the effort, since later in the day, people ended up waiting in line two or three blocks away! Because so many people were in line, dealers were allowed to start setting up at 3:00 a.m. and at 9:00 a.m. (instead of the scheduled 11:00), the line got moving, and we were admitted into the hotel.

After passing the admissions desk, we saw the first surprise of the day: the original USS *Enterprise* captain's chair, and an original bridge chair (supposedly Uhura's). These were accompanied by a variety of Federation ship models, models of phasers and other weapons, and a small, working bridge model (in a tabletop viewing box).

Most fans quickly entered the Grand Ballroom to get good seats to see and hear the scheduled speakers. This room was *big*!—it had over 1,000 seats in at least forty rows. If you came early enough, you could get seats up front or in the center; those arriving later had to sit in the back or at either end. Even with so many seats, there was standing room only when several of the guests spoke.

After the official opening and introductions, Majel Barrett Roddenberry was the first guest to appear. She read unfilmed portions of the *Star Trek IV* script and showed part of the famous Star Trek Blooper Reel, including private scenes that had never been seen at any convention before. She ended up by answering questions from the fans.

By this time, most fans had managed to make a first visit to the dealers' room, and were hit by the sheer size of it. There were hundreds of dealers in 18,000 square feet of table space, offering every Star Trek item possible. Dealers, like the fans, came from all across the United States, as well as from other countries, including England, Japan, Canada, and China.

Back in the speakers' room, Rick Overton, an actor and comedian, took over as convention host. Now, we were divided on the idea of having a comic hosting a convention (especially this event), but this man was fantastic! His spoofing of the Star Trek actors and other stars was a real hit with the fans. Rick continued to entertain, as well as keep things moving, all weekend.

Next up was Eddie Egan of Paramount Pictures, on hand to talk about *Star Trek IV: The Voyage Home*, accompanied by slides, footage, and a brief Paramount promotional film. He appeared on both days of the convention, making sure that every fan got to see this preview.

Alexander Courage, the composer of original Star Trek music, appeared briefly onstage to answer questions, then graciously stayed around in the dealers' room to sign autographs, answer questions, and chat with fans.

A panel featuring writers Dorothy (D. C.) Fontana and Paul Schneider and set designer John Dwyer looked back on the series and answered endless questions about it.

Next Nichelle Nichols hit the stage looking as good as ever. She answered questions about *Star Trek IV* and her singing career, as well as her work for NASA. She played a short Star Trek film featuring her singing as the background, followed by a question-and-answer session. Mark Lenard appeared briefly after Nichelle, also answering questions.

Up next was the no-minimum-bid auction. Among many other exciting items, a pair of original Spock ears, with a card autographed by Leonard Nimoy, went for $395! At the auction, cohost Gary Berman announced that this was the best-attended Star Trek convention in ten years. Estimates of attendance over the two days ran as high as 5,000.

Leonard Nimoy himself was the last guest of the day, welcomed by a standing-room-only crowd. From the time he went on stage to the time he left, an entire hour, flashbulbs went off in full, blinding force constantly! It was distracting, and I got a terrible headache from it, as did others. The reason for all the picture-taking could have been the beard that Leonard was wearing. He discussed his starring role in, and direction of, *The Voyage Home*. There was an hour-long intermission after Leonard spoke, and it was needed—for air!

Wrapping up the first day's activities were trivia and costume contests, a short Star Trek play, a Star Trek magic show, and finally a Star Trek wedding! Yes, Star Trek fans Ray Tayner and Holly Nowell were actually married onstage at the convention. The groom, best man, and minister were dressed in Starfleet uniforms, and the bride and ring bearer were dressed as Vulcans (including pointed ears). Everyone enjoyed it very much, and agreed it was the perfect ending to this first, fantastic day.

The second day was as good as the first. The crowds were a bit smaller, and it was somewhat easier to move around the dealers' room and find seats in the auditorium. Still, the marketplace was mobbed, just as it had been on the first day. A new feature was two women who were selling Star Trek Cabbage Patch dolls! (Most of the stars were presented with dolls in their image.)

Programming started with a selection of Star Trek music and images (with music by Nichelle Nichols) and an entertaining look at twenty years of Star Trek as contrasted to the real-life exploits of NASA. A small presentation by fans talking about fanzines and clubs included a talk by Walter Irwin of *Best of Trek*. Following this was the repeat of Eddie Egan's *Star Trek IV* preview.

The next guest to appear was Walter Koenig. The highlight of his talk was the famous "Pavel Chekov vs. Walter Koenig Debate"— live. Walter started the debate calmly, but then with Chekov's line "Without me, you wouldn't be famous" came Koenig's line "Without me, you wouldn't exist!" It was fantastic how Walter was able to present both sides. At the end of the debate both Chekov and Koenig were really going at it, louder and louder until someone from off the stage picked up Walter and took him away—with him still yelling at "Chekov." Walter returned to answer questions, of course.

Shortly thereafter, Mark Lenard made his second apperance. (He was the only actor to appear both days, as well as the only actor to sign autographs at this event.) According to Mark, Sarek and Amanda met "in the parking lot at Paramount." He answered many questions at fan club tables, as well as onstage.

The auditorium filled up again for DeForest Kelley's appearance. The roof was raised when he stepped onstage, a repeat of the greeting given to Leonard Nimoy the day before. After waiting for the crowd to quiet down, Kelley read a humorous poem he had written especially for the occasion, and it was enthusiastically received. He then displayed a shirt from an animal shelter he actively supports, saying, "In this place, none of the animals die. They all find a home." He answered many questions, gave the cameras another "muscleman" pose, then left the stage in a continuous roar of applause.

A second no-minimum-bid auction came next, and a copy of Nimoy's book *You and I*, autographed by the entire main cast (except Shatner), went for $351. This money went to the Alan Nimoy Memorial Fund.

After this, I entered the dealer's room and was surprised to see Roddy McDowall of *Planet of the Apes* fame. He was just another fan passing through.

Another big highlight of this convention was the original *Galileo Seven* shuttlecraft! It was curtained off behind the dealer's room, and a $1 admission was charged to see it, all proceeds to go toward making further repairs on it. Fans thanked a boat builder for salvaging the wreckage from the desert (thrown in the back lot of Paramount after its "usefulness" was over) and completely restoring it—right down to the painted numbers, lighted back end, and opening door! A set of photos in front of the shuttle showed before, during, and after pictures of the repair process. This was one fantastic sight! People were signing petitions to get this full-sized prop put into the Smithsonian Air and Space Museum—right next to the *Enterprise*, of course!

The final event of this historic convention was the appearance of Gene Roddenberry and the showing of the one and only Star Trek pilot film, "The Cage," starring the late Jeffrey Hunter. Gene talked about mind control and the effects of Star Trek on society (and society on Star Trek), and the origins of the series and of his "Great Bird of the Galaxy" nickname. He also spoke of his wife, Majel, the start of her Star Trek involvement, and the problems that went along with it. Finally, Gene was presented with an Industrial Light and Magic matte of the new *Enterprise* in orbit around Earth, and a bottle of champagne. Gene's glass was filled, and his toast was: ''May you go through the next twenty years with honor, dignity, and love.''

With this toast—and a few hundred more pictures—the Twentieth Anniversary Star Trek Convention came to an end. Nobody wanted to leave, but it seemed everyone had to rush to catch buses, planes, etc. The big event was over, but it will go on forever in the memories of the people who were there.

MY LIFE IN THE TWENTY-THIRD CENTURY

by Madeliene Merritt

As you can see in our Trek Roundtable section, we get many, many letters, more than a few of which discuss how Star Trek has affected the writer on a very personal level. Over the years we have been deeply touched by many of them (as well as by an occasional article). Seldom, however, have we seen the sheer beauty and power of hope and faith, as reflected in Star Trek and its ideals, that Madeliene Merritt describes below.

For a long time, I was puzzled. What could suddenly turn an educated, semi-sane, thirtyish woman into a rabid Trekkie? What is this great power?

I had every chance to make the conversion in my youth. My teenage friends told me there was this great show about all the stuff we believed in, with these great characters on a spaceship. However, since I had declared from my lofty tower that I Didn't Watch Television, it was some time before I could be persuaded to watch an entire episode. That episode turned out to be "The Way to Eden." I was embarrassed.

That was my last brush with Star Trek for years, except for those odd times when seemingly normal friends would announce, "Star Trek's on," and plop down in front of the tube until the final credits transported them back to their own time.

The first movie was reputed to be for fans only, so I didn't see it, even though a friend had recently given me a book by a guy named Heinlein.

By the time of the second movie, I was a real SF buff. I'd independently discovered Sturgeon's Law (90 percent of science fiction—or anything—is garbage), but that didn't keep me from scouting the book racks every week. So of course I'd see *Star Trek II: The Wrath of Khan*. I enjoyed *Star Wars* and *Doctor*

Who, didn't I? And *Wrath of Khan* was a good show. Good story, lots of action, fine acting.

When the third movie came out, I said, with no particular urgency, "Sure, I'll see it. I have to find out how the story comes out, don't I?"

"And the Human Adventure Continues . . ." Over already? What a short movie! They've just begun the story. (I don't want to leave the theater with my cheeks wet.)

Two years to wait before the next movie! There's only one thing to do: See it again. And again. At the bargain cinemas, on cable, on a VCR. And, hey, look what's in the bookstore. . . .

I had gone to see if those old *Star Trek Log* books I remembered and had rejected from years past were still there. They weren't. But there were movie novelizations, original adventures, and even entire books about Star Trek. I began conservatively with Joe Haldeman's *Planet of Judgment*, but *The Best of Trek #4* showed me I was, well, not normal, but crazy like other people. And everyone could get into the act. You could write your own stories, publish your own fanzine, write songs, play games, join a club, go to conventions, build models, etc. I'd never heard of such an active fandom. I didn't want to do all those things, but I loved the cafeteria atmosphere.

But why did this happen to me? I've told you about Star Trek and me. Let me tell you about me.

Since Star Trek first aired, I'd acquired a couple of college degrees, a husband, a baby, a house, two cars, and other trappings of middle-class existence, as well as some embryonic career successes. Before *The Search for Spock*, I was struggling with the diagnosis and treatment of brain injury in my child.

I'd been told there was nothing I could do; I should resign myself to watching my child in special education all his young life, but of course I should take him to a clinic three times a week. Everyone avoided mentioning the rest of his life, and I wondered where was the special world my child would graduate to from his special education.

I didn't like it. I knew of a place where brain-injured children got well. Not all of them all the time, but there was enough positive evidence to encourage me to try it.

"If there's the slightest chance . . ."

Unfortunately, this place was not the Fountain of Lourdes. It didn't deal in miracles, but in hard work. Parents were expected to work around the clock with their children, with a little time off for biological requirements . . . but not much.

How wonderful, though, to have an answer. My doctor told me they were quacks, my husband told me there was nothing wrong with the kid, every therapist of every conceivable nature said, "Don't bother—it's too hard, and it won't work." All these statements were based on no experience, but everyone I came into contact with said at least one of them. The clinic itself was even not very encouraging, because the staff wanted to be sure that all applicants understood clearly what was required of them.

"The word is no. I am therefore going anyway."

I had registered and was waiting for my appointment when I saw a movie about a man who gave everything he had for his friends; one dead, one suffering. He hoped to see the one suffering cured, but he expected no other gain than that, except for the knowledge of having fulfilled his responsibilities as completely as he could. After seeing this movie, I read and watched Star Trek voraciously.

Once we'd been to the clinic and received our therapy program, life as we knew it went on hiatus. Every minute of every day was regimented. To find out where I was wasting time, some days I made a by-the-minute cassette recording. It always began, "Captain's Log, Stardate . . ."

Many volunteers are necessary for a program of this nature. They're called "patterners" because their job is to help move the child's body in a mobility pattern that he has trouble performing, such as crawling. Over one hundred people helped us. Teams would arrive three times a day.

My little boy thrived on the program. The silent, withdrawn baby burst into childhood at warp speed, quickly regaining the ground he'd lost. It was exciting, exhilarating—exhausting.

I didn't fare as well. True, I was using my faculties to the fullest, but long days of therapy followed by long nights of making materials and equipment began a steady debilitation. I lost some "good friends" who didn't understand what I was doing, why I couldn't do the things I used to do, and why the mental health department didn't put me on a leash. My church turned an elegantly indifferent shoulder. My debtors exhibited no such indifference, though their brand of attention was not precisely what I needed.

Of course, things weren't all bad. Remember the one hundred volunteers? Most of them I either hadn't previously known or had only a slight acquaintance with. My heart was warmed when they would show up week after week to do a not particularly interesting job for a child who was not uniformly grateful for their efforts. And then there were the ones who went the extra miles: recruiting other volunteers, helping with the endless materials requirements, doing double duty in emergencies.

Through it all, I led my team (though in my past life I'd been a professional end-of-the-line follower), keeping as bright and confident an air as I could. I buried my torturous doubts, because if I faltered, with all my training and knowledge, what could I expect from anyone else?

Lenore Karidian described the dilemma and burden well. Captain Kirk seemed to appreciate her understanding.

Some people sensed my trials. One woman—of another race and very different background, who shared a profession with me but little else—always seemed to know when to offer another way of looking at things, a trait I came to cherish. Then there was the woman who didn't believe in what I was doing, and freely said so, but did everything she could to ease the burdens, including keeping my child and doing his therapy when I had to go out of town for my mother's funeral.

You can't go too far wrong with friends like that. "Friendship in the balance," as Joyce Tullock would say.

Time, our insidious enemy, continued to pass, despite all evidence to the contrary. My father-in-law fell ill. We kept going. Traumas erupted in another branch of the family. We expressed our sympathy and returned to our work. My profession (music) suffered gravely. I wanted to scream at everyone that my son's future was at stake. "Isn't that worth a career?"

My mother committed suicide. I began succumbing to illnesses. It wasn't hard to determine their source. But the only time we couldn't keep going was when my son broke his collarbone and couldn't perform the physical exercises.

I've always had a lot of sympathy for Spock in "The Galileo Seven," when no one shared his extremely logical priorities of getting out of a bad situation with all possible speed.

An unexpected snake reared its head the closer we came to our goal. I had no idea that the one thing I could never cope with would be success. When I traced the source of my increasingly frequent anxiety attacks to this nasty root, I had to give up some deep-seated obsessions.

It seems to me I've seen a movie, and more than one TV show, where a man's obsessions threatened to destroy not only himself, but the others for whom he was responsible.

Finally, it was over. The last lap was full of suspense as we wondered if my failing health would claim me before my son's health was established. But he reached his goal in a series of performances not possible for a child with damaged circuits in his brain. (As a brief scientific note, I'd like to add that we weren't trying to cure or revive dead brain cells, but trying to engage some of the remaining ten billion cells.)

At the graduation party, I looked over the company of people who had worked with us. I saw a lawyer, an accountant, a masseuse, a computer programmer, a journalist, a TV cameraman, a musician, a fireman, an artist, a marketing director, a reflexologist, a salesman, teachers of various grade levels and varying specialties, social workers, secretaries, students, a bank teller, and a meter reader. The youngest patterner was seven; the eldest was talking about her great-grandchildren. I saw preschoolers, too young to pattern, but eager to do the physical workout and the intellectual exercises right beside my son. The elementary-age children were desperate to contribute. ''They're too young,'' I'd heard voices say, but I'd become used to ignoring voices, and after patient training, they could work. Some of the staunchest patterners were under ten years old. The teengers, blissfully confident in their youth, were a different breed from the obnoxious airheads given so much publicity. The future is safe in the hands of these thoughtful, responsible young people. There were other mothers, grateful they weren't in my shoes, knowing they could be someday. And the older people with so much to give found someone who needed them.

''You have all done remarkable service under the most difficult of conditions.''

They certainly deserve Starfleet's, or anybody else's, highest commendation. They saved a life, though they speak only of what they have gained from the experience.

Today my son is in the mainstream of life, in a normal classroom, declared and observed to be a normal child. I am beginning to pick up the pieces of relationships and career, and doing all the thinking I didn't have time for in the past.

''If there's the slightest chance, it's my responsibility.''

''What I have done, I had to do. If I hadn't tried, the cost would have been my soul.''

In *The Best of Trek #9*, Harvey Greenberg calls these virtues ''adolescent.'' That sufficiently explains why I didn't seek help from professional counselors. Mature acceptance would not save my son. I'm sure Dr. Greenberg and his colleagues would agree with Starfleet Commander Morrow:

"Your life and your career stand for rationality, not intellectual chaos. Keep up this emotional behavior, and you'll lose everything."

Kirk does lose. In the series, rarely did he have even a regret, much less a price to pay, for his decisions. Part of the reason for that was his distance from Earth; Starfleet treated him as a final authority in situations he encountered, instead of breathing down his neck and playing Monday-morning quarterback. But in *The Search for Spock*, his mission takes him into the heart of matters that are the legitimate province of Starfleet Command. Kirk knows what he is doing, knows the price he is paying (his career and the careers of his friends), but he does not hesitate at all. When the coinage turns more personal, the anguished Kirk still pushes ahead. It seems to me that he has no place else to go. He achieves his goal: McCoy is saved, and Spock, instead of resting peacefully in death, is given a tenuous new beginning in life. Standing in the ruins of his life, Kirk has what he wants.

One doesn't have to turn to fictional heroes for powerful examples. History presents an impressive array of heroes who accomplished deeds their times deemed impossible: Jesus; Sts. Peter, Paul, James, John, etc.; Father Damien; Semelweiss; Lord Lister; Van Gogh; Bach . . . In any field, the list is long. But history's lesson is clear. Most of these people did not live to see their successes; the reward for infinite diversity is martyrdom, leprosy, insanity, suicide, poverty, and obscurity in your own time. At least in Gene Roddenberry's mythical future we can cherish our differences and dare to dream.

Everyone knows brain-injured children will never be even averagely capable. Everyone knows warp drive is impossible. Asimov explained this to us, saying that faster-than-light travel is a storyteller's convenience. Then he added, "But it won't be discovered by someone who doesn't believe in it."

Star Trek is someone's dream of how we can be, how we should be. Those of us who believe with Gene Roddenberry can make sure it comes true. We have only two centuries left, so we'd better get started right away. Everyone can help. We'll have to stop putting limits on ourselves, stop blindly believing what "everybody knows." In the past, new limits were created when the old ones were exceeded. Let's try to forget the concept of restriction, and, instead, learn to say with Mr. Spock, "There are always possibilities."

A REPLY TO MARK GOLDING

by Tom Lalli

One of the things we enjoy most about editing these volumes is the ongoing dialogue our writers and readers carry on, not only with us, but with each other. Right from the very beginning of Trek, we've encouraged debate and discussion, and it's a rare volume that doesn't contain at least one article rebutting, answering, or discussing an earlier one. This time around, prolific and popular contributor Mark Golding gets taken to task by Tom Lalli, whose article speculating on Star Trek IV was one of the most popular entries in The Best of Trek #9.

In the universe of Star Trek, there are many annoying inconsistencies, discrepancies, and plain old brain bogglers. As one watches the episodes time and again, these problems can be solved with a little research and imagination (as in Leslie Thompson's "Mysteries" articles), but mistakes keep cropping up. Some have tried to resolve all of Star Trek's inconsistencies in one fell swoop. In his article "Alternate Universes in Star Trek" (*The Best of Trek #3*), Mark Golding proposes that the adventures of the *Enterprise* occur in various alternate universes, rather than in a single, continuous one. Thus he explains away all discrepancies between different Star Trek adventures by theorizing that they occurred in various slightly different universes.

Though it may sound wonderful, closer examination reveals that the faults of this theory far outweigh its potential benefits. First of all, the creators of Star Trek obviously meant for all the episodes to be seen as occurring in the same universe, and they did their best to keep things consistent. Considering their task—creating an entire future world from scratch—they were largely successful. We should honor their efforts and use our *own* creative powers to do away with what hanging threads remain. It seems to me almost too easy to impose on Star Trek a multiple-universe theory, simply because the show is science fiction. Most fiction has inconsistencies. If Shakespeare, for example, describes one character as being both short and tall within a play, we do not assume that the different acts take place in separate, nearly-identical universes! Star Trek's science fictional nature is no reason to treat it any differently.

It is highly doubtful that anyone has watched Star Trek all these years with the view that each episode was taking place in a different universe. Our opinions of the *Enterprise*, her crew, indeed of everything in the show take into account information absorbed from *all* the episodes. It would be impossible to separate the information given in one segment from that given in all others. For example, suppose the Captain Kirk we see in "Amok Time" never knew Edith Keeler, because "City on the Edge of Forever" happened in another universe. How could we possibly differentiate the two in our minds? Even worse, suppose the Kirk of one universe made poor decisions, or even committed crimes, that we cannot be aware of because the only view we have of *that* Kirk is from the one episode?

Yes, the alternate-universe theory does solve problems such as Kirk's habit of continually risking his own life and those of his officers. If Kirk actually beams down only a few times in each universe (as Golding proposes), he is more realistic, true, but also less experienced, less knowledgeable, and, ultimately, less heroic. In other words, he is no longer the Jim Kirk we knew. We must now create a new mental image of the character Kirk, one that is less daring but more practical, less romantic but more believable. Obviously, it is virtually impossible to perform such mental acrobatics while watching an episode. And there is no need to, as we can find other ways to solve Star Trek's mysteries.

One useful method is to "stretch" the seventy-eight episodes so that they encompass the full five-year mission of the *Enterprise*. We can thus reduce the improbability of the *Enterprise*'s series of exciting and important adventures. One tends to chronologically arrange the episodes according to the original broadcast dates, but this is illogical. Why consider the events of successive episodes to have occurred a week apart, simply because that's they way they were broadcast? In the case of "The Menagerie," we can be certain there is no week of "Star Trek time" to correspond to the week of real time which originally separated the two parts (they actually overlap). And we must adjust the time frame of the episodes anyway, to do away with the gaps between seasons. This is certainly preferable to presuming months of inactivity between "Operation: Annihilate" (which ended the first season) and "Amok Time" (the first show of the second year). So we should feel free to view the seventy-eight episodes as having happened over a five-year span.

If the episodes occur at regular intervals, we can space them about twenty-three days apart, but it is more effective to stagger the dates to account for changes. For example, "Where No Man Has Gone Before" obviously predates "The Man Trap" by at least a few months. A similar "buffer zone" can be installed after "Balance of Terror" to account for changes in phaser procedure, and so on. Using this system, the ship's adventures (as related in the episodes) occur on the average of once every three weeks. The time between episodes would be filled with more routine missions, repair operations, and shore leave. (The seventy-eight adventures we see are those which are the most exciting or significant. It should be remembered that some of the episodes actually begin as ordinary assignments, such as "The Man Trap" and "Metamorphosis," then develop into dramatic stories.) Assuming that each mission takes an average of five days, the *Enterprise* has the potential for 365 missions in five years! So it is not so unrealistic, after all, for the seventy-eight we see to occur during this time.

In his article, Mr. Golding calculates the odds against the crew successfully completing all of their missions (in one universe), and they turn out to be astronomical. He bases his calculations on the odds against Kirk and Spock in "Errand of Mercy," which Spock states as "over seven thousand to one." Now, I must assume that Mr. Golding has never watched "Errand of Mercy" very carefully, because it is clear in the episode that there was no possible way for Kirk and Spock to beat those odds, but for the fact that the Organians were ensuring their safety. The last lines of the episode are: Spock: "We did beat the odds, captain." Kirk: "Oh, no, Spock, we didn't beat the odds—the Organians raided the game!"

In several episodes in turns out that the odds against the crew were not as great as they first seemed. In "The Squire of Gothos," "Shore Leave," and "The Corbomite Maneuver," they are under the watchful care of advanced aliens and, as in "Errand of Mercy," are never in any real danger. In "Court-Martial," "Whom Gods Destroy," and "Turnabout Intruder," the odds are against the villain because he or she is mentally ill. In "Assignment: Earth," there was no way for Kirk and crew not to succeed, since they were trapped by time into doing the right thing; the same might be said of "City on the Edge of Forever" and "Tomorrow Is Yesterday" (depending on whether one believes history can be changed). There are also many episodes in which the status quo is regained, but at tragic cost, such as "Charlie X," "The Alternative Factor," "This Side of Paradise," "The Paradise Syndrome," "Requiem for Methuselah," and "The Way To Eden." It is debatable how successful these missions were. And, in retrospect, Kirk is only partly victorious in "Space Seed," as his actions later come back to haunt him. Although Star Trek may not be strictly realistic, it is not as if the *Enterprise* crew were constantly engaged in glorious triumphs.

In "The Captain Kirk Revenge Squad" ("Enterprise Incidents" #10), Mark Golding takes another route to solving Star Trek's mysteries. Here he has the adventures of the *Enterprise* all occurring in one universe, but introduces a mysterious "unseen force" which is working against the Federation. This force explains (1) the number of potentially galaxy-destroying things which the ship encounters, and (2) the failure of Federation scientists to develop a practical technology for human immortality. Another, "good" unseen force is helping the *Enterprise* to counter the evil force. Mr. Golding makes a valiant attempt to eradicate all the improbable or inconsistent elements of Star Trek (again he mistakenly uses the example of "Errand of Mercy" to show phenomenal odds against the *Enterprise*), but, as before, he arrives at a scenario that is much more unlikely than Star Trek is to begin with.

The mysteries raised in this article can be solved without such extreme adjustments in the Star Trek universe. The galaxy-destroyers, like those in "Operation: Annihilate," "The Doomsday Machine," and "The Immunity Syndrome," are probably not the result of one malevolent force. Each of the menaces has been wandering space for eons, and any race which had designed them to combat the Federation would have had to calculate our achievement of space travel far in advance. Any race this powerful could surely find more efficient methods of doing away with humans. Also, we cannot presume to say that the appearance of these things in our galaxy is unlikely. Equipped with only a limited knowledge of our own solar system, how can we speculate on what might be found in our vast galaxy? As Gene Roddenberry has pointed out, the things we eventually will find will be at least as astounding as anything dreamed up for Star Trek.

Mr. Golding also finds it inconceivable that Federation scientists have failed to implement a practical immortality system, like those in "What Are Little Girls Made Of?" and "I, Mudd," without being prevented from doing so by some evil force. He admits that, in this case, the "force" might be simple human fear of the unknown, since the Federation obviously has the technology to make people immortal in artificial bodies (at least, after the above-mentioned episodes they do).

Perhaps, though, it is wise caution rather than fear which is at work here. The Federation may not feel capable of dealing with the myriad problems immortality would bring. Some people would probably fight to prevent the Federation from "playing God," perhaps even to the point of causing civil war. There would also be those who would try to use the technology for their own purposes, like Roger Korby or Mr. Flint of "Requiem for Methuselah."

Even if these problems were circumvented, the larger question remains: Is immortality desirable? Flint did not seem thrilled with his longevity, and in "Metamorphosis" both Cochrane and Kirk note that "immortality consists mainly of boredom." Mr. Golding writes as if immortality would be an easy and natural benefit to humankind, like an abundant food supply, when actually it would result in endless questions and complications, ultimately leading to the emergence of a new race of beings whose nature we could not predict. The citizens of the Federation may be lucky that their leaders are wise enough (or frightened enough) to put off immortality.

"Obviously, a person who is alive is far happier than a person who is not alive." Unless Mr. Golding has died and come back to life, he is unqualified to make such a statement. The attitude that death is an evil to be avoided at all costs inspired Mr. Golding's criticisms of the Prime Directive; it prevents the Federation from preserving and extending the lives of the "more primitive" peoples of the galaxy. He assumes that it is only the quantity and not the quality or dignity of life which matters. By intervening in the affairs of the non-spacefaring peoples within their domain, the Federation would destroy the delicate evolution of those races and their cultures. The Indians of North and South America were brutalized and devastated by invaders who thought themselves "superior." What glorious heights would Native American civilizations have reached, and what unique contributions would they have made to humankind, had they not been killed off and absorbed? Though the Federation's aims would be benevolent, the result would be the same: The individuality of the subject cultures would be eroded and eventually destroyed.

To say that we are responsible for the well-being of alien races on other planets, who may very well have value systems totally different from our own, is as absurd as the notion that we should sail the seas of Earth searching for shipwreck victims to save. The Federation has learned the hollow and self-serving nature of missionary zeal. Indeed, Mr. Golding refutes his own argument by showing why Kirk was wrong to "free" the Feeders of Vaal in "The Apple." The races which are far advanced above those of the Federation (the Organians, the Metrons) prefer not to tamper in Federation affairs, and the Feds are wise to follow their example.

The ultimate reason for refuting Mr. Golding's proposals is simply that they detract from, rather than add to, the internal consistency of Star Trek. There is nothing in the episodes to suggest that they occur in various alternate universes (despite the fact that such universes exist in Star Trek's reality). Nor is there any evidence of unseen forces of good and evil fighting for the fate of the galaxy. Indeed, it is clear that Gene Roddenberry and his crew sought to suggest the opposite, that we are the masters of our own fate. With a little imagination and work, most of the discrepancies within Star Trek can be satisfactorily resolved without resorting to these farfetched scenarios. Though Mr. Golding's proposals are interesting and stimulate debate, they conflict with what we already know about the Star Trek universe, and are therefore unacceptable.

In his article "Immortality" (*The Best of Trek #4*), Mark Golding goes into more depth about the concept and its importance in Star Trek. Though this piece is comprehensive and well-written, Mr. Golding again ignores the implications of practical immortality; he is obviously more interested in the technology involved, and only gives lip service to the enormous ethical and psychological changes its advent would entail:

"Korby [in "What Are Little Girls Made Of?"] stated . . . that he was going to improve on human behavior by so constructing the robot brains that they would be incapable of feeling the negative emotions, so that they would be rational and logical. Kirk was really twisting things to state that such a beneficial plan would be a form of enslavement."

The unconditional approval of Korby's plan implied here displays a lack of understanding of basic human psychology. Simply stated, without cruelty there is no kindness, without hate there is no love; this is the message so eloquently stated in "The Enemy Within." Without his negative emotions, the power of command eludes Kirk; he realizes we humans need our negative side as much as our positive side. And just as physical pain is necessary as a warning to prevent bodily harm, psychological pain (part of our "negative emotions") is vital for healthy self-direction. Far from being a beneficial plan, the eradication of our negative emotions (assuming the impossibility of separating them from the positive ones) would be closer to suicide, since without them we would not be able to function.

Mr. Golding goes on to say that the type of being Korby suggests would be "like Mr. Spock," intending this as an endorsement for the plan. He ignores the fact that Mr. Spock (in the TV series) is an emotionally retarded individual with serious difficulties relating to reality. Because of his suppression of emotions, he cannot operate at full efficiency (which seems to be the goal of Korby's robots); rather, there is a great potential for emotional breakdown (as in "The Naked Time"). As Spock himself realized in *Star Trek: The Motion Picture*, logic without emotions is absurd and empty. Without emotion, without desire, logic is useless. Thus, implementation of Korby's plan would amount to enslavement, since the robots would need programming to direct their emotionless lives.

Mr. Golding goes on to describe the various benefits of implanting human minds into androids and computers. One would be that Captain Kirk would be able to command a ship from inside a computer, thus having direct access to all information, and to any advice the computer could give as to a course of action. Of course, the unasked question is, would Jim Kirk *like* living inside a computer? Unless he was brainwashed or adapted to believe that this was his natural state, the knowledge that he was living inside a machine would quite probably drive Kirk (or any other human) insane. No matter how much we may be annoyed at the inconvenience of a physical body, to be suddenly without it, and to be conscious inside a mechanical device, would be an incredible shock. The evolutionary changes which would allow humans to experiment in this fashion are nowhere in evidence in Star Trek's twenty-third century.

Assuming, though, that Jim Kirk wanted to have his consciousness transplanted into the computer—and assuming he survived—would this be a good idea? Mr. Golding writes that Kirk would be a much better commander as an M-5 computer than as a man, based on the relative success of that device in

"The Ultimate Computer" (despite the use of the engrams of the mentally unstable Dr. Richard Daystrom). However, we must remember that *anyone* is capable of mental instability or even insanity (indeed, there are those who see Kirk as quite neurotic), and as we saw in "The Ultimate Computer," anything less than perfection could be calamitous where the power of a starship is involved. Also, as Spock says in that episode, "a starship also runs on loyalty, to one man. . . . I have no desire to serve under a computer." This is not messy sentiment but well-informed logic; without at least a human figurehead to follow, no human crew could be expected to perform competently. Only a fully mechanized ship could be commanded by a computer.

Star Trek's message was that immortality is unnatural, a trap that must be avoided. Mr. Golding equates the rejection of immortality with murder and suicide. Both sides of the argument have their points. What is inarguable is that immortality would create fundamental changes in the nature of human beings. The psychological changes, and the adjustment of our attitudes toward life, would be so far-reaching that the immortal beings would be *beyond* human. Whether they would be better than, worse than, or simply different from us is impossible to say.

Everything we do, everything we think, is influenced by the knowledge that we will eventually die. Indeed, it could be said that death *defines* life. The transient nature of this existence, and our ignorance of any existence prior to or following this one, forces human beings into a certain perspective. Immortality, life *without* death, would obliterate this perspective and force the creation of a new one. Mr. Golding believes that the search for immortality is the only real problem of life. This is an understandable (though extreme) point of view; however, immortality would make it impossible to answer another great question: What is death? Despite the authors claim that death is "nonexistence," the uncomfortable truth is that we have no idea what death is.

Star Trek's aversion to immortality (and to paradise) reflects a hatred of stagnation. Perhaps humans, if given immortality, would simply sit and rot, since there would be no reason to do anything now rather than later. The absence of death, the root of all the obstacles we confront and are thus strengthened by, would cause the deterioration of the human spirit. Of course, it is quite possible that the human race would adapt to immortality and go on to incredible heights of achievement because of what it allows. The point is this: Immortality would demand the further evolution (or devolution) of the human animal. Mr. Golding seems oblivious to this fact. By proclaiming immortality an uncomplicated boon to humankind, Mr. Golding is, at best, being recklessly optimistic. At worse, he is pointing the way to our spiritual and moral self-destruction.

STAR TREK LIVES IN MY LIFE

by Jacqueline A. LongM

Walter had the pleasure of meeting Jackie LongM at Swamp Con in Baton Rouge in February of 1986, and being interviewed by her for the public-access television program she hosts and coproduces (also titled Star Trek Lives in My Life.*) The following excerpts are from Jackie's ongoing series of personal reflections on Star Trek, science fiction, fandom, and life and the world in general. We enjoyed them immensely, and found ourselves nodding in agreement and empathy; we think you'll feel the same way.*

The Great Bird of the Galaxy

When I was a young child growing up in a suburb of Washington, D.C., all I knew was that my daddy worked for the government. (He still does.) Later in life I discovered that he actually worked as a drafter-designer for the National Security Agency and was not allowed to talk about his job when home. However, during those years it never dawned on me to ask; Daddy just went to work in the morning and came home at night. We would have dinner, then Daddy would read the paper and watch news, a documentary, or some sports event on television. Nothing of real interest, at least not to me.

My two sisters and one brother were very close in age and had to do everything together. Therefore, Daddy took us all to the circus and to the park. He took us all to the doctor and shopping for Mother's Day. When we all missed the bus and got stranded after school, Daddy came and got us.

He was blessed with only one son, and for a brief interim he took my brother aside to teach him sporting skills. Unfortunately, Mama insisted that we all play together. So the next day following each session, my brother would show us what Daddy had taught him the day before. For two years in a row, my brother got to attend the opening game of the professional baseball season. My sisters and I cried until an unprecedented move for women's liberation took place (considering it was the late 1950s): My mother said, "You have to take the girls."

In what now seems like a brilliant revelation for one so young, I discovered that excitement did not come from seeing the Washington Senators lose to the Baltimore Orioles. The thrill was telling my classmates that my daddy was coming in the middle of the school day to get me, and seeing their faces light up trying to sneak a peek at my handsome father.

As time marched ahead, I late-blossomed into a Star Trek fan. I say "late" because my viewing began during the third season. The movie theater closed at 9:00 p.m., and I was underage for clubs, therefore Friday nights at 10:00 p.m. were fine for me. Plus, my parents had purchased a second TV set by then. I'd simply shut their bedroom door and enter my own private world of the twenty-third century.

Another four or five years passed. I was home from college for the summer. One afternoon my Mom sashayed into my room and dropped a *Washington Post* ad page on my bed. By this time she had established an intimate, one-on-one communications relationship with each of her children; words were not necessary. I gazed at the particular ad she had turned up. It read, "The World of Star Trek: Featuring Creator and Producer Gene Roddenberry." My excitement was spontaneous. "The Great Bird of the Galaxy appearing fifteen minutes away at the Capital Center. I can't believe it! Of course I'm going!"

As the family gathered for dinner, Star Trek became the topic of conversation. My daddy asked me questions about Gene Roddenberry and I shared the limited information I had. Out of the blue, Daddy remarked, "He sounds interesting. I think I'll go too."

Noah Webster has yet to catalog a word to describe the emotional enthusiasm that remark aroused in me. When the big event came, my daddy followed my lead as I explained what conventions were and how Trekkies act. I whispered background information on inside jokes and comments that Roddenberry made. I even stood up and asked an intelligent question. Needless to say, I was happily beaming with pride and joy.

After the affair, we went to eat and talked about our thoughts and feelings stirred by the presentation. Star Trek incorporates such a broad scope of subjects that we talked politics, religion, social science, psychology, the military, and relationships—as well as science and fiction. Our discussions and debates ran on for weeks. Suddenly there was really something to talk to Daddy about. Also, talking to him now seemed to be easier.

As a black female, I could give several accolades to Gene Roddenberry, for I truly believe Star Trek played a part in the acceptance and advancement of both my race and sex. However, major changes are made only after a lot of minor encounters where people sit down, talk, understand each other, and relate.

Therefore, my real thanks go to Roddenberry for creating Star Trek, which provided the opportunity for me to better relate to the "Great Bird" of *my* galaxy—my daddy.

The Chekov Psychology

I was deep into "black tow," penning a difficult Spock scene in my unpublished Star Trek novel. Shockingly, from the bedroom came cries of "No! No! No!" My characterization supervisor, J.B., barged out waving an earlier Chekov/Sulu chapter in mid-air: "Chekov is wrong!" she wailed. "I won't let you do this to him. It's wrong!"

Hardly offended, I mildly remarked, "I call it like I see it," then proceeded to accuse her of identifying with the situation, not the character, since she had endured a similar real-life incident. Outraged, J.B. called me a heartless, unfeeling Vulcan and yelled "Spock!" in an offensive tone as she slammed the bedroom door.

After the slow count to ten and the deep breaths, I went to apologize. While J.B. remains constantly a female "Bones," she caught me in a moment of "Spock." Still, the confrontation brought home one painful revelation—I did not truly know Chekov.

Two months later: Delta Con '85 in Baton Rouge, Louisiana. Special guest: Walter Koenig. Yes, I was there! Koenig's presentation opened with an original dialogue between himself and Pavel Chekov. Dropping into a Russian accent to play Chekov, Koenig comically debated the fantasy life of his created character versus the actual life of himself, the talented actor.

The extraordinary presentation revealed two facts. First, Walter Koenig is a remarkable actor. The rigid, proper, often hyper and intense chief navigator of the *Enterprise* is not the playful, easygoing, conspicuous, sexy personage of Koenig. *He acts!*

The second point made clear was that both what we are perceived to be and what we are can coexist simultaneously. When the perception is our own, we often debate ourselves.

For example, I say to myself, "Self, I want to be a writer."

Self says, "If you want to be a writer, you have to write."

"How can I write when I have nothing to write about?"

"You saw Walter Koenig this weekend. What did he say that struck you the most? Write about that."

"What struck me most is that he has a degree in psychology, but, of course, says he was never a psychologist."

"Well, what does a psychologist do?"

"A psychologist makes a person think and then act on those thoughts."

"Hasn't he just made you think and act?"

"Self . . . you're right. Walter Koenig is a psychologist."

"Yes . . . and you are a writer."

I Am Not Spock

I am not Spock . . . but I'd like to be.

I long for the practical discipline of logical thinking, the certainty and stability of a structured life, the understanding that accompanies scientific, mathematical, and technological knowledge. I want to use reason as my motivating force and have order as my ultimate goal. However, my limited existence has been marred by emotionalism, chaos, and a D in math! Regardless of my longings, I am not Spock.

I am not Spock . . . but I try to be. I attempt to evaluate each situation on its own merit without interjecting unrelated personal influences. I strain to render fair decisions without prejudgment and prejudice. I subscribe to the high ideals of dignity, honor, and truth that form the basis of the Vulcan society. Yet it is difficult for me. There are times and situations when I discover that I can tell a lie. This only reinforces the fact that I am not Spock.

I am not Spock . . . but I need to be. I need the loyalty and certainty that results from the mental linking of true friends. I desire the total abandonment of mind, body, and soul immersed in the onslaught of ecstasy, fantasy, brilliance, and boundless energy that accompanies *pon farr*. I would gladly sacrifice countless nights of sexual sparring and social role-playing for one night of unadulterated, honest bliss once every seven years.

During my later college years I served as secretary to my Greek organization. The president was a strong-willed, flamboyant Scorpio with significant leadership abilities. The vice-president was a Leo—cold, quiet, calculating, and expressionless. At a national meeting we recessed for a chapter caucus. I heard myself argue animatedly for the feelings of our members and the perpetuation of our spirit and goals at all costs. All I needed was a hypo, medical scanner, and DeForest Kelley's voice. Dr. McCoy would have been proud! Although my cause was just and I made my point, in retrospect I wish I had been more logical, like Spock . . . but then, I am not Spock.

Back on campus I worked as the first female chairperson of a particular special committee. After thorough preparation I stormed into the Dean of Students' office wheeling, dealing, and negotiating for the decision most advantageous to me and my organization. Upon returning to the dorm, I related my recent triumph to my roommate. The "Jim Kirk" gleam in my eyes did not go unnoticed by her; she pointed out the parallel: Kirk vs. Starfleet Command. While proud of my accomplishment, I questioned my procedure. Could a more controlled, logical approach have worked?

I confessed my hidden delusions to a close friend, describing my ability to act totally on instinct without forethought. Although my actions yielded the appropriate results, I still wanted to be like Spock!

He replied, "You are like Spock, Jackie. You have so attuned your emotional instincts with your mental abilities that you now 'feel' what is the logical thing to do."

I wasn't sure I completely agreed with him, but it was food for thought. I've since realized that I am not Spock, nor am I Kirk or McCoy, either. I'm just me.

Yet, that is the true beauty in the Star Trek universe: Infinite Diversities in Infinite Combinations.

Death and the *Enterprise*

Captain Spock's death at the climax of *Star Trek II: The Wrath of Khan* brought silent, solemn tears to my eyes. But the self-destruction of the *Enterprise* in *Star Trek III: The Search for Spock* caused a churning in my stomach as if my guts had just spilled out. My lungs gasped for air as if I were hanging in the vacuum void of space, clinging to my last fragments of life. For a few seconds, I sat in that movie seat literally sick.

A couple of years ago, I purchased my first automobile, a

Volkswagen Rabbit I called Crusader. The two of us zipped up and down I-95 between New York and the Carolinas, boldly going where this woman had never gone before. If there was a friend in need, a crisis to solve, an important ceremony, or a meeting to attend, Crusader and I were there. Finally, after five years and 180,000 miles, Crusader gave out. My husband peered into my eyes, shaking me by the shoulders, and cried, "Give it up! She cannot be repaired!" Although devastated, I yielded to the logic.

I can't help but compare the death of the *Enterprise* with the loss of my car. Fortunately, I have yet to endure a close personal death. My parents, intimate friends, even my grandparents are still alive. When my puppy was struck by a car, I was 1,000 miles away. However, I have come to accept what happened to the *Enterprise*. She was a machine, the same as my automobile. Machines break down or become obsolete.

They will someday build another *Enterprise*, just as they resurrected Spock and Volkswagen built more Rabbits. Still, through it all I have learned a very important Star Trek lesson: Not only do you turn death into a fighting chance, but you accept death as part of life.

Someone to Scream With

There is always someone to scream at. There are times when there's someone to scream to. Often, there is someone to scream about. But rarely is there someone that you can really scream *with*. Usually, when the need to scream arises, pride, public image, responsibilities, or circumstance makes you overcome the natural urge.

Take for example the case of James T. Kirk in *Star Trek III: The Search for Spock*. Pretending calm, he sat in the Starfleet Officers' Lounge awaiting a response to his personal request of Fleet Commander Harry Morrow. The body of Kirk's dearest friend, Spock, had been left on the newly formed Genesis planet. The soul of Spock, his *katra*, had been placed in another of Kirk's friends, Dr. Leonard McCoy. The separation was killing both friends.

"Harry, give me back the *Enterprise*!" he pleaded. Morrow refused.

You could see the scream anchored with Kirk's chest hammering to be hauled up. But high-ranking officers of a superior fleet are not prone to emotional outburst. Therefore, he curtailed his anger and converted it into determination.

There can be no greater anguish than to survive the earthquake, then get hit by the aftermath tidal wave. That is how Kirk must have felt when Saavik's voice sputtered, "Admiral . . . David is dead."

That was a moment truly worthy of screaming, but Kirk had no time to mourn his son. He faced a deadly Klingon enemy and the safety of Project Genesis rested squarely on his shoulders. Balling his fist and violently cursing, Kirk turned the anger into an act of desperation.

The final self-destruction of the Starship *Enterprise* struck a blow for human endurance. Reformed on the surface of Genesis, Kirk, unwillingly, looked up. He saw his life. One minute, a glorious blaze; the next, black and empty.

Have you ever been so consumed with an internal scream that your vocal cords refuse to vibrate, your lip muscles won't conform to the proper position, and your mind can't issue the appropriate command to deactivate your nerve endings? All Kirk could do was whisper, "My God, bones . . . what have I done?"

I can identify with James T. Kirk because I saw *The Search for Spock* at a strange theater, in an alien state, with unfamiliar people and a newlywed husband. In my effort to maintain the proper public image, I held in my screams each time Kirk held in his. After the film, my husband placed his arm around my waist to escort me from the theater. He thought he was being chivalrous, but I knew my body lacked the emotional strength to propel itself out. The latent screams were still trapped inside me.

Days passed, but the kinetic screaming remained. Then I remembered my former roommate. We had seen *Star Trek: The Motion Picture* together and talked all the way through it, happy to see the *Enterprise* and our old friends again. We saw *Flashdance* and sang the soundtrack together as the movie progressed. Also, we watched a little-known film named *The Fish That Saved Pittsburgh*. It was about basketball and starred Julius "Dr. J" Erving. My roomate and I stood up in our seats, yelled, jumped, screamed, and cheered as if we were in Madison Square Garden. It was she I needed.

Although I had moved five states away, I knew she had not seen *The Search for Spock*. She was saving every available dime to return to school, and the local theaters in her area had increased the price of admission because of Star Trek's vast popularity. Also, there was no one with whom she could see it because her new roommate hated science fiction. Therefore I sat at my desk, addressed an envelope, stuffed cash money into it (which the post office discourages), and wrote this note:

"Take this money and go see *Star Trek III: The Search for Spock* on your Wednesday day off. When you see it you will want to scream. I saw it with the husband and couldn't. I will call you Thursday night, 9:00 p.m. sharp, so that we can scream together. Love, J. L."

That Thursday night at 9:00 I dialed her phone number. At 9:01 she picked up her receiver and immediately started screaming. I joined in. We screamed and screamed and screamed! She was standing—I could hear her jumping up and down. I was on my bed, rolling around screaming. Our screams turned into hysterical laughter, then tears of relief. We eventually settled down and discussed the movie after my husband declared us both terminally insane.

A lot has been written in the annals of Trekdom concerning friendships and relationships. Is it the primary motivating factor in the characters' lives? How will they develop or affect the future? How much strain and pressure can our heroes' bonds withstand?

I can't begin to answer or analyze these deep matters of friendships and relationships. All I can do is offer a piece of wisdom derived from my personal experience. I'm sure James T. Kirk can relate.

"Once you find the someone you can truly scream with, you will have found your *t'hy'la*."

Amazing Grace

"With love, we commit his body to the depths of space." Captain Sulu moved from the line. "Honors: hut." The ships company saluted. Mr. Scott began to play his strange musical instrument. It filled the chamber with a plaintive wail, a dirge that was all too appropriate.

Star Trek II: The Wrath of Khan

Every Sunday evening at six my mother would turn on the inspirational gospel radio station and listen to *The Mother's Hour*. It was an hour of popular religious hymns played on a single organ. Once, when my sister and I were home from college, the song "Amazing Grace" came on the program. Mama began to hum along and finally remarked, "You know, I really love hearing that song. It is truly one of the best songs ever."

This brought on quite a negative emotional reaction from my sister and me. "Ugh! I hate that song!" "Every singer who's ever sung has done that song, and ninety percent of the time done it wrong!" "That song has been played on every instrument including bells, zithers, and kazoos!" "I am sick of that song!" "If I never hear it again, it will be too soon!"

Having survived our teenage development stage, Mama was used to having us disagree with her. Still, the magnitude of our reaction to her simple comment surprised her. Indignant, she stated, "Well, you might as well prepare yourself to suffer through it one more time because I intend to have it played at my funeral before they put me into the ground!"

Fortunately she is still alive and we have yet to endure that scene. However, we were party to another shockingly unexpected one more than ten years later.

By the time *Wrath of Khan* was released, we had both married and I had moved to another state over 1,000 miles away. We saw the film separately in our own home towns with our respective husbands. A few months passed before I visited for a holiday. When the initial greetings were over, Star Trek become one of the first topics of conversation.

"I could not believe it," my sister exclaimed, "After Spock gave his life for the *Enterprise* and crew, and Admiral Kirk gave his most deeply moving eulogy, Scotty had the audacity to pick up the bagpipes and play 'Amazing Grace'!"

I responded with equal horror. "Just think, two hundred years from now, people will still be playing that song."

My mom is not a Star Trek fan; she considers it to be like the weather, something that's there all the time and that people talk about. So when we told her that "Amazing Grace" was used in a Star Trek movie, she mildly replied that it was probably appropriate.

Still, as the pallbearers lifted Spock's black coffin into the launching chamber and the missile was fired, I did not wish to hear the national anthem. Nor would a modern "I love you, baby" tune have filled the emotional void of that cinematic moment. Somehow, "Amazing Grace" did.

I have been known to be dogmatically stubborn at times, but

when reviewing centuries of past religious culture and faced with its obvious reality in the future, I yield to the logic. So when I die, ''Amazing Grace'' can be played at my funeral, too. If it's all right for Mom and Spock, it's okay for me.

THE VULCAN HEART, THE VULCAN SOUL

by Nancy Hardenberg

It seems that fans never tire of delving into the endlessly fascinating and offtimes confusing depths of the Vulcan psyche. Although we've featured several articles in the past discussing pon farr *and other aspects of Vulcan sexuality and mysticism, no one else has ever approached the subject from quite the same angle as Nancy Hardenberg. By the way, this article began life as two separate pieces submitted by Nancy, who graciously agreed to combine them into one. We think the result proves the old saying about the whole being greater than the parts.*

The *pon farr* . . . the *katra* . . . Vulcans and their culture are a never-ending source of fascination for Stark Trek fans. The *pon farr* as depicted in ''Amok Time'' is one of the most intriguing concepts of the original series, and the *katra*, introduced in *Star Trek III: The Search for Spock*, further whets one's appetite for understanding the Vulcans. First it is discovered that this almost coldly logical species is not so frigid after all, having a most intense mating ritual, and then we find that even in death we haven't heard the last of them. By looking at circumstances surrounding the occurrences, some conjectures can be made as to the workings of Vulcans and their culture.

When we, the viewers, are first introduced to *pon farr*, we learned that Spock must ''return home, take a wife, or die.'' Kirk pledges his friendship with his career, disobeying Starfleet orders by taking Spock to Vulcan. We are convinced that Spock's plight is real; he must return to his home planet or die.

When he gets to Vulcan, however, things do not go smoothly. T'Pring chooses the challenge instead of marriage to Spock. Here we have a contradiction in the story of *pon farr* as Spock explained it to Kirk—Spock is challenged, fights, and does not consummate the sex act. What happens? Nothing! If the drive

41

were truly biological, a drive to mate or perish, then why didn't Spock die? Assuming that Spock's *pon farr* was a true one and that when Dr. McCoy examined him he was in danger of dying, the turn of events does not make complete sense.

We are led to believe that *pon farr* is the drive of the male to mate, which logically implies the activation of sex hormones (part of Dr. McCoy's diagnosis includes the fact that Spock's metabolism is upset because of hormone imbalance). A plausible reason for this would be that the drive indicates fertility. In humans, the pituitary gland is responsible for secreting sex hormones, so it is reasonable to assume a similar gland is responsible for the arousal of the Vulcan male at *pon farr*. This gland has its own biological clock and first becomes active when the male reaches sexual maturity. When that is, at what age, is difficult to discern, because Spock's age at his (presumably) first *pon farr* in "Amok Time" is quite different from his age at its first occurrence in *The Search for Spock*.

At whatever age sexual maturity occurs, the Vulcan male's sexual hormones become active and he starts to act irrationally; he's in heat. It would seem that sexual intercourse, and that alone, would relieve him of his madness. Yet Spock's experience in "Amok Time" is different. If we believe that Spock really experienced *pon farr*, then what the heck is going on?

My proposition is that the emotionally agitated state which accompanies the drive to mate is the cause of the irrationality, and eventual death, of a male Vulcan rather than the need for sex. In humans, the pituitary gland secretes other hormones than sex hormones; this is also the case with Vulcans. Another hormone, which acts as a stimulant, is released simultaneously with the sex hormones. It is this hormone which is the cause of the emotional and irrational behavior; triggered by the presence of the sex hormone, it acts as an impetus to action and is "turned off" by the physical and emotional releases of the sex act.

In Spock's case, he must have an outlet or he'll die, so he does as Vulcan tradition dictates, and is drawn to *koon-ut-kal-if-fee*. But—and this is a crucial but—instead of consummating the sex act, he must fight his captain and best friend. To begin with, this is an emotional predicament, but then to think he's killed this person . . . well, isn't that an emotional experience? Couple that with the exertion of battle, and it is entirely possible that Spock would have no more desire for T'Pring. His sex hormones could still have been active, making it possible for him to sire children, but he'd already had his emotional and physical releases, relieving him of the madness. At that point, to Spock, the thought of holding T'Pring would have felt terrible, even revolting.

So Spock survived his first *pon farr* without having sex. If we are to use the films as a guide, he survived further episodes as well, because he is apparently thriving by the time he gains his captaincy (*Kolinahr* notwithstanding but I'll get to that later). He seems to have reached a state of serenity; he says things like "I have no ego to bruise," and "The needs of the many outweigh the needs of the few." He's doing okay. But then he decides to be heroic, and we're introduced to the *katra*.

Just what is the *katra*? According to Sarek, it is "the living spirit," "all that is not of the body," the "essence" of an individual. It contains all that individual's knowledge. From this description, it seems to be the counterpart of the human soul. A question comes to mind, however: Can an individual function without his soul? If the answer is no, the question then becomes: What did Spock give to McCoy in his final mind meld? ("Remember.") If it was his one, immortal soul, then Spock could not have performed his life-saving function for the *Enterprise*, or told Jim Kirk of his friendship. The only apparent alternative is that the mind meld merely prepared McCoy to accept Spock's soul as it fled his body in death. Then Spock's soul in its entirety would have been present in McCoy. If this were the case, then why didn't Spock regain his full memory immediately upon receiving back his *katra*? Why did he need Kirk's prompting?

A more likely explanation is that McCoy received a *copy* of Spock's knowledge and memories. By transferring this knowledge to some device or receptacle in the Hall of Ancient Thought, Spock would indeed attain a measure of immortality. This also would have enabled him to perform his heroics after the mind meld, and would account for the need to tap newly embedded knowledge when he got his "marbles" back.

The mind meld itself can be seen as an electrical process, since brain activity is such a process. In order to perform melds, Vulcans would have to have attained a highly developed control of neural impulses. Upon entering into a mind meld, electricity would pass through the fingers to the recipient's brain, with the resulting perception of shared consciousness by both. The final meld would leave impressions by exerting an extreme force that is damaging or exhausting, and therefore desirable only at death. This would explain why the concentration of so many Vulcans was needed to reverse the process. In "The Immunity Syndrome," it was demonstrated that Vulcans can transmit thoughts over great distances. They are probably able to convert their electrical brain activity into some sort of transmittable signal—like radio waves—under extreme circumstances. In short, the concentration of many, resulting in great force, was needed to erase Spock's *katra* from McCoy.

When the process is complete, it is obvious that McCoy is none the worse for his trouble, but Spock is somewhat in the dark. To understand the aftereffects of removing the stored information from McCoy, it is essential to know how it was stored in his brain. It was probably stored in his unconscious, as are memories and experiences that are not readily retrievable. The human mind is limited in its working memory and cognitive processes, being able to process only from five to nine chunks of information at one time. There is much more information in an individual's brain at any one time than he can think of. McCoy has some extra information in his brain, but he doesn't have easy access to it; after all, he didn't put it there. It does influence his behavior, however, and in a rather classically Freudian way. He has no control over it; it just comes out when he's not aware of it.

The information was probably compacted—there was an awful lot of it. The problem is how to get it out of McCoy and back into Spock. Another copying process, this time coupled with a delicate erasure. The Vulcans did fine with the erasing, it would seem, but not as well with the implant into Spock.

Considering the information is thirdhand, if you will, this could account for Spock's difficulty remembering. Two other sources of the problem present themselves. One is that the compact form of the information did not easily lend itself to "unpacking." The other is that the rejuvenated Spock's barren mind did not know how to access the information. Perhaps all three reasons played a part. After all, Spock's body had not been alive long and had few experiences. Adults are experts at interpreting, storing, and accessing information. Infants are not. And, experience-wise, Spock's mind was an infant's.

Will Spock ever remember what happened on Genesis (specifically the *pon farr* with Saavik)? Difficult to say. The absence of language would have made symbolization, and therefore the storing of experience in a meaningful way, unlikely. However, Spock's mind, although immature, was practiced in receiving information, so there are always possibilities. One would have to consider the pain of superfast aging, and the emotions of *pon farr* as detrimental to his ability to recall anything, however.

Regardless of the final result of the *katra* ritual upon Spock, we now have another clue to the incomplete story of Vulcan culture. The *katra* ceremony is apparently an ancient practice; when Sarek requests "the *fal-tor-pan*, the refusion," the reply is: "What you ask has not been done for ages past and then only in legend." Luckily for us fans, it works.

It is not only the *katra* ritual which is ancient, so is the *koon-ut-kal-if-fee*. "What you are about to see comes down from the time of the beginning," T'Pau told Kirk and McCoy in "Amok Time," "This is the Vulcan heart, this is the Vulcan soul. This is our way." What intriguing words! They impart an awesome sense of heritage, an irrevocable link to the past. We know that Vulcans have long ago given up their violent ways for the peaceful pursuits of logic and knowledge, but their rituals retain elements of mysticism and violence, remaining unchanged; it is as though if they did not remind themselves of what they once were, they would fall forever off of their narrow chosen path of logic and peace.

When you stop to think about it, the Vulcans and their culture had to have been shaped by their environment. As James Kirk said in *Wrath of Khan*, survival is the first order of business, and, for a species, reproduction is the first order of survival. The seven-year cycle, although an oddity to humans, has a logical source: It is evolutionarily adaptive. Giving birth to viable offspring is of the utmost importance; it is they who go on to perpetuate the race.

As Spock indicates in "Return to Tomorrow," it seems that the race was placed on Vulcan during an early stage of its development, or, because of extenuating circumstances, reverted to an early stage. At any rate, we know that "in the distant past, Vulcans killed for their mates," and such a past indicates a less-than-civilized society. Also, scarce resources lead to competition, and the scarcity of food and water on Vulcan is a likely source of the warrior tradition.

The question we must now ask is: In this violent environment, what adaptations are necessary for the children to survive?

One possibility is that Vulcan offspring had a better chance to survive if there were fewer of them. Male fertility only every seven years would definitely limit the number of children conceived. Another reason might be that Vulcans were forced to mate at specific times by the climate; favorable conditions occurring every seven years providing adequate nutrition for babies. By the time the next mating drive came about, the children born of the previous time would be nearly self-sufficient. This cycle could also be the source of the timing of the *Kas-whan* ordeal depicted in "Yesteryear." Through this trial, children prove themselves adult—if they survive. Either way, they remove themselves from the need for complete protection and care by their parents.

And what of women in this scenario? Their fertility would of necessity and efficiency be linked to the males'; there is a causality between the males' need to mate and the women's fertility, therefore drawing both to the mating process.

It is necessary that both the male and female (especially the female) be ready to participate when the cycle arrives. This is accomplished by bonding. "One touches the other, in order to feel his thoughts." Can it be that this process was born out of the necessity of survival, the drive to mate? Of course. It is quite logical. Males, sporadically driven to mate, sired viable offspring only when females were available at the proper time. On such a harsh world, all of life would have been intense, especially mating. Perhaps the intensity and volatility of the Vulcans produced the conducivity they have for the electrical activity that is thought. Out of their need, the dependence of the males on an available female, and the passion, grew the mind meld.

It was most likely discovered by those unscrupulous early Vulcans who tried to use the mind meld as a weapon that extreme force of one mind upon another resulted in the death for the aggressor, and insanity, and eventual death for the victim. Violent as the Vulcans were, they were never stupid. As time passed, melding became a very personal, private thing, little used, and then usually restricted to bonding.

Others, however, had to be trusted to use the great burden of the mind meld wisely—healers. They would be the spiritual Indian leaders of the clans, as were the medicine men in some American tribes. As the only members of their clans with the knowledge of how to control a meld, their psychic as well as physical help would be necessary in many cases. Perhaps they instigated the healing trance before most Vulcans learned to do it themselves. The healers, possessing the necessary disciplines to control melds, would have known of and recognized the important of the *katra*. The concept of keeping knowledge and control grew with passing generations, and eventually a place arose for this purpose: the Hall of Ancient Thought.

Surak could have come from the class of healers. Raised in their traditions, he would have been an exemplary Vulcan, but a logical extension of the best in all healers. Through their trade, healers became sensitive to suffering, learned to abhor violence, and became interested in the spiritual and the intellectual. Surak had wisdom—through his upbringing and training, his experience, and his access to the Hall of Ancient Thought—but he also had good timing. He lived at a time when his race was on the edge of extinction; it was this final threat which allowed his message to be heard. In his reforms, he specified that life should be guided only by logic, but also that everyone should be instructed in the ways of healers, and become skillful at the mind meld and the healing trance. Also, all should have access to the Hall of Ancient Thought.

This development had a sobering effect on Vulcan society. The realization that one's knowledge would be preserved for the betterment of all Vulcans created a sense of responsibility. One would have to choose wisely what to do with one's life, and the choice of mate was equally important. Evidence of this sense of responsibility is found in Sarek's behavior at the beginning of "Journey to Babel." If he merely disapproved of Spock's choice of career, Sarek's behavior (not speaking to his son for over eighteen years!) seems petty. But if the effect is not merely personal, but in a larger sense affects all of Vulcan, disobedience to a parent's wishes takes on a more serious tone.

The same can be said for taking a mate. The choice would not be left up to the whims of emotion or the drives of the body; rather the choice would be made early, so that such considerations would minimally disrupt life.

The *Kolinahr* discipline is the absolute extension of the rules which guide Vulcan society. It can be argued that such training is necessary to gain control over the *katra*, since we heard nothing of it, nor did Spock ever attempt to transfer it in times of danger, before he had some training in *Kolinahr*. Regardless, the striving for pure logic in this discipline is the ultimate commitment to the Vulcan way of life.

When it comes down to the nitty-gritty, though, the Vulcan way of life is contradictory. It's highest achievement, the *Kolinahr*, is a denial of the physical and the animal. Yet their most cherished ceremonies, the bonding, the *koon-ut-kal-if-fee*, are constant reminders of those traits. One has to wonder if the Vulcan solution to the problem of controlling themselves, what they are as a result of biology and evolution, is any better than Spock's solution to his dual heritage in the original series: having a part of their lives they wish to deny, but cannot.

Humans, at least, acknowledge their emotions and try to live with them. Vulcans try to live without them, with their emotions under such tight control that to even show them is considered bad taste. By human standards—and perhaps even by Vulcan standards—their peace was bought at a high price.

TOMORROW MAN

by Joyce Tullock

It suddenly occurred to us that we, and our readers, have been enjoying a unique privilege. Over the past few years, we have been witnessing, firsthand, the evolution of one individual's philosophy about Star Trek and its worth, meaning, and ultimate significance to we "real" humans. As Joyce Tullock continues to delve into and refine her thoughts about Star Trek and its universe in each successive article, she takes us along with her on her journey of discovery. How suitable, then, that she now turns her attentions to comparable journeys of Kirk, Spock, and McCoy.

All the universe surrounds us. An infinity. In this galaxy alone, there are more things to see, to wonder about, to discover, than we can know in a thousand lifetimes. But we feel driven to continue to try, because experience and discovery are so essential to our kind. It is our nature to seek. And so we travel the roads of outer and inner space, constantly in search, as if to verify or even justify our existence. It is the human way.

Star Trek's journey through outer and inner space has become symbolic to a whole generation. And as it moves into its second generation, it expresses humanity's need to grow beyond the being it is now, to discover its own greatness. It is a journey to adulthood, perhaps, a quest of the highest sort. In fact, it may well be that Star Trek's major theme involves man's greatest adventure—the discovery of himself.

In Star Trek, nothing is greater than the individual human being—except, perhaps, what the human being can become. Those who need a label would call it the humanistic approach, and that fits, for science fiction as a whole is the genre of humanism. It tends to put humanist questions of every nature to the forefront. Are we greater than the animals? Are we animals? What is the nature of the human soul? Is there some absolute code of conduct by which all human beings should abide? What is the "moral" thing? Are we the subjects of some greater, unknown being? Or—could it possibly be—are we creation become self-aware?

Those questions can be frightening; for some, even threatening. But they will not go away. We can hide from them, as some do, behind theological, sociological, or political doctrines. We can ignore them if we want to, or we can even deny that such questions exist. But they will continue to exist, as ideas tend to do, beyond all the walls we build around them, waiting for the day when one person will have the courage or innocence to ask a question.

The creative minds behind the evolution and production of Star Trek know about these questions. They can't help but know for two reasons: They are versed in the themes of science fiction; and they are human beings.

Humanity was cooked from the same brew as the stars. Everyone knows that. But through the eons we became different from the stars, and that is what sent us, in the fictional Star Trek, at least, on the road to self-discovery in space—like children looking for the place from which they came. But first off, we have to overcome some prejudices. We had to evolve as a species and get some things out of the way.

Star Trek begins with an assumption. At the time of the *Enterprise*, racial prejudice does not exist on planet Earth. That puts us one big leap from the starting point of our own time. While the theme of racial prejudice apparently does exist in Star Trek, it does not seem to thrive where Terrans are concerned. Not on the literal level, that is, but it is surely discussed time and again when Kirk, Spock, and McCoy encounter alien societies. But, on the *Enterprise* itself we can at least assume that racial prejudice is pretty much a thing of the past (excluding an occasional "throwback").

In Star Trek we're dealing with another kind of prejudice, worse than racism, worse than sexism, more ridiculous and difficult to overcome even than religious bigotry. It is the feeling man has, the one he has been brought up with from the infancy of humankind, that he is somehow not "worthy." It is a fear, really. Man's biggest enemy. We see it expressed in many different ways, but always at the root is the theme that man is "inferior," either because he is inherently so, or because someone or thing wants, quite frankly, to lord it over him. And each episode that deals with this fear directly helps overcome it a little bit more.

In a goodly number of episodes we see this theme approached in various ways. "All Our Yesterdays," "The Apple," "Bread and Circuses," "The Enemy Within," "The Empath," and "The Return of the Archons" are just a few, a cross section of the type of theme that relates to man's discovery of, first, his prejudices about himself, and then, ultimately, the revelation of his own value. It is a slow process, like a theme-journey that travels through virtually every episode of Star Trek, culminating, in different forms and on different levels, in the movies. It's highly unlikely that it was a conscious effort on the part of Roddenberry or anyone else. That simply isn't necessary. The topic of man's inner conflict and self-discovery is such a vital theme in science fiction that it really cannot be avoided. It is always there, like the spirit of some haunted, disembodied soul. It cries for attention. And it has many voices, many faces. Sometimes, to see it, you have to look very carefully, and with love.

There is what we might call the "reversionary" man, the Jekyll and Hyde. We see this approach to man's inner debate about his worth in episodes like "Mirror, Mirror," "The Enemy Within," and "The Alternative Factor." Each of these stories dissects the very nature of man in an effort to explore his dual, good/evil existence.

In "Mirror, Mirror" we have an alternate-universe *Enterprise*, and what we call a "distorted" image of our crew; their opposites, or, some might argue, their inner, darkest selves. Kirk, caring, insightful, and clear-thinking in the Federation's universe, is shown to be a cruel tyrant in the alternate universe of the Galactic Empire. Perhaps "tyrant" is too kind a word, for this Kirk seems to have no conscience. He is willing to kill anyone who gets in his way, without hesitation. In fact, we may assume he does so with glee. The Kirk of the Galactic Empire is greedy for power.

But he isn't alone there. Everyone on the alternate-universe *Enterprise* is greedy for power. They're even worse. We know, for example, that the alternate McCoy's sickbay is nothing less than a torture chamber. It's all very appalling to our kindly Federation McCoy, and it leads one to wonder what kind of vile demon lies within the body of that Galactic Empire McCoy whom Spock has locked up aboard the Federation *Enterprise*.

In fact, Spock is the only one of the "mirror" characters who seems to have any redeeming qualities at all. Strangely enough, or predictably enough, both Spocks figure out the transposition and eventually cooperate in a kind of separate unity to make things right. In the meantime, we are treated to glimpses of the savage Kirk, Scotty, McCoy, and Uhura snarling in their cell while their kindly mirror personalities try to make their way back home.

It's a curious point that while the mirror Spock looks sinister enough and sports a devilish beard, he is not all that different from his Federation-universe counterpart. Kirk and McCoy recognize this, and at the moment of escape, McCoy risks his only chance of returning home in order to save this mirror Spock from death. Kirk understands McCoy's compassion, acknowledging that this Spock does "remind" him of their own Mr. Spock. So the similarities are striking, and the mirror image is incomplete. At worst, it is a flaw in storyline; at best, it is a paradox. Of course, *someone* had to save the day, and that is probably the reason for the kindly alternate-universe Spock. But it could also go to prove what Spock has maintained for so long, that Vulcans truly *are* different from humans. Vitally so. Perhaps, even in a mirror universe, they respond differently than humans, with greater control, striving to find logic in a chaotic world? How compelling. For the negative world of the Galactic Empire hardly seems the kind of place to nurture any creature devoted to order. And yet "Mirror, Mirror" ends by telling us that there is hope, even in the dog-eat-dog universe of the Galactic Empire. Hope, that is, if logic and honor are allowed a formative hand.

"Mirror, Mirror" is a good story. It is fun, it is nasty, it is vigorous and strangely compelling to watch. Both the episode and the topic it discusses are popular material for fan writers. There have probably been volumes written in the fan literature about the Kirk, Scott, or McCoy of that dark universe. Not simply because it is fertile ground for the amateur writer, but because of the almost hypnotically enthralling nature of the subject. All writers, whether they admit it or not, write in part as a means of self-discovery. Writers need to understand what makes people the way they are, and there is no better way to do that than to look at people as they are not. From the Bible to Milton to Stephen King, we have marveled at evil, perhaps even been secretly enchanted by it. Perhaps that is because evil, for all its destructive power, is something we need.

Which brings to mind another Jekyll/Hyde episode: "The Enemy Within."

In this episode, there is no temporizing; we *need* evil! Or at least, to be fair, we need the qualities of human nature most of us would equate with evil. We need our darker side, our aggressive side (which the creators of this episode equate, rightly or wrongly, with our animal nature). According to "The Enemy Within," this is the side of us that makes us build skyscrapers and spaceships and venture to the stars. The animal, aggressive side is the part of man that makes him forge ahead, unendingly, almost without forethought, into new territory. Very much like Milton's Satan, come to think of it. Very much indeed.

Kirk has another transporter accident in "The Enemy Within." Only this time, instead of being shot to an alternate universe, unwelcomed and mistrusted, his atoms come back home a little, shall we say, readjusted. He gets split in two. We will not dignify the science in this episode with a discussion of the possibilities or impossibilities of such an accident occurring. Somehow the set number of atoms it takes to make one Jim Kirk come apart in a most miraculous manner and fashion themselves together again to form not one, but *two* starship captains. We will suspend disbelief, if we have any doubts, and venture on to the greater good. For this story is a honey. And the accident had to happen if it was to be told.

There are two Jim Kirks, then. One is good, one is evil. That's the literal interpretation. Let's start again. There are two Jim Kirks. One is animal, one is spiritual. Oops! That's not quite right, either. One more time: There is one Jim Kirk, and he is split into two tenuous, unsuccessful entities. He will not be truly human until he is put back together.

For the sake of discussion, let's borrow from a statement above, from our bank of ideas about the human creature, and find a way to discuss the two independent and conflicting halves of Jim Kirk. Let's call the negative half his "animal" half (though in the course of our discussion we may find that it is not as "negative" as it seems) and let's call the positive half his "spiritual" half (though in the course of our discussion we may find that it is not so positive as it seems). Language can be confining, especially when we're dealing with paradox. And the more we get into man's discovery of himself, the more "paradoxical" it all becomes!

Jim's animal half appears on the *Enterprise* alongside his

spiritual half, and all hell breaks loose. The distinction between the Kirks is immediately apparent, but the implications of their differences are not quite so clear. At first, the spiritual Kirk seems normal enough. A little lackluster, perhaps, even boring, but certainly the concerned, caring Jim Kirk we have all loved for so long. He is very worried about being split in two, plus other worries concerning a landing party which is freezing to death on the cold planet's surface because the transporter doesn't work.

The spiritual half gradually beomes aware that his ability to make command decisions has become strangely impaired. He has lost his usual emotional vigor and drive. Before long, he recognizes that he needs what the other half has—aggressiveness, animal drive, the will to prevail.

But there's a problem. The animal half is dying. And he is dying in an angry, animal, wild-eyed rage. He virtually storms the *Enterprise* while he is still able, jealous of the spiritual Kirk, even murderous toward him. Where the spiritual Kirk is sensitive and caring, the animal Kirk is insensitive and totally unconcerned with his fellow man. He is a lusty fellow, and his animal passions lead him to attempt to rape Yeoman Rand. No doubt had he been allowed, he would have destroyed Kirk's beloved *Enterprise* and everyone on it.

The important thing about this story, though, is how Jim Kirk comes to know and appreciate himself. He had to get over some prejudices about himself, too. This is something which only the spiritual Kirk is capable of doing. And it is an excellent example of man's need to understand and overcome the unthinking, destructively aggressive side of his nature. For Kirk, the only way to survive, to be the person he was before the accident, was, ironically, to regain that part of his nature which had become so repulsive to him in the personification of the animal Kirk. He goes through a great deal of soul-searching in this episode as he tries to reconcile himself to the fact that the "animal" Kirk is just as much a part of him as is bone, muscle tissue, and blood. He must understand, respect, and thereby control that in himself which is repellent to all he holds dear. And if he and those he loves are to survive, he must learn to use it, as well.

It is nothing less than human destiny. In discovering the mysteries of space, time, and all the universe, we must also discover the richness and complexity of what we are. We can't turn away from it and survive.

"The Enemy Within" provides us with a very gentle, human discussion of the value and beauty of being human. Kirk discovers that humans, not only himself but all humans, are neither pure nor inherently righteous. Neither are they evil or simply naturally wicked (the odious teaching of original sin). They are a mixture—a *good* mixture. The tiny atom is an innocuous thing, until it is split. When its whole is divided, havoc ensues in the form of fantastic energy. On a less powerful scale, that is what happened to Jim Kirk. And in "putting himself together again" he learned to value and channel those qualities, both animal and spiritual, which make him a man. He was a fortunate man, in a way, for he was forced to come to a point of truce with himself; face to face, he met and conquered the demon in his soul.

But before we become bogged down in clichés, let's look a little deeper. Kirk did more than face the "animal" side of his nature. At the very end of the episode, when Kirk takes that last daring chance on the transporter (we aren't sure at this point if it will bring back a whole Kirk or a whole "dead" Kirk) he embraces himself, soul to soul, as a brother would embrace a brother. He feels love for that being he had earlier despised. And in doing so, he comes to love and value all that he is.

Often unnoticed by the fans, it was one of Kirk's most courageous moments. And it pointed the way, early on (the fifth episode), to the path Star Trek would take in its entirety.

"The Alternative Factor" deals with the Jekyll/Hyde theme as well, but with an important difference. The "evil" double in this episode is more than just warlike and aggressive. He is mad, totally insane. And he is a fanatic. His name is Lazarus, and unlike Kirk in "The Enemy Within," really two people. One, the lunatic, is from our universe, and he is obsessed with killing his mirror Lazarus (a sane, kind, decent being) who is from an alternate, antimatter universe. If the two should meet it would mean the destruction of both universes.

It should not go unnoticed that the fanatic Lazarus from our universe has become mad through the simple knowledge that he has an exact likeness in another parallel universe. Like some bold, single-minded crusader from another time, he ventures out in his spacecraft (which is also sort of a time machine) in order to annihilate this one human who is his double. That says reams about hate. And it is an unmatchable commentary on the process and rationale of prejudice.

As an episode, "The Alternative Factor" moves slowly, mostly because what it has to tell is so concise, and the rest of the story must be padded out with action and the "winking" in and out of the two alternate Lazaruses. Like the other Jekyll/Hyde stories, it is heavy with paradox. The crew of the *Enterprise* is once again experiencing the results of positive/negative behavior in mirror beings. Only this time, they are the observers, confused at first, trying, and almost failing, to understand. But the ultimate answer to Lazarus' problem is not so different from the mirror Spock's answer to his universe or the split Kirk's solution to his divided essence. The good Lazarus had to find a way to restrain his mad alternate self from destroying two entire universes.

"The Alternative Factor" is much like the stories of old mythology, and Lazarus becomes a godlike being, cast into a lonely void between universes where he must eternally fight the good fight of sanity over madness. It is a lonely battle indeed. And whether we are aware of it or not, it is a fight experienced by every human being since the beginning of time.

The mad Lazarus was filled with many negative qualities: anger; fear; hatred; prejudice. He was the embodiment of all destructive human drives. He would wipe out two universes so that he could be the only Lazarus. He was filled with ultimate prejudice—against every living thing. The good Lazarus' positive answer to the problem involved tremendous love for all existence. And he made the grand sacrifice of spending all time in the void with a madman.

Symbolism is the name of the game when viewing and discussing "The Alternative Factor." But when viewed symbolically, it reveals ideas very similar to "Mirror, Mirror" and "The Enemy Within"—the key to life, to human existence itself, lies in the ability and downright *need* to come to terms, or at least control, all aspects of human nature. To respect the enemy in some cases, to even go so far as to love him in others. The eternal struggle of the two Lazaruses is realistic, when viewed as the human struggle with self. Kirk's answer offers more hope on a personal level. He is saying, essentially, that control (like Spock, like Lazarus) is necessary, but that it can be taken yet one step further . . . to love.

Before we leave the Jekyll/Hyde episodes, we should mention an interesting side note: "The Enemy Within" is considered by some to be a kind of starting ground, or establishment episode, for the Kirk, Spock, and McCoy friendship. There is so much interaction and character examination going on in the story that it brings them all closer together. In this episode, they become solid friends, and their affection for one another is most apparent. For that alone, we owe Richard Matheson a great deal, because the Kirk-Spock-McCoy friendship has become the very cornerstone of Star Trek. The way they complement each other and their collective desire to understand and deal with the unknown are also essential elements in the humanistic theme that runs through Star Trek. And with Kirk at the head, the triad friendship is certainly busily doing the job of discovering just what it is to be human.

And don't they do it well! Twenty years of Star Trek has brought a great seasoning to the relationship of what we have now come to call the Big Three or the Triad. We have come to look at them as the collective man. And as the collective man, Kirk, Spock, and McCoy have had a few prejudices to overcome themselves. About themselves. And about one another.

What, you say? Kirk has prejudices about Spock or McCoy? Look back on the episodes and see. You might be surprised at what you find. Kirk *does* have his doubts from time to time. His opinion of McCoy in the series' first episode does not exactly reflect confidence. Nor does it display a great understanding or insight into what the man is all about. In "The Man Trap" he is angry with McCoy, more than once implying that the doctor's behavior is less than professional. Not that Kirk is particularly wrong, mind you. Only that he—well—doesn't know or doesn't quite trust the physician yet. He seems to see him as a good enough doctor, not a bad Joe, but perhaps too involved in his own feelings. This is a good example, though, of the kind of internal prejudices wrapped up inside every human being. We call them self-doubt, and they are not necessarily a bad thing. As long as we know how to approach McCoy's "feelings"; that is, his very emotional nature.

McCoy is *always* involved in feelings, as we discover during the series' unfolding saga. But never again, after "The Man Trap," does he reveal anything about his personal past to Kirk. At least, not for us to see. But then, if we'd been allowed to see more of his personal friendship with the captain and less of his professional one, it would have been a different series, wouldn't it? A little more soap than space. There are other times throughout the series, of course, when Kirk and McCoy come to harsh words; "Friday's Child" and "A Private Little War," to name a couple. And they show their relationship has been through great strain at the beginning of *Star Trek: The Motion Picture*. Soon enough into the series, however, we find that although they may be at odds, with squabbles and even a kind of peevish mistrust, it is primarily the healthy kind of contention that must exist from time to time in solid friendships.

As late as *Star Trek: The Motion Picture*, Kirk is challenging McCoy's opinions, perhaps feeling the doctor should keep his own "prejudices" to himself. When McCoy dares to question Kirk's motives for rejoining the *Enterprise,* the admiral darn near throws him out of his quarters. But this has more to do with Kirk's independent nature than with his friendship for McCoy. Kirk and McCoy are both completely human, after all. And they can both be very pigheaded, when it suits their own prejudices. Like anyone, they have their blind spots.

What about McCoy's prejudices? He has a slew of them, especially about the Spock part of the collective friendship. And he has more squabbles with the good Vulcan than we'd care to relate here. Everyone knows about the great Spock/McCoy logic/ emotion debate. It's common knowledge, too, that the famous debate is lodged in a unique, powerful friendship. From the view of the collective Kirk, Spock, McCoy friendship, it can be seen as being not so different from the Jekyll/Hyde paradox discussed earlier. (Most likely Spock would like that allusion, since he was the rational side of the Great Internal Debate. But maybe we'd better keep the analogy from McCoy.) The two, as part of the symbolic human personality set up with the Big Three, must of necessity *always* be a little bit at odds. It's healthy psychology, good writing, and just plain fun. We wouldn't have it any other way. But, oh, how the two do squabble at times! No doubt Spock could feel great sympathy for the eternally struggling Lazarus.

But the "prejudices"? They entail McCoy's view of humanity: what it should be; what he'd personally like it to be; what he believes it *is*. McCoy is something of a cynic, on the surface at least. At times he seems a little embarrassed by the human race. Perhaps, when upholding its virtues to Spock, he feels a little defensive. Whatever the case, from the collective friendship standpoint, the McCoy/emotion part of the friendship is always nagging the Spock/logic part to ease up a bit, enjoy itself. Maybe McCoy sees in Spock too much of himself, as well. All the more fitting that the debate goes on. None of us *really* feel comfortable about confronting ourselves with total honesty.

But in Star Trek, the characters work at facing one another—practice for facing themselves. It's part of the process of discovering their own worthiness, which, let's not forget, is what this whole "prejudice" thing is all about. Self-doubt, actually, of the worst kind. The kind that has been "taught" and "learned" throughout the ages. Humans are brought up with it from the time they first begin to understand that they are greater than the other animals. It supposedly works to keep them in their place. At least as far as religious training is concerned. *Like yourself, human, but not too much.* To be too happy with what we are is somehow against all that is holy and good.

If that's the case, our Vulcan Mr. Spock has been a good human. From the collective-friendship point of view, he is the one who holds that naughty human nature—you know, the part that lusts and carries on—in contempt.

And so we have Mr. Spock's "problem." He has some trouble accepting the likes of Leonard McCoy. No one really blames him, either. It's hard to get a handle on the kind of personality who says one thing while actually meaning another. It takes Spock some time (perhaps all the way to "The Empath," or even beyond to his encounter with Vejur) to fully understand what makes McCoy tick. He is so alien to the Vulcan. And as part of the collective personality, he represents the part of "self" most commonly held in mistrust.

McCoy, who constantly derides Spock's love of logic and emotional restraint, knows, as any human must know, how important Spock is to the *Enterprise.* But here's a question for someone to answer: Does McCoy *know* how important Spock is to the friendship of the three of them? How self-aware is that collective personality? Or is it aware at all?

One thing is certain: If the friendship *is* in any way self-aware, it is through the personality of James T. Kirk. He is the overruling mind, the living spirit, not only of the Friendship, but of the *Enterprise.* And there's a good reason for that: Despite any problems he may have with Spock or McCoy, he is able to maintain an overall objectivity that neither of the two can quite achieve. They aren't "allowed" to do so, if they are to represent the struggling elements of logic/emotion.

And as the "overseeing" mind of the collective personality, Kirk is at a level where he can see them both most clearly. His early "prejudices" about McCoy gradually evolve into an understanding of and affection for the man. He knows that McCoy, for all his sometimes caustic human ways, is responsible, loving, at times even heroic. Kirk is the part of the collective mind which is able to most easily "forgive" McCoy his cynicism and sharp tongue. As a fellow human, Kirk is the cerebral "crossover"; he knows through conscious experience what Spock must gradually learn through a trial-and-error friendship.

Kirk, too, knows about Spock. He understands and respects and has affection for that stupendous, logical, ordered mind. He worries sometimes about Spock's detachment, but for the most part he leaves that job to McCoy. After all, as ship's physician and as the fire-spitting emotional aspect of the collective mind, McCoy is most suited to the task of gadfly. Kirk tends to stay out of the fighting for the most part, acting as mentor for Spock and referee for McCoy. It seems to work.

Kirk has no prejudice where Spock is concerned. He lets McCoy do the doubting while he does the encouraging. He knows how vital Spock's contribution is to the *Enterprise* and to the Friendship. And he is not wrestling with himself to the extent that Spock and McCoy must. In a figurative way, he is more complete. He has to be, as a leader and as the man cast in the role of supreme adventurer. When he does doubt, he is able to turn to Spock and McCoy for help. It's a true symbiosis.

So although the collective friendship of Kirk, Spock, and McCoy has its usual prejudices about itself and its motives, and, at times, even its worthiness, the strong, willful mind of Jim Kirk leads it on, defying old traditions of self-doubt. *He* trusts himself. He trusts his friends. And so he is able to move forward, one of those rare, dynamic individuals who dares to trust the future.

The Friendship has a life of its own. And a new kind of measure is set up. Not just the measure of a man, but the measure of combinations. It is a matter that is finally discussed openly in *Wrath of Kahn* and *The Search for Spock*. Which is greater, the part or the whole?

Depends on what you're talking about. If you're out to solve a problem, it'd be handy to have Kirk, Spock, and McCoy working on it collectively. One of them alone, or even two of them, might have some blind spots, develop a little trouble in finding the right answer. But if you have all three . . .

They don't work by committee. That's good, too, because nothing ever gets done (or at least done properly) by committee. What happens in the collective mind is this: All there make their contributions, then the one whose field of expertise dictates action makes his move. In a sense, he uses the other two to gather information for him and offer support. But when the point of decision-making comes along, he is usually on his own.

We've seen all three of them work this way in different episodes. Many is the time that Kirk and Spock have served as "aides" to McCoy, keeping the ship and crew in line or gathering scientific data while the doctor went about the business of developing an antidote for the disease of the week. This is the case in "Miri," "The Tholian Web," and "The Deadly Years." In these episodes (and many more), McCoy's knowledge and decision-making abilities come to the fore. The ultimate answer to the *Enterprise*'s problem rests in his hands, because the solution is a medical (or emotional) one. Kirk and Spock can act as support and advisers, but they must also stand back while McCoy uses what he knows to figure out an answer.

Sometimes, as in "The Empath," he makes a decision totally alone, even against the overt advice of his friends. Sometimes even against orders. But it is still clear that his decision is the result of the Friendship and Kirk's and Spock's influence on him.

The influence of one friend for the other is always strong. While Kirk wasn't present in "The Tholian Web," his advice and guidance lived on to help the other two. Interesting to note, isn't it, that the collective mind seems to have the power to almost outlive the individuals who make it up? (We see this again in *Star Trek: The Motion Picture*.)

At other times, McCoy and Spock have stood by while Kirk was the man of the hour, giving his advice, making their services available according to their talents. This is what we see in episodes like "A Private Little War," "The Devil in the Dark," and "The Ultimate Computer." In all cases, the ultimate resolution is in Kirk's hands, but it is the advice and support of his friends that leads him to that point.

McCoy's part in "A Private Little War" was that of devil's advocate. In a balance-of-power situation, McCoy, as the emotional one and the physician, sees only that more weaponry will bring more pain and destruction. He tells Kirk so in no uncertain terms. Very much a humanist viewpoint, it is perhaps Star Trek's sanest moment, a cry for help from our own times.

The irony of it is that Kirk, though he agrees in principle, cannot agree in fact. If he were to step out of the situation and do nothing, it would mean the ultimate destruction of the hill people, and it would mean that the Klingons would eventually establish power over the planet. So in this case, while Kirk listens to McCoy's views, and probably respects them, he can use them only as feedback. The ultimate decision is his and his alone. It is a military decision.

In *Star Trek: The Motion Picture* and *Wrath of Khan*, Mr. Spock has to make some decisions on his own. The first Star Trek movie finds all three of the characters "alone," struggling once again to discover their friendship and build it into a unit. They accomplish this by the end of the film, but before that happens Spock must make a personal decision. Without the overt support of Kirk and McCoy, he ventures into the loneliness of Vejur, the living machine. He is on a journey of self-discovery. And though he goes it alone, it is only after the fact that he discovers just how vital his friendship for Kirk and McCoy has become. If it were not for those two, it is unlikely that Spock would have been so instinctively "driven" to discover what it was that seemed to be missing within himself. It is his friendship that drew him to Vejur. We are told that he somehow "sensed" a danger to his friends, and to his mother Earth. Sensing strange emanations from the area in space occupied by Vejur, he left Vulcan and joined the *Enterprise*. We can only assume that the investigation of Vejur was always on his mind. Once he enters the alien's territory, he experiences the questions which are tearing Vejur apart. "Is this all I am? Is there nothing more?"

In an awe-filled moment, Spock understands. And it is at that time that his friendship for Kirk and McCoy reaches full maturity. Their human, dynamic influence on him had changed him during his five-year tour of duty. When he sensed the threat to their lives and world, he responded, just as though he were a part of them. Even the distance of time and space and personal differences had not separated them. He had tried to run from them once, but found, through Vejur's loneliness, that he was running from himself. His decision to meld with Vejur, however, was a personal one, guided by the influence of his friends. Never, not even in *Wrath of Khan*, would he ever be alone again.

He made two vital, solitary decisions in *Wrath of Khan*. One was to give his life for the ship and its crew. The other was to give his essence, his *katra*, to McCoy.

"I'm sorry, doctor, I have no time to discuss this logically."

Uh-huh, Spock. Bones is sorry too.

Wouldn't it be great to have just two minutes with Spock, to ask him about that time in his life, and about what led to the two decisions he made that day. No doubt he would tell us they were both totally logical solutions to two distinct problems, one of a military nature, one of a personal nature. And if we caught him in the right frame of mind, we might even dare to ask, "But what *moved* you to rest your essence within the mixed-up, irrational, sometimes chaotic mind of Leonard McCoy?"

The answer he would give, if he deigned to respond to such a forward question at all, would go something like this: "It was a practical decision, based more on what was convenient than what was purely logical. I assure you that there was nothing emotional about the matter."

There is nothing emotional about wanting your essence to live on after the body's death? There is nothing emotional about choosing as the vessel for your soul a human being who has been your friend for twenty years?

But Mr. Spock has us just the same, for his decision is such a clever combination of logic and feeling that we can never untangle it. It is the best kind of decision, perhaps. Balanced, sensitive, productive. It's the kind of decision-making he learned from Captain Jim Kirk. And it's tempered with the quality of insight seen so often in Leonard McCoy.

So we've seen what the individual can do. We've seen what the whole can do. Which is better? Which is most productive in the search for understanding? Which is of the greater value to human society?

It's a paradox again. Or perhaps, as we said earlier, it's a matter of perception. The question is raised in *Wrath of Khan* and *The Search for Spock*. In *Wrath of Khan*, Spock says, "The needs of the many outweigh the needs of the one." Kirk and friends disagree in *The Search for Spock*, and the admiral explains in answer to the Vulcan's question "Why would you do this?": "The needs of the one outweigh the needs of the many."

For Kirk there is no longer any separation between himself and Spock and McCoy. They are a unit. We cannot even be absolutely certain who the "one" is: Spock or McCoy? They are both in big trouble. As individuals, they are important. That's what Kirk means by "needs of the one." In that way, then, the parts are each considered to be greater than the whole.

It's the humanist idea come full circle. A sort of fundamentalist approach to a liberal-minded concept. And it gives the Friendship a symbolic and surrealistic maturity. It puts it on a grand scale and allows the science-fiction approach of Star Trek a greater depth and breadth, so that, if we want to, we can examine each episode in retrospect, allowing ourselves an imaginative and interpretive freedom which is seldom provided in science fiction, fantasy, or any kind of episodic adventure.

In Star Trek the questions of the needs of society and the value of the individual are essential. They make up the bulk of material, covering a wide range of stories and storyline "types," from the banished Zarabeth of "All Our Yesterdays" to the happily stagnating subjects of Vaal in "The Apple" and the brainwashed followers of Landru in "Return of the Archons."

Often the conflict between the inner "needs" of the one and the practical requirements of society play a part. These stories sometimes involve class struggles, such as we see in "The Cloud Minders." Here is a classic example of a stratified society. The citizens of Stratos oversee the Troglytes, who are miners and farmers of the planet. While the symbolism is so obvious that it rather rudely hits us over the head, it still makes a good point and reminds us that we are only fooling ourselves if we don't recognize the same problems in our own society today.

Most real cultures are stratified, of course, whether we like it or not, whether they proclaim themselves to be communist, socialist, fascist, capitalist, or somewhere in between. But in the case of Ardana things have gotten a little out of hand. The Troglytes are little more than slaves, and the pseudo-intellectuals of Stratos have managed to rationalize the whole situation— believing in their own way that the Troglytes are best suited to the working-class life through some kind of inherent intellectual inferiority. Of course, we know better, but it takes the imagination of Kirk and the medical skill of McCoy to figure out that the Troglytes are suffering from—are you ready?—pollution of their environment. The Troglytes mine a substance called zienite. Somehow during the extraction process a gas is released that impairs the intellectual capacities of the brain and can even cause one to become violent (as if the conditions under which the Troglytes lived were not enough).

Eventually Kirk proves this to the leaders of Stratos and they begrudgingly come to understand that all Ardanans are created equal. Would that it were easy! Nevertheless, it is an excellent example of how Kirk and his crew work on a humanist level. Suddenly, through interaction with the *Enterprise*, the "lower classes" of Ardana are able to celebrate their equality and self-worth. We can imagine that the Ardanans' society will have some rocky times after the *Enterprise* moves on, but such is the pathway of growth.

Kirk meets many elitist cultures along the way. Some are small, such as in "Plato's Stepchildren," where the planet Platonius is ruled by Parmen, another pseudo-intellectual who, by virtue of his greater psychokinetic powers, rules as a kind of mad-hatter philosopher-king. The only true "unequal" on Platonius is the dwarf, Alexander, who is made to serve as court jester and all-around scapegoat. He has no special powers, you see.

Once again McCoy and Kirk work together to make things right. McCoy discovers that Alexander lacks the psychokinetic powers only because of a difference in how his body assimilates a substance called kironide. After Parmen and company prove to us how sadistic and childlike tyrants can be, Kirk and Spock turn the tables on him, allowing themselves to be injected with enough kironide to have powers of their own.

The true humanist hero of this episode is Alexander. He refuses McCoy's offer to inject him with the power-engendering substance, because, quite simply, he doesn't want to "be like them." Not only does he discover his self-worth, he understands the responsibility and power that go with the discovery. As the episode ends, Alexander leaves Platonius and begins a new life. He is eager to experience new worlds. He has left hatred behind.

In "Who Mourns for Adonais," we come across a very small elitist society indeed. A society of one. The lonely, tyrannical god Apollo is in search of subjects. He is an outdated creature, however, unable to come to terms with the equality of peoples (as are the citizens of Ardana, or even, to a minor extent, the pitiful "philosophers" of Platonius). When Kirk and company prove to him that it is their inherent right and will to live as free individuals, poor old Apollo just gives up and casts his spirit upon the cosmic winds. The world of human self-esteem and equality is not for him.

The story of Apollo opens up another area of discussion where the needs of society and the needs of the one come into conflict. Religion.

In Star Trek, as in all science fiction, religion—organized religion, not the belief in a superior being—is a negative. Like it or not, that's the way it is. Look at just the most obvious episodes where Kirk, Spock, and McCoy are confronted with real or sublimated religious questions: "Who Mourns for Adonais?"; "The Way to Eden"; "For the World Is Hollow and I Have Touched the Sky"; "The Apple"; and Star Trek: The Motion Picture. Each of these episodes deals with the tendency of religion or high-held religious leaders to rule their subjects through hypnotic, charismatic, or just plain heavy-handed means. In every case, the "god" or religious ruler may have been at one time well-intentioned, but has become outdated, stagnant, even cruel. Any attempt to excuse their behavior always finds itself limited to the literal or surface interpretation of the episode. It is quite a different matter when observed under the powerful, multifaceted lens of science fiction.

"For the World Is Hollow and I Have Touched the Sky" is the most classic, most undilutedly obvious example. It's a classic in that sense, complete with McCoy as the "runaway" who is searching for solace in the face of death (he's just diagnosed himself as suffering from a rare, uncurable blood condition). He finds his solace, he thinks, on the seed ship *Yonada*, where he falls in love with the beautiful priestess Natira. He quite frankly abandons ship. Whether this is proper or not, considering his condition, we do not know. It may well be that the diagnosis of a fatal illness allows an officer to resign from the fleet. But McCoy does jump ship in hope of finding some last days of "happiness" by marrying Natira. He is looking for paradise, and for a metaphysical answer to supposedly unsolvable physical questions. The secret of religious obedience on Yonada *does* have a physical answer, however: To be a member of the society ruled by the all-wise computer Oracle, McCoy must allow himself to be implanted with the Instrument of Obedience, a small device inserted above the temple. He does allow it, and eventually pays the price.

Religious obedience, it seems, just isn't in the ol' Southern boy's blood. Out of necessity, he finally rebels. He finds a way to change Yonada's orbit (it's heading for a crashing rendezvous with a heavily populated Federation planet) and contacts Kirk about it through his communicator. With all good intentions and earnestness of a religious zealot, the Oracle tries to kill him. Disobedience is not allowed, even for the consort of a priestess.

Kirk and Spock, of course, come through. They risk a lot to save him, too, because Kirk has just been ordered to speed *Enterprise* along on another mission. When they enter Yonada's secret control room, they also discover a cure for McCoy's disease. We find out later, by the way, in Gene Roddenberry's novelization of *Star Trek: The Motion Picture*, that the whole experience will have a profound effect on McCoy's life and on his influence in Starfleet medicine.

So McCoy makes some self-discoveries here, as do the people of Yonada. Once the outdated, superstitious bonds of the Oracle are broken, they can move on to find their destined homeland. And they can live a as a growing, productive, free society. Once they are freed from the brain-controlling influence of the Oracle, they are able to discover their own potential and self-worth.

There are other episodes which deal with the theme of blind, unthinking obedience to some master being or master plan and its tendency to destroy the society it was supposed to protect. Tyranny is tyranny, whether it be clothed as religious, military, or political government. But in every episode where we find this kind of oppression, we find that the story wants to focus on one or two individuals who have the courage to break away. Again, the needs of the many versus the needs of the few. The individual is important, not only for his contribution to the whole, but for who and what he is as an entity.

Whether it is Kirk, himself, outwitting a machine—as he so loves to do—in episodes like ''The Apple,'' ''The Ultimate Computer,''and ''The Changeling,'' or whether it concerns nonregular characters who desperately seek their freedom, like Alexander in ''Plato's Stepchildren'' and the underground freedom fighters in the Nazi episode ''Patterns of Force,'' no storyline pretends to put the value of the individual beneath the needs of his or her society. But episode after episode does show us circumstances under which such extreme ''prejudices'' exist.

Star Trek seems obsessed with showing us the individual's struggle for identity and freedom. The day may come, as every human suspects, when the struggle against the computer-god Landru in ''Return of the Archons'' does not seem so farfetched. ''Return of the Archons'' is an interesting study, in fact, because it embraces any kind of oppressive society you choose to name: religious, political, scientific, what have you. Somehow, they're all wrapped up in the same package as far as Landru is concerned. He/it doesn't care about the fine line of definition. You're either ''of the Body'' or you're not. And if you're not, don't worry, you soon will be.

The bottom line in ''Return of the Archons'' parallels those of other stories we've discussed. The people who are the victims of the highly ''prejudicial'' society or tyrant are ultimately given a choice. They can remain as they are, ofttimes rather contented (but not always, and not everybody), or they can dare to learn what is wrong, try to correct it, and go on from there. We leave the people of Beta III in a mess, but a very healthy mess, according to Kirk. And we might as well take his word for it; he knows a good bit about growing pains. He's grown a great deal through his adventures, and as part of the Kirk/Spock/McCoy friendship, participated in the painful growth of others. And he's learned to be careful about how he assesses his friends.

He's learned, for example, that the sometimes abrasively emotional McCoy who "thinks with his glands" in "The Man Trap" is also the McCoy who thinks with his heart in "The Empath." When McCoy defied the wishes of both Kirk and Spock and offered to trade his life for theirs, he demonstrated to the Vians that humankind, with all its supposed "inferiority," has the very enviable ability to love. The Vians said of McCoy, "His death is not important." They implied it was for "the greater good."

They were fools. They didn't understand the value of the individual human being. How could Kirk explain? Is there even a language that has the capacity to describe what we all instinctively know? McCoy had already explained it, by showing the kind of love one human can have for his friends. In "The Empath" Kirk learned to respect the power and great stature of that kind of love and to value the emotional personality behind it.

He has also seen how Spock's drive for logic and order eventually led him to journey deep into the cold, lonely heart of Vejur. Only Spock could have done it. And the information Spock gleaned on that fact-finding journey not only helped to save a world, it helped to save Spock himself, and the friendship of the three. The Vulcan learned, finally, that his own fearful prejudice against human emotion was what kept from being a complete individual. The learning process was painful, but not nearly as painful, Spock discovered, as the emptiness of the entirely logical machine-god Vejur. It's probably quite true that had Spock not journeyed into Vejur and come face to face with the transcending value of human emotion, he would not have been able to entrust his own spiritual essence to McCoy in *Wrath of Khan.*

Everything is tied together in Star Trek. Or it can be, if we care to examine things closely. But nothing compares to the complementary alignment of the Kirk, Spock, and McCoy personalities. They have overcome a multitude of prejudices in order to direct their attention to the larger questions humanity is destined to ask. Their adventures are ours, because where one leaves off, the other takes up, giving us a complex, well-rounded view of humankind's journey in the universe. And its discovery of its own value and potential. In discovering their own self-worth, their inherent *right to be*, our fictional Star Trek friends have found the key, unlocked the door, and taken the first step into man's future. Through their experiences, we can examine who we are and why, we can look objectively at others, we can even dare to challenge ideas which, rightly or wrongly, rule whole worlds. We can defy definition. It's a human break-through, really, a journey into a universe of ideas and exploration. And it never ends.

KEEPING THE FAITH, OR HOW TO LIVE THROUGH A STAR TREK CONVENTION

by Ingrid Cross

If you are among the fans fortunate enough to have attended a large Star Trek convention, you know how much fun and excitement is generated during the course of a weekend. Everything seems to go so smoothly, and everyone seems so happy, that you may have been struck by the thought that you could organize and put on such a convention yourself. If you're seriously thinking of doing so, take heed of the following article. And if you wouldn't dream of organizing a convention yourself, perhaps reading about the difficulties involved will cause you to appreciate the next con you attend all the more.

The idea to put on a Star Trek convention in Baton Rouge, Louisiana, was actually born in Omaha and St. Louis. Joyce Tullock and I had attended conventions in those cities in 1983, and, while we were there, one of those deceptively insane ideas crept up on us when we weren't expecting it.

Why not put on a Star Trek convention in our own city?

Both Joyce and I had attended several Star Trek conventions through the years, ranging from informal "fan-oriented" cons to those with one or more of the series actors. We thought we had seen everything: soaring successes; raging disasters; cons where an actor was supposed to attend, but hadn't been paid and therefore quite logically didn't show up; committees that cared about the fans and put themselves out for them; extravaganzas promising the moon and delivering a meteor; cons where professional investors became involved and absconded with the money. As fans we had been enthralled when meeting other fans; we had enjoyed innovative events; and more often than not, we had been bored by routine programming. We had thrilled to the chance of seeing those people who had made Star Trek possible, who had given a tenuous concept life and breath.

We had seen it all, we thought. And then people who knew us as McCoy fans started asking when we were going to put on a convention and have DeForest Kelley as a guest.

First we sneered at the idea. Or we simply smiled politely, ignored the question, and walked away. But the idea simmered in our minds until the fateful drive back to Louisiana after the marvelous St. Louis experience.

Why couldn't we put on a convention? We were smart enough to pull it off, we had a lot of friends around the country who seemed interested in attending a con in the Deep South, we even knew people who might be interested in appearing as guests! And we knew how to advertise.

These were key concerns to us. There were others, of course: money (the biggest of our worries at the beginning and the nightmare beast to plague us until the conclusion of Delta Con), the time required to put a large convention together, the necessity of having enough staff members to help, et cetera.

Looking back, it seems as though we spent more than a year and a half working with the project. We enjoyed it, in the end. But would we do it again?

Perhaps that's the essential question to use as a starting point.

Star Trek conventions ("cons") have been around since 1972, when a group of New York fans thought, "Hey, wouldn't it be great if we had a gathering of other Star Trek fans? We'll get together at a hotel with a hundred or so people, talk about the show, swap ideas for stories! It'll be wonderful." A lot of people know the rest of that story: Several hundred fans showed up. And a new trend was born.

We shouldn't blame early organizers; they meant well. But they started Star Trek fandom on a path few convention organizers should have followed. Conventions have since been held all over the country—indeed, all around the world. The number of attendees totals in the many thousands (there are no accurate attendance figures). Cons have been held at universities, in hotels of all sizes, and even in huge convention centers. Their success has been measured mostly monetarily (by organizers), but by other factors as well: Did the convention live up to the committee's expectations, and to the attending fans' expectations? Was the programming interesting enough? Did the guest actors live up to the crowds' expectations?

Conventioneering is largely a matter of expectations. Committees set out with some sort of objective (although this is questionable at times), and the fans attending also have hopes, realistic or not. (From our experience as organizers and attendees, these hopes are generally unrealistic.) And when the hoopla is all over, idealistically all these expectations should have merged together and been accomplished.

Idealistically. A lot of things can go wrong between the instigation of an idea and the realization of it.

Perhaps you're one of those people who has thought about organizing a convention. Maybe you've been to other conventions and had the idea creep up on you that you could do a better job than others did . . . that you could put together a convention that would blast everyone's socks off.

We won't discuss sanity at this point. To make the decision to put on a convention is to invite yourself to the nearest mental institution—speaking from experience, of course.

On several levels, the convention we put on, Delta Con, was a success. People enjoyed themselves, the programming went off as planned, and a lot of wonderful things happened to us while planning it and during The Weekend.

Joyce and I had several objectives when we planned the convention. We estimated attendance at 600 to 800 people—a good medium-sized convention. DeForest Kelley and Walter Koenig were our invited main speakers. Other guests included Walter Irwin and Edward Spiteri, a NASA scientist. Connie Faddis, a fan writer/artist/editor, was our guest of honor.

Why do people commit themselves to such a project? You have to be motivated by *something* in order to make the decision in the first place. Let's be straight about one thing immediately: Anyone who does it for the chance to make "big bucks" had better get out before starting.

Money is not a good enough motive. But more on that in a moment. Trust us on that point for the time being.

Fame? What fame? Organizing a convention is sheer back-breaking, exhausting work, if you want it to come off halfway decently. There is no "fame" associated with being a convention organizer. How many convention chairmen appear as guests on a network talk show? How many work the lecture circuit or get interviewed by Dan Rather? If you're motivated by the notion of being "someone," you're in for a big disappointment. When it's all over, you'll look around and say, "I'm the one who did the convention! Aren't you impressed?" If you're lucky, people around you will yawn. More likely, they'll say, "What's a convention?"

In short, in the real world outside of fandom, having organized a convention means nothing. It might look great on a résumé—if you want to own up to it in the "mundane" world. You have contributed nothing of lasting value to the evolution of mankind and the pursuit of world peace.

Most of the people who attend a convention could care less whose name is behind the project. The majority of people want a party and you supply it. Like any host, you'll be fortunate if they pick up their trash as they leave.

To this day, we're not sure we had any tangible reasons for putting on a convention, short of promoting Star Trek in this part of the country. Baton Rouge is a long way from the Midwest, which is where most of the better conventions take place. Part of our motivation was that a purely Star Trek convention had never been done here before.

And part of the motivation was the challenge of doing something we had never done before. We wanted to prove we could do it. (It's not clear to whom we were trying to prove this point.) And we wanted to prove we could do it in ultraconservative Baton Rouge.

Partly we wanted to share the enjoyment in Star Trek we had experienced with others around us in the city, and around the country.

We'll assume those were good enough reasons. They sufficed for our purposes.

So one of the first steps is to make sure you know *why* you're putting on a convention.

You have to make several key decisions as soon as you decide to do the convention. What kind of weekend do you want to have? Do you want to pay actors to come and speak, or will it be a weekend where fans just get together and talk Star Trek? Do you prefer programming that is laid-back and loose, or do you want to program an event or several events concurrently for twelve to eighteen hours? Will it be an extravaganza, complete with a huge dealers' room, charity dinner, parties, autograph sessions, and so on? Or do you envision your con to be an intimate, quiet three-day get-together?

If you lean toward the quiet get-together, you're better off inviting several Star Trek friends to your house and playing videotapes for seventy-two hours straight. But if your visions take you on a wild extravaganza replete with actors and the entire freewheeling experience of a major convention, your needs will be accordingly greater.

One of those major needs is money. Money, as some wise philosopher once said, makes the world go around. It also fuels a successful convention. Conventions are like dinosaurs: They need a lot of food in order to survive. Except in the case of cons, read "money" for "food."

The first step when planning a convention is to work up a budget. Let's say you want to invite two actors, two writers, and a NASA representative. The actors do not come free. This is only right, since the convention circuit is a part of their working life. They appear at conventions in order to enhance their visibility to the public, of course, and they do it because they love Star Trek. But they also do it for money. Whether or not you agree with the idea—and there are a lot of people who can't quite grasp it—it is a fact of life. In addition to speaking fees, you'll probably be paying for their air transportation and hotel costs.

Your other guests have requirements, as well. The writers and NASA rep will have to sleep somewhere. Even if they don't charge you for their speaking services (after all, a writer generally makes public-speaking appearances to promote his work and name), you will most likely be responsible for their hotel costs and perhaps meals. Some things can and should be negotiated—but some items in a speaker's contract are immovable.

Okay, you'll need money for speakers. Let's use a ballpark figure of $15,000 to cover speakers' fees, hotel rooms, and incidentals (hotel rooms and so on).

Did a collective "gulp" just resound from the audience? Probably so. Wait until close to the convention when you get phone calls from people wanting to attend and they balk at the ticket price, which ranges from $10 to $40 for an entire weekend. Try explaining to people that the speakers cost money. One trial of a convention organizer's patience is listening to that refrain—even from friends—over and over again. But it gets worse.

Your initial estimated figure was $15,000. That won't quite cover it. As one chairman of a successful Midwest convention told us, take that figure and double it, or you'll be in for a terrible ordeal when it's all over and you're in bankruptcy court. When planning for a medium-sized convention with professional actors, a budget of $30,000 is adequate. Barely.

So in order to decide whether or not you should make the commitment, what's the next step? Realistically estimate your attendance. If you are a hard worker and you can hustle enough, you might feel you can pull in 800 people. Now divide your total budget by the number of people to get the ticket price you should charge.

And then you need to really think. Expect to stop and think about any major step in planning a convention. The question to ask yourself here is: Would *I* attend a convention that costs as much as what I need to charge? If you can honestly answer yes, go on to other considerations.

If the answer is a shaky maybe or no, perhaps it's best to bow out immediately. Either drastically rethink your plans or scrap them completely and plan on attending other people's conventions . . . but please keep that experience of budgeting firmly in mind as you enjoy yourself at their conventions.

How do you get your hands on the $30,000 you'll need to put on your convention? If you're a property owner, you can mortgage the house. If you're a hustler, you can probably get a lot of your up-front money by getting people to pay admission early. You'll still have to come up with more money, though, as most people don't plan a year and a half in advance when going to conventions. And most of your income will come from "at the door" attendance. You will have bills to pay long before then, so you'll need cash flow, and the best possible way to get it is by talking to a banker. A business loan is another big commitment— another opportunity to think, as you leave the loan officer's office, about whether or not you really want to go through with the convention. If the answer is again yes, keep going.

There are a lot of *major* concerns involved with putting on a convention, as you have probably already guessed. For example: Who will be in charge? If a club is planning to put on the convention, someone will have to take ultimate responsibility. If individual fans are putting it on, the same applies. It is helpful to have a core committee that oversees the entire operation and makes all the decisions. The smart con organizers will realize that the person or persons who put up the money should have the decision-making power. Otherwise, you run the risk of losing friends—especially if the person who is given major responsibility is not the person who signed on the dotted line of a legal document.

Something else to consider is that should you make any money on the convention (highly unlikely), the persons who put up the money should be the first to be repaid, after all outstanding bills are settled.

The ideal delegation of responsibility is to give the core committee the ability to make those tough decisions and be able to enforce them. Some friends who had put on conventions before told us the chances of breaking even were practically nonexistent on a first-time con. Since we were the ones who would have to make up the difference after it was all over, we were the ones who made the decisions. It was that simple. It goes without saying that you have to know yourself and your partners well enough before you give them a sizable responsibility, especially where money is concerned.

Each person on the core committee should have a job description. In other words, each key person's role must be delineated. Think of the major categories required in the project and assign each to a specific person. They will probably have others under them to help carry out the objectives, but someone has to be in charge of each committee.

A good example is programming. Decide what you want fans to do during the weekend and go from there. At Delta Con, we had speakers, video rooms, an art show and auction, a gaming room, panel discussions, a charity dinner and auction, and more. We did not divide up the work so much as check on one another constantly to make sure that each item was being followed through on. As we made our plans known, several friends around the country were tapped on the shoulder (or begged) to be in charge of something.

This caused some problems, however. For example, the person in charge of the art show and auction lived in Virginia. She could not attend any committee meetings with us, which might have made her job easier. Instead, she was thrown into the situation the weekend of the convention. And while the art show and auction went very well and was a successful, integral part of our overall programming, it was not fair to her.

So another key to success is to have local people who can help you.

And that brings up the subject of workers. You will need warm bodies when actually running the convention: people to assist the committee chairmen or to relieve them once in a while to eat or sleep; security people to keep overenthused fans from whatever dangers might lurk around the corner (e.g., excessive partying that threatens to demolish the hotel); and gofers, to take care of just about everything else.

A good rule of thumb is ten ancillary people for every one hundred people you expect to be attending. And, of course, those seventy or eighty people working during the convention cannot work twenty-four hours straight (as the convention organizers seem to), so you will need some scheduling genius to help get everything covered at the same time.

A good way to find people is to check out local clubs—Star Trek and science fiction. If you can find fans in your area, half the battle is won, because there is a good chance you and they will be speaking almost the same language. And if there is some common interest you all share, it makes it easier to work together during The Weekend, with all the other pressures crushing everyone involved in running the convention.

And by the way, the persons who are running the project should be prepared to deal with every kind of person. Diplomacy and tact unfortunately go only so far sometimes. A con organizer needs to have a strong backbone. It's difficult to coordinate forty to seventy people and make sure they're doing what needs to be done. You'll have to worry about personality clashes between the committee and the workers, and among the workers as well. If you make it clear up front who is taking the ultimate responsibility and who has the final word, things should run more smoothly.

Money, core committees with responsibility, and ancillary people to work the convention. What next?

Where are you going to hold this wonderful event? Let's assume you'll be holding the convention in a hotel. First step: Find a hotel that is willing to host the group. This involves examining *your* needs, as well. How many meeting rooms will you need? Does the hotel have a ballroom that will hold the number of people you're expecting? How much does the hotel charge for using its facilities? Does it have special convention rates for its guest rooms?

Finding the answers to these questions requires research; and after talking to many (or all) of the hotels in your city, you'll have a better idea of where to hold the convention.

We were lucky with Delta Con. There are five major hotels in Baton Rouge. Two contenders were eliminated after simply looking in the Yellow Pages, where we discovered their convention facilities were limited to 400 people or less. One hotel was crossed off the list for various reasons, among them the fact that it was stuck in the middle of nowhere, with no restaurants or tourist attractions nearby. (After all, most people are using vacation time to attend a convention; why not give them the chance to explore your city?)

We scouted out the fourth hotel and discovered we didn't care for the atmosphere; the hotel caters mostly to businessmen. It was nice, but *cold*; we wanted a place with the Southern charm that Louisiana lays claim to.

The fifth hotel had many things going for it. It was located on the Mississippi River, was close to the airport, had enough meeting rooms for our programming, and was possessed of old-world charm and history aplenty. And—almost too good to be true, according to friends who worried about our sanity at times—the sales staff were a joy to work with. We worried needlessly about silly things, and the hotel staff graciously laid those fears to rest. After all, they have dealt with conventions since the 1930s. In other words, they had experience.

Still, they had never hosted a Star Trek convention and were probably blissfully ignorant of what to expect. We kept trying to warn them about the costumed fans, excitement, and strange things that would happen. They would just smile. So despite our worries that they didn't know what they were getting into, we worked out negotiations and moved on.

It is essential that you can talk with the sales staff and that you get along with them. If they seem inflexible from the start when you're checking them out, they will be inflexible during The Weekend—something you can do without, considering all the other problems you will encounter. Make sure you are comfortable with them, that you can ask them anything. And treat them with respect.

There is only a limited amount of negotiating you can do with the hotel. You can argue over prices all you want, but the sales staff must go along with management's price list. The hotel is in business, too. There are other points which might be more negotiable—for example, the price charged for meeting rooms.

With conventions, hotels make their biggest money on the number of guest rooms booked. Usually, the more rooms you book, the less you will be charged for the meeting rooms. As with anything else in the discussions, get everything in writing. That way, you will face less headaches when you settle the bill and you won't have to rely on word-of-mouth deals made a year or so before.

Nothing involving the hotel is too minor. You will need to know if it has another major convention booked the same weekend as your con. If it does, consider selecting another date. You don't want to have mass confusion reigning, plus the worry of checking more badges at the door than is necessary. And you want to make sure your attending guests will be able to get a room at the hotel. Ask the hotel about its policy on security personnel. Do you need to "rent" a guard for the weekend, or does the hotel take care of it? (And who pays for the service?) Is there a doctor on the premises, or at least someone who knows first aid and CPR?

In short, you need to know if you can work with the hotel staff. You're going to be involved with them for at least a year, and you'll practically be living with them during The Weekend. The weekend of the convention is not the time to find out they're impossible to deal with. An excellent way to ensure good working relations is to meet with them on a regular basis, increasing the frequency of the meetings as the convention date approaches. Just calling them every other week or so helps. It shows you care about your project—and it will help them care, too.

So you have a budget, a committee, an idea of programming, workers, and a hotel. You're ready to set a date and let the world know about it.

There is nothing minor about these details. In fact, you're probably getting the idea that nothing at all is "minor" when putting on a convention, aren't you? Good. That's what you should be thinking.

It *sounds* simple, "setting a date." Far from the truth. Somehow you have to know when other major conventions are taking place and where they will be held. To start off our consideration of dates, for example, we ruled out November through February. November and December are holiday months; not many people are in the mood to go to a convention around Thanksgiving or Christmas. Besides, they generally don't have enough money to spend on air fare, admission, and in the dealers' room. January and February are bad months for bills; everyone is paying off holiday debts. We wanted to be able to draw students from nearby colleges; that ruled out the summer months. That left March through May, and September and October.

We had two other major reasons why we didn't want the summer months if we could avoid it. First, there are a lot of conventions in the Midwest and on the East Coast during the summer—we would be competing with established conventions. That was a dangerous prospect. In addition, the summer heat in Louisiana is devastating to people who aren't used to it. And since we needed to bring people in from around the country—not just our state—we didn't want fans collapsing in the streets from heatstroke.

That narrowed it down to September and October. September is not as rainy as October—if you've never attended a convention over a rainy weekend, take my word for it: It's depressing. And college kids would have more money available to spend earlier in the semester. Plus, WorldCon was held over Labor Day and other conventions had been held during the summer, so maybe fans would be ready for another convention.

We thought we had settled every angle. And we were pleased with a late-September date—until we realized that the first home football game of the local university (LSU) was on the same weekend. Normally, we don't worry about things like that; sacrilegious as it sounds, neither of us is into football. But in our city, football is *sacred*. Especially the first home game.

It affected our attendance on Saturday, but it wasn't as bad as it could have been. Believe me, when we first found out about the game, it was a frightening notion to think we had spent eighteen months planning and maybe no one would show up.

This just goes to show that you cannot plan for every contingency. But we darn well tried. Sometimes we came up with reasons why we shouldn't use a specific date that now seem ridiculous. But if they sounded good enough at the time, we decided on the basis of our gut reaction. (Another good quality for convention organizers: If you can't trust your own visceral reaction to an idea or potential problem, you will face worse problems all the way down the line.) All of this leads to the fact that you need to think about the date and all possible problems involved. For example, you don't want to schedule your convention—especially a first-time con—for the same weekend as WorldCon, the biggest science fiction convention of all, because it's been around a long time and you'll be competing against its reputation.

Now you know when you want to hold your convention. The next step is to let people know that you're going to have a convention.

By this point, we were accustomed to the idea of the convention. We had a good idea of what was going to happen that weekend, but we had to translate it to paper and advertise it; several major chores had been taken care of before we committed ourselves in print.

First, we had signed contracts with DeForest Kelley and Walter Koenig, and we had made agreements with two of our other speakers. Not many people seem to do things in this order. If someone is flying in to attend your convention, he is making the conscious decision to come based on your guest list. Putting an actor's name on a flyer and other advertising is making a commitment; if a contract has not been signed or a definite agreement in writing made before that advertising goes out, it is, in my opinion, tantamount to lying. You are leading people on and getting them to commit their time *and money* to a fiction.

An example: If a fan decides to attend Con X where William Shatner and Leonard Nimoy are billed as attending guests, that fan has an interest in seeing one or both of them. If a convention committee accepts money from a fan before contracts are signed, and then negotiations happen to fall through, the fan will be disappointed.

There are other repercussions beyond disappointed fans. The word has already gone out that these actors will be at Con X. When they don't show up, you can bet the committee is not going to take the blame. The organizer will not come out and say, "Well, we didn't have them under contract in the first place." That would be admitting to lying and false advertising. More than likely, the *actors* will be blamed by the committee. ("They just didn't show up" has been heard about more than one actor in just exactly these circumstances in the past.) Such actions damage the actors' credibility, and affects every other convention that legitimately went through negotiations and signed contracts. Con X's greed smears every other convention organizer and causes general distrust among fans.

Another tactic for attracting fans is a bit more nebulous. This involves the practice of putting out a flyer with a long list of "invited guests." This is not outright lying, of course. These writers, actors, or other speakers probably have been *invited*; the implication is that these "invited" guests will be signing a contract and are expected to attend. While it's not a deliberate falsehood, it is still misleading. Major companies would be called up before federal agencies for "false and misleading" advertising if they were to engage in such practices. Convention organizers using this ploy should wait until contracts are signed; negotiations don't have to take forever. But they *should* be started early!

So before you put out a flyer, you'll want to have a very definite idea of what programming you are offering fans. We could have used the invited-guest routine; we certainly approached enough people about speaking at Delta Con. The list would have been impressive to a lot of people, perhaps more impressive than our final guest list; it depends on your perspective. But our reputation was important to us. If were going to take someone's money, we wanted to make sure that person knew exactly what would be happening that weekend.

It seemed as though a lot of people had been burned before by less savory tactics. We received many letters from people wanting assurances that Mr. Kelley and Mr. Koenig would definitely attend before they sent their money. So it was with a clear conscience that we could reply, "Yes, we have them under contract."

Negotiating with the actors was an exciting, interesting process, but, as we'd heard from other people, there were no major problems dealing with them. They each have idiosyncrasies and requirements. Each Star Trek actor has a set price for his speaking fee and each requires payment of the hotel room. Most of them require air fare. From there on, everything diverges according to the individual. Meals and other considerations are negotiated on an individual basis.

We knew we were underway for sure when we received the signed contracts back in the mail. It was a heady feeling. Now we had committed ourselves and the convention was a reality. Now we had to tell other people about it.

There is nothing simple about designing a convention flyer. Everything has to be on that little piece of paper—without boring everyone who reads it to tears. The same rules apply to a con flyer that apply to any other piece of advertising. You ask yourself the basic questions, then answer them: who, what, when, where, and why. Include clear and accurate directions to the hotel. Put it all together in an attractive manner and mail it out. Of course, this description of the entire matter is rather brief; I won't go into the headaches of editing material to fit onto the page. (Of course, there is always more you could tell . . . but you have to get the reader interested. Anyone can read about a convention. You have to make fans want to *attend* the convention and see it for themselves.) Make the flyer *enticing*!

Probably the most difficult part of getting ready to do the convention flyer is choosing a name for the event. There are no rules about this procedure, except that you don't want to use someone else's name—you don't want to trade off of some other group's good reputation, or bad reputation, if its con happened to be a bomb. The majority of the conventions around today use something about their geographical location to describe the convention. The New York Star Trek Convention sums it up nicely. Or Coast Con, the Gulf Coast convention in Biloxi, Mississippi. Also, some Star Trek terms lend themselves to good convention names: Archon, Con-stellation, Nova Con (although why anyone would want to have a convention named after a catastrophic astronomical event is beyond me). As with any other product, you want a name that catches the imagination, pulls the reader into the concept. There were a lot of choices available to us, most of which were too silly or too difficult to pronounce. We finally settled with Delta Con because Baton Rouge lies in the Mississippi Delta region, and it *sounded* strong and substantial.

After you have the flyer prepared and printed, you figure you're ready. Well, as long as you have someone to send them to, yes, you are ready. Now you have to find your market (something you should have considered before this point, really). You could advertise in different genre-oriented magazines (*Starlog, Twilight Zone*, etc.). You could also ask local bookstores to distribute your flyers. (A national chain store probably will not, since it usually has a policy against endorsing products. This is a shame, but understandable, since such stores don't want to lend their reputation to something that could be, as far as they know, of questionable integrity.) You could even plaster them against windshields at a local mall parking lot.

But the best bet is direct mail. And that entails a mailing list or two. If you know a lot of other fans around the country, you could ask them to send your flyers around to their friends. Ask nearby conventions if they would be willing to let you use their mailing lists. (This can be a touchy matter—we found one well-known convention group to be jealously uncooperative.) Also, mail batches of your flyer to other conventions; after all, if people attend *that* convention, you have found part of your market, right? At least they know what conventions are. And check with Fandom Directory (Post Office Box 4278, San Bernardino, CA 92409); it has a mailing list service at a reasonable cost.

We found that direct mail worked best. With current postage rates, though, mailing out 10,000 flyers first-class was an unbearable expense. After talking to different people who used bulk mailing, we decided to get a permit. We saved 9.5 cents on each flyer that way.

Nothing was more pathetic than seeing our small group doing the first major mailing of about 3,000 flyers. We spent the money to have the printer fold the flyers for us (saving us about three to four hours of labor), but we had to put labels on each one and then sort them by zip code. The living-room floor was a hopeless cause—as it would be for many weeks to follow. Five of us sorted the flyers by zip code destination, tried to figure out the postal regulations, and somehow managed to put the right labels on each bundle.

Then we dragged the bags to the post office and worried while they checked the forms. Thankfully, we had guessed correctly at the sometimes vague wording in the regulations. The first bundle was off!

What celebration! It sounds easy enough doesn't it? And yet, one of our earliest concerns was becoming a reality. That first mailing took approximately one hundred hours to complete, when you consider the time spent by the artist to design the flyer, writing, typing, and laying out the copy, pasting labels on each flyer, and sorting and bundling. With everyone involved in the convention also holding down a full-time job, you can see how the time required to do things right would begin to mount up and eat a hole into our lives.

And that was only the beginning of advertising. Starting a year before The Weekend, we took out ads in both professional and fan-oriented publications. We printed a total of 15,000 flyers, all of which were mailed out, sent to other conventions, or distributed locally. We ended up with maybe 300 left over.

Four months before the convention, we began working with the media. One of the most critical phases is sending out the press releases at the best time—in other words, not too early and not too late. Anything more than four months before the convention is too soon; the media won't care. And if you haven't let them know you're around with less than two months left, you might as well forget it. By that time, you'll have too much else to do to give enough attention to local publicity. About three months before the convention is the right time to *begin* with your publicity, but don't forget to follow up right until the day of the con!

We sent releases to every newspaper and radio and television station in Louisiana, eastern Texas, Arkansas, western Mississippi, and a lot of major colleges in the country. After all, this was a Big Event in our area—the first time in this part of the Deep South that a Star Trek convention would be held. And with two of the actors attending, it made for good news copy.

There was some excellent early response, mostly from small-town newspapers. We didn't sneer at any of the coverage; even if it was a three-line blurb, it was free publicity. (The word "free" is what counted most.) Most of the media people worked well with us. There were, as always, some exceptions.

One of the biggest problems a Star Trek convention faces is the public's ignorance of what is involved. You may have noticed, if you're a hard-core fan, that if you mention the words "Star Trek fan," most people will visualize a person who wears poorly made pointed ears and carries a phaser. The media are no different. So you have to try and keep things in perspective. The most common question we heard when talking to reporters was "Is Dr. Spock coming?" Second most common was "Well, what do you do all weekend? Watch reruns?" As they say in politics, we had an image problem. Some media people never did quite catch on to what was happening; we saw some reporters aimlessly wandering the hotel halls with blank expressions. But on the whole, the media treated us generously. We managed to set up radio and television interviews with some of the guests and had a large group at a press conference.

We also bought radio time on a local station. We booked one week of spots; we should have booked two, but even the one week helped immensely. Walter Koenig graciously agreed to tape the spot for us in Los Angeles, and it was put together in Baton Rouge. We managed to get a lot into a thirty-second spot: time, place, what a convention is, and our phone number.

The phone calls started about two months out and steadily increased. We took it as a good sign that the phone was constantly busy; it meant the message was getting out. Overall, we had excellent advertising.

So we were pulling in the people who wanted to come see the strange events. At the same time, we were trying to hustle around and get dealers to come in as well.

Dealers are a strange breed. You can't put on a big convention successfully without them, but some are a pain to work with. Dealers are usually people who sell memorabilia full-time. They go around the country to a different place almost every weekend peddling their wares—an extremely competive, cutthroat business.

We wanted a large dealers' room, which meant selling fifty tables. The cost of a full table included a three-day membership. We made sure we mailed flyers directly to dealers. And those we didn't reach saw our flyers at other conventions.

We got the number of dealers we wanted. But we also got a lot of headaches. There should be a booklet on the care and feeding of dealers, because handling them was a challenge. As I mentioned, they're in a competitive business; after all, there are only so many Paramount-licensed Star Trek items to sell. As a result, despite our pleas to bring other items, nearly every dealer showed up with what everyone else had.

This did not make them happy. While we could appreciate their dilemma (some of them had come from as far away as New York State and weren't moving a lot of merchandise), it was difficult to be sympathetic with a group of grown men and women who whined and complained.

Overall, the majority of them were well behaved. But there were a few that the committee and some of the fans attending the con wanted to restrain with a chair and a whip. Of course, I hasten to add that these characters are in the minority. Unfortunately, they are a very vocal minority and tend to give you the impression that all dealers are obnoxious. Most of the dealers at Delta Con were helpful and cooperative.

If you're putting on a convention and want dealers, be prepared for every possible problem. Just keep reminding yourself that you are sane, and that you are doing them a favor by holding this convention so that they will have a market for their wares.

For a year and a half you are working toward one goal: The Weekend. Time rushes past in a blur and you find you are becoming quite adept at working late hours and learning to constantly worry. The strangest details are a source of worry before a convention. I was worried about getting the actors in and out of the ballrooms safely. That went well. But there were other surprises.

For example, I hadn't anticipated the incident of the lost pants. I walked into the gofer room to hear someone asking, "What happened to [the actor's] pants? Who has them?" With remarkable calm, I asked what was going on. When they saw my furrowed brow, they made it clear that no one knew which dry cleaner his pants had been sent to. Fortunately, the actor wasn't out walking the halls in his underwear.

By a month before the convention, a lot of details should have already been settled. First of all, your contractual obligations should be fulfilled at specified times. The actors and other guests usually set up a payment schedule. You should have paid first and possibly second installments on those contracts by this time.

(Otherwise, you might not have some of your promised guests. Why should they show up if they have not been paid as promised?) Most notably, you should have mailed out press kits, scheduled as many of the interviews and television appearances as you possibly can, and made sure that your guests have been kept up to date on the convention's progress.

By this time, you should be planning and practicing a lot of things. Don't use this valuable time for something you could have take care of much earlier.

Registration is a big concern. Do you know how it will be set up to get people in as quickly as possible? Is there someone you can trust in charge of the money? (Don't laugh. People at other conventions have learned the hard way.) When will you be open? Go to the hotel and walk it through. Fix problems you can foresee. But practice it!

Program books should be completed by now, ideally. There is no excuse for collating and stapling program books two nights away from the convention.

Convention badges can be ordered and printed months ahead of time. Your preregistration system should have been ironed out and working smoothly. Letters of inquiry should have been handled as they came in. As mentioned before, the press should know what's happening by this time.

What's left, less than two weeks from the con?

Well, all the thousands of details that couldn't be taken care of earlier than this. Final arrangements with the hotel (finalizing any banquet arrangements, if you have one; floor plans; chair setup requirements). Interviews with the press. Getting your radio spots to the station(s) on time.

I don't remember the final two weeks before Delta Con. Well, I know they happened; I just don't remember what I actually did. I know we were busy all the time with final concerns. Last thing I knew we had three weeks to go and then it was the day before.

Moving into the hotel was a mess. Living about twelve miles from the hotel created problems. Not only did we have to get the actors and other guests from the airport, we had to get everything from our living room into the hotel. This ended up happening Thursday night from 9:00 p.m. until about 1:00 a.m. Despite all the checklists we had made up, we still forgot things.

Like the convention T-shirts. We got everything to the hotel and someone realized the shirts weren't there. We looked everywhere for them all day Friday as people were coming in and registering.

They were back at the house, waiting patiently in the back room.

Friday was a nightmare. We had plenty of people to help set up the convention, it was just that some major problems developed. We had difficulty with art display flats for the art show. The poor art show director wrestled with inferior and decrepit flats and managed to get them in order by late Friday afternoon. No one will tell me with certainty, but I think they were building those flats as artists were entering their work.

The hotel people had neglected to tell us about fire regulations in the dealers' room. The arrangement we had set up to keep everyone happy had to 'be changed two hours before the room was to open for setup. Then when we did open the room, dealers were arguing about their locations. I was lucky; I was about to scream when our chief person in charge of the gofers stuck his head in the door and offered to help.

Joyce and I were halfway to the airport to pick up one of the guests when we realized a local TV station was going to be at the hotel for a live spot at the same time we had to be at the airport.

That worked out well; Walter Irwin saved our necks and handled the press very nicely.

Every time we turned around, someone had a problem. I had not foreseen having so many problems—after all, we had been planning this for so long. The object lesson here is that there is no way we could have planned for *everything*. That's why it's a good idea to start working on a convention so early. At least we had managed to plan on possible contingencies in certain emergencies. We had something to fall back on, even if we hadn't actually gone through a specific crisis that weekend. In addition, we were lucky to have an excellent working staff and guests who were willing to pitch in and help solve problems.

Friday is a blur, and mercifully will remain that way until the end of my life. Saturday and Sunday went very well; the major problems we had anticipated months before didn't materialize (of course, others did, but they weren't as bad as they could have been). People at the convention kept telling us they were enjoying themselves, and that was what counted. Registration was very good, and that was important, as well.

The convention workers seemed to have a good time. The key committee members appeared to be moving with the flow of

events, for which we were grateful. The guests were happy—
they kept telling us they were, and that was nice to hear.

And yet I remember looking at some of our main workers and
saying very calmly, "Never again." They didn't take me seriously . . . then. They could see no particular reason for me to
say that, and so they laughed.

I was deadly serious.

The idea started creeping up on me early Friday morning (at
about 6:30, sitting in a local television studio); a mutinous
thought, really, that didn't take full form until Sunday afternoon.
Little sleep for three days before The Weekend, very little sleep
and no food to speak of during The Weekend . . . and that
mutinous thought burst into full flower.

"Never again" was a private motto for some of us that weekend. Sure, it was fun for everyone—except that the organizers
were running out of enthusiasm. Neither Joyce nor I operate well
with two to three hours of sleep a night and maybe two solid
meals all weekend. Plus we were the ones who heard the complaints and handled the problems. Don't get me wrong—we had
not expected to be able to enjoy the convention at the time. (We
began to realize this about six months before.) But we also didn't
realize how much of an overwhelming experience it would be.

But we managed to pull it off. The people standing in the
registration lines were proof of that, as well as the constant
media coverage all weekend. We had "done it." We had put
Baton Rouge on the map for a very new, different, and positive
reason.

But was it worth it?

Even before the convention we asked ourselves that question
over and over and we could not find any convincing reason to
answer yes. We ran up against a lot of people who wanted
something for nothing; we weeded those people out.

We also met many people who wanted to attend the convention for free. We simply could not make certain fans understand
why we had to charge admission. I guess they felt it was their
divine right to see the actors for nothing. (By the way, we found
there are a *lot* of people out there who think the actors owe them
something.)

By the end of the convention, we were in awe of all of our
guests: their patience, diplomacy, enthusiasm, overwhelming kindness, and courage. By the end of Delta Con they had become
like a family, devoted not only to the task at hand but to the ideal
Star Trek represents. They acquired a deep mutual respect for

one another, a kind of warm comradery that may be rare in most cons, but was beautiful to see. It was our greatest personal reward for Delta Con.

We had so many problems behind the scenes that at times it tried our patience; and we had been developing enormous amounts of patience all along. We simply started to run out.

It is impossible to total up the time Joyce and I spent on Delta Con, beginning with the very early vacillating discussions ("Should we or shouldn't we?") all the way through The Weekend and even after (writing the final checks). We didn't work twenty-four hours a day on the preparations, true. But a conservative estimate shows that we probably spent a total of five months preparing the convention, including all the detail work and the actual running of the weekend.

And so, you might ask again: Is it worth it to put on a convention? If you measure success in terms of fame and fortune, no. But if you're looking for other things (if you're still thinking of putting on a convention, please pay attention to this), the answer is yes. There were many things that made it all worthwhile.

We met a lot of people who are the salt of the earth; we wouldn't have had the opportunity to meet and work with such fine people if it hadn't been for Delta Con. We learned a great deal, as well: how to borrow money, how to work within a tight budget, how to beg for materials at times, how to talk to reporters, how to organize thousands of details and shape them into a three-day extravaganza.

You can't put a price on those things. I wouldn't want to try. But, in the balance, was it worth it?

Well, here is a list of what we accomplished:

1. We wanted a convention *for the fans*. Joyce and I had been to a lot of conventions that seemed to be put on for the benefit of the committee. We wanted to do one where the fans were the important people.

We succeeded. We were told over and over that Delta Con was the friendliest, warmest convention people had ever attended. And nobody got kicked out of the autograph lines.

2. We wanted to gain the experience of managing something like a large convention.

We certainly succeeded there, as well. The convention is something we can put on our résumés, an event that might someday help us in our professional lives.

3. We wanted to celebrate Star Trek.

Delta Con was more than a party. It was a gathering of friends, people who shared a common interest and love of Star Trek. There was a spirit that weekend of pride in being involved with something as positive as Star Trek . . . and that attitude seemed to come through even to the media.

4. We wanted to bring the Star Trek experience to the Deep South.

Again, this was accomplished. Nothing like this convention had ever been seen in our part of the country before. It set Southern fandom on its collective ear, without any apologies. A lot of people in other parts of the country don't understand and therefore are a little afraid of the South. We made it possible for them to look at us a little closer and realize that the South has a lot to be proud of.

5. We learned—and watched as our friends learned—to give without stint.

We saw many heart-warming examples of this; our workers were by far the best group of people brought together to work on a convention. They proved themselves over and over again, going beyond what was asked of them. There was the worker who knew someone who wouldn't be able to attend on Sunday and get her autograph on that day. Rather than saying ''tough luck'' (which happens at other conventions), this worker stood in line on Saturday—using her assigned card and giving up the chance for her own autograph so that one of our attending fans could get the actors' signatures.

There were the gofers, who were assigned to specific time schedules, coming back for extra duty when they thought they would be needed—without being asked.

There was the guest speaker who took care of an attending member's rambunctious kids so the mother could listen to De-Forest Kelley's talk without distraction.

There was everyone's quiet determination to see that everything ran on schedule—unheard-of at a majority of conventions—so that when an event was to start, it started *on time*.

Those accomplishments mean a great deal to us. They are what Delta Con was all about. They were its reason for being. And to be frank, they are probably the most tangible rewards anyone receives from a convention. Those who might think being a con organizer gives them prestige are only kidding themselves. And eventually they will pay a heavy price in sweat and money with relatively little thanks in return.

Putting on a convention is one of the few things a person can do that reveals humanity in black and white. At cons you'll meet some small people, true. But you'll also have a chance to meet and work with the best of people. For us, Delta Con was a sharing between guests and staff. We wish everyone could have seen what we saw, and felt the warmth of caring between participants. They really were all a family.

If you do put on a convention, we wish you the best of luck and hope that your experience will be as uniquely rewarding as was ours.

YOU COULD GO HOME AGAIN: STAR TREK SEQUELS

by John Wicklund (with Walter Irwin)

The following is a fine example of an article which is based on an idea and research submitted to us by one of our readers. Frankly, coming up with a fresh, new approach to Star Trek is fairly difficult—we're continually surprised ourselves at how inventive and insightful our contributors are—but the sheer work of gathering up the facts and examples from the programs and films themselves is the hardest part of writing. No, we're not trying to scare you off—the ideas and the work are also the most rewarding parts of writing, as well.

Sequels have always been an important and integral facet of moviemaking, but over the last few years, they have become a major part of the business. Sequels are considered even for films which have only a moderate amount of success—blockbusters like *Star Wars*, *Raiders of the Lost Art*, *Superman*, and *Rocky* (to name only a few) continue to generate sequel after sequel, almost all of which are as commercially successful as the original. Only straightforward, one-story dramatic films (such as *On Golden Pond* or *Places in the Heart*) are immune from the urge to produce a sequel and cash in on the popularity of the original.

Of course, not all sequels are motivated out of simple greed. The *Star Wars* films were intended to be a trilogy; *Indiana Jones and the Temple of Doom* presented the character to us as a "prequel," an adventure taking place several years before the events of the first film. But it is unlikely that these films, or any of the other aforementioned sequels, would have been made if the original had not made tons of money. The risk, in terms of both money and time invested, is simply too great.

Years ago, however, it was somewhat different. Studios controlled film production with an iron hand on both cost and quality, and sequels were commonly made to even moderately

93

successful pictures. To keep their contracted theaters filled with product, the major studios had to turn out two or three films a week! So it's unsurprising that tried and tested formulas were snapped up and used again and again. When a sequel proved successful, another was quickly made, even more economically, for standing sets and "stock footage" could often be used. This practice led to the invention of the series film, in which the same characters returned again and again in similar situations, for one film after another. Well-known examples of these are the Charlie Chan and Sherlock Holmes mysteries, and the Blondie and Andy Hardy comedies. When television came along, elements of these series films were combined with those from radio's continuing dramas, and the television series as we know it was born. In essence, each weekly episode was a sequel of sorts to the last, as each contained elements found in earlier episodes.

The odd thing about television series, however, is that although they contain continuing elements, they can also present sequels to individual episodes. The best-known example in Star Trek is, of course, the return of Harry Mudd, from "Mudd's Women," in "I, Mudd." Almost as well known is the abortive plan to have Captain Koloth return in the fourth season as a continuing nemesis for Captain Kirk.

Star Trek: The Motion Picture was an even stranger breed: it was both a continuation of the series and a sequel to the series as a whole, and, through the character of Will Decker, an indirect sequel to "The Doomsday Machine." *Star Trek II: The Wrath of Khan* and *Star Trek III: The Search for Spock* are also part of the series, sequels to the series, and, even more confusingly, *The Search for Spock* is a direct sequel to *Wrath of Khan*, and, through the character of Sarek, an indirect sequel to "Journey to Babel." Whew!

Now that Paramount has loosened up its strictures on the novels published by Pocket Books, we are also beginning to see both direct and indirect sequels to various episodes in novel form. For example, one of the most popular novels of recent years, *Yesterday's Son*, by Ann Crispin, is a direct sequel to "All Our Yesterdays."

It is fun to sit down and consider what other, if any, Star Trek episodes lend themselves to a sequel, and, if so, how readily. (Of course, *every* story can have a sequel if you're willing to stretch far enough. Here we are only considering the use of elements in the show itself to launch a sequel.) I've prepared the following list of episodes, each with a rating on a scale of 1 to

10—1 being little adaptability to a sequel, 10 being excellent adaptability. Along with each is a few comments on why or why not a sequel is possible, whether or not such a sequel should be made, and some random thoughts.

"Where No Man Has Gone Before" Rating: 4

Further investigation of the barrier at the edge of the galaxy and its effects on humans would naturally be undertaken, but probably not by the *Enterprise*. Gary Mitchell could conceivably return, but his death and its effect on Kirk is so important to Star Trek lore that it would have to be an exceptional story, one which would enhance Kirk as a character.

"The Man Trap" Rating: 1

The alien creature died at the end of the episode. As it was purportedly the last of its race, a sequel which brought another "salt monster" back would provide nothing new, and kill the point of the original episode.

"Charlie X" Rating: 2

Going back to visit Charlie and/or the Thasians wouldn't make much sense, and having Charlie aboard the *Enterprise* again would just be a rehash of the original.

"The Naked Time" Rating: 4

The rating is this high only because the "cold mix" matter-antimatter formula was used in a later episode, a sequel of sorts, and is now part of Star Trek lore. To have the crew again affected by the "uninhibiting virus" would be redundant.

"The Enemy Within" Rating: 1

The freak transporter accident which created the duplicate Kirk should never happen again. Besides, the story was successful because it was thoughtful and succinct; a sequel would only water down the message.

"Mudd's Women" Rating: 9

As mentioned above, Harry Mudd returned in a later episode, "I, Mudd," proving himself a popular and adaptable character. Also, the science behind the Venus drug is worth exploring, as is the system of smuggling and underground sale of it and other proscribed substances.

"Miri" Rating: 6

We wouldn't mind learning how Miri grew up and what she would think of Kirk and the others these days. It would also be interesting to see how these 900-year-old children reacted to civilization, as well as learning how and why a duplicate Earth developed in deep space.

"Dagger of the Mind" Rating: 4

The general theme of the episode is always worth looking at again (as in "Whom Gods Destroy"), but specific events cannot, and should not, be duplicated.

"The Corbomite Maneuver" Rating: 9

What ever did happen to Balok and Bailey? Why isn't the First Federation allied with the UFP? Why aren't Kirk and his crew flying around in a mile-wide *Enterprise*? This episode raised many more questions than it answered, and is wide-open for sequels, both direct and indirect.

"The Menagerie" Rating: 3

"Was the survival of the Talosians ensured by Pike's arrival?" is only one question raised at the end of the episode. But since the planet is off-limits, any story involving it would probably be more concerned with the consequences than with what happens there.

"The Conscience of the King" Rating: 1

Kodos is dead, Leonore is insane, Kirk is avenged. Story's over.

"Balance of Terror" Rating: 4

Even though this was the episode which introduced the Romulans, direct sequels to it would be impossible, for the particular enemy was destroyed. Maybe we could see Stiles again and learn if he really did overcome his bigotry. Wouldn't be a bad idea to go back and do a few prequels based on events mentioned in this episode.

"Shore Leave" Rating: 5

There was the animated episode as direct sequel to this one, of course, and it left open the possibility for more adventures. However, it would be difficult to come up with any kind of conflict now that we know it's a pleasure planet and the main computer is cooperating.

"The Galileo Seven" Rating: 1

This is another self-contained episode, the events of which don't leave much of an opening for a sequel. Besides, it was such a strange, illogical show that it's doubtful anyone would want to bother with a sequel.

"The Squire of Gothos" Rating: 8

We know nothing of Trelane and his race, and would like to know more. Since they seem to have a moral code, it's possible they, like the Organians, might take a hand if things were desperate enough. Also, many people took a liking to William Campbell in the role, and would like to see him again.

"Arena" Rating: 7

The events of the episode cannot have a direct sequel, of course, but there is a wealth of unknown information about the Gorn. They and the Federation could go to war at any time, ally at any time, ignore each other for centuries.

"Tomorrow Is Yesterday" Rating: 1

The *Enterprise*'s return to the 1960s later in the series ("Assignment: Earth") was unlikely enough; we don't need any more episodes involving this kind of time travel. And after all the trouble Kirk and company went though putting Christopher back into his proper place in time, they certainly wouldn't want to bother with him again.

"Court-Martial" Rating: 1

Another self-contained episode. The only way we'd ever see Ben Finney or his daughter again is in a flashback to Kirk's past, which would hardly qualify as a sequel. We've also seen enough court-martials, although we'll probably see (or at least hear about) another in *Star Trek IV*.

"Return of the Archons" Rating: 2

It might be slightly diverting to see the development of the post-Landru culture of Beta III, but there's really nothing to hang a sequel on.

"Space Seed" Rating: 10

Gee, I wonder whatever happened to Khan and his people? Seriously, this episode offered great sequel potential from the beginning. Even Spock said it would be fascinating to come back and see how things turned out.

"A Taste of Armageddon" Rating: 6

What would be the consequences of a united Eminiar and Vendikar being admitted to the Federation? Or what would happen if they really did go to war? How would Kirk feel? How would the Federation react? How would the Federation punish Kirk (if at all)? Lots to speculate about here; a good opportunity to have Kirk once again pay a real price for one of his snap decisions.

"This Side of Paradise" Rating: 2

The spores were destroyed and Leila Kalomi is probably so mortified she'd never again come within a 1,000 miles of Spock. However, once again we have a prequel story which most fans would love to see.

"The Devil in the Dark" Rating: 2

The question remains of what more we can learn from the Horta, but now that the creature is no longer considered a menace, it's just another interesting but familiar alien race.

"Errand of Mercy" Rating: 9

The Klingons, introduced in this episode, are still very much around, as is the Organian Peace Treaty, which was a direct result of events in this episode. James Blish wrote a sequel to this episode—"Spock Must Die!"—but it is now generally considered to be an alternate-world story. This episode contains much that is worth coming back to: the Organians and their powers, etc., the delightful and scary villainy of Commander Kor, the forces which were driving the Federation and the Klingon Empire to war, and much, much more.

"The Alternative Factor" Rating: 1

It's possible that the twin Lazaruses could return from limbo, but it would spoil the only good thing about this episode, the good Lazarus' sacrifice—and who really cares, anyway?

"The City on the Edge of Forever" Rating: 7

Although no one really wants to spoil a beautiful story by having a sequel involving Edith Keeler, the time portal itself offers myriad opportunities for additional stories. "Yesteryear," the first of the animated episodes, was one such, and many more are possible.

"Operation: Annihilate" Rating: 2

Should the flying parasites show up again, the ultraviolet-light process should deal with them quickly. The only reason this episode gets a 2 is that it's possible we'll see Kirk's nephew again one of these days.

"Amok Time" Rating: 7

Much of what little we know of Vulcan culture was shown or hinted at in this episode. In a way, almost all of the stories and articles discussing *pon farr* etc. can be considered inspired by this episode, if not actual sequels. It's also very possible that we'll be seeing T'Pring again one of these fine days. Additionally, this episode provides much fertile ground for prequels, as well.

"Who Mourns for Adonais?" Rating: 1

The mighty gods have fallen, and we shan't see their like again. But if the network had allowed the original ending to this episode to air, we definitely would have sequel possibilities. If you'll recall, Carolyn Palamas was carrying Apollo's child, who should inherit his father's godlike powers. What if somebody from the *Enterprise* crew—Scotty!—ran across this child, say, fifteen or twenty years later?

"The Changeling" Rating: 1

No more Nomads . . . sterilize! (Besides, if you really want a sequel to this episode, go watch *Star Trek: The Motion Picture*.)

"Mirror, Mirror" Rating: 5

It's intriguing to think about having the *Enterprise* crew make a return visit to the mirror universe. We'd also like to know how the revolution—if any—went over there. But as attractive as these storylines are, the rating is low because any such stories would necessarily take more than one episode or movie to tell well.

"The Apple" Rating: 3

Again, there are story possibilities in the effects of freedom on the inhabitants now that Vaal has bit the big one.

"The Doomsday Machine" Rating: 2

Commodore Decker gave the giant "vacuum cleaner" permanent heartburn. Seriously, the episode is just fine as it is, and any sequels would only water down the effect of the original. This episode receives a 2 rating rather than a 1 only because Decker's son, Will, shows up in *Star Trek: The Motion Picture*, thereby providing definite continuity. (Out of the scope of this article, but worth mentioning, is the fact that one of the Star Trek role-playing games features a scenario called "The Return of the Doomsday Machine.")

"Catspaw" Rating: 3

The creatures from another dimension could return (Sylvia would probably love to have another go at Captain Kirk) if they are still alive. Then again, they could show up in a Lovecraftian horror tale.

"I, Mudd" Rating: 7

Harry Mudd appeared again, up to his old tricks, in the

animated episode "Mudd's Passion," and we will always welcome seeing him again. Besides, wouldn't you like to know how he fared on a planet with several hundred Stellas?

"Metamorphosis" Rating: 5

Did Zefrem Cochrane and the Commissioner/Companion really live happily ever after? Did they have children? Why do we suspect that Kirk and Spock pay regular visits to that planetoid . . . could it be a new transwarp drive that looks suspiciously like the work of Zefram Cochrane?

"Journey to Babel" Rating: 9

The story is exhausted, but we would like to see more of the many races both featured and mentioned in this episode, as well as more of the interaction between them in the interworkings of Federation government. That rates a 3; what pulls it up to 9 is the fact that this episode introduced Spock's parents, Sarek and Amanda, who appeared in "Yesteryear" and *Star Trek III: The Search for Spock*. More important is the role these two have played in all kinds of Star Trek fiction and articles . . . they're as important to Star Trek as the *Enterprise* crew.

"Friday's Child" Rating: 4

The planet is an intriguing place, what with its stringent codes of honor and honesty; some exciting adventures could happen there, and its people would make an interesting addition to the Federation. We also can't believe that Leonard McCoy wouldn't make an opportunity to visit his godson and namesake just to see what kind of man and leader he's turning out to be.

"The Deadly Years" Rating: 1

Another disease, another cure.

"Obsession" Rating: 2

Another creature, another cure. (Seriously, there are prequel possibilities in the relationship between young Kirk and Captain Garrovick.)

"Wolf in the Fold" Rating: 2

Argelius is a very interesting place, obviously perfect for shore leave, and perhaps another story could take place there. But "another creature, another cure" applies to Redjac, as well. (Even though Redjac returned in a story published in the DC Comics Star Trek book.)

"The Trouble with Tribbles" Rating: 3

The lovable Tribbles showed up again in an animated episode

("More Tribbles, More Troubles"), as well as making a cameo appearance in *The Search for Spock*. But popular as they are, Tribbles really only do one trick. There's not a heck of a lot of story possibilities inherent in them.

"The Gamesters of Triskelion" Rating: 4

It might be interesting to go back and see what happened after "Kirk freed the slaves."

"A Piece of the Action" Rating: 7

Lots of story potential here, both as sequels and prequels (what were the imitative people of Iotia like before the USS *Horizon* arrived?). Besides, who could resist the chance to stop in and play another hand of fizzbin?

"The Immunity Syndrome" Rating: 1

Another monster-menace taken care of. Enough of that.

"A Private Little War" Rating: 4

The little planet of Neural offers some intriguing scenarios. Maybe Tyree and Rambo can take the planet.

"Return to Tomorrow" Rating: 1

Sargon and Thalassa are gone for good. As far as the Spock-Chapel elements of the story, well, let's not get syrupy here.

"Patterns of Force" Rating: 4

Discovering how the Ekosians dismantled the Nazi government (if indeed they did) and patched up things with Zeon would be interesting to see. Surely there were fanatics other than Melakon around. . . .

"By Any Other Name" Rating: 6

What will happen when the true Kelvans finally show up? What happened to Rojan and his people? Why haven't we seen any of the technological advances developed by the Kelvans used in Federation ships? There's more going on here than we've been told.

"The Omega Glory" Rating: 4

Again, we'd like to revisit and see what became of the opposing forces on Omega IV.

"The Ultimate Computer" Rating: 5

Technology, once discovered, won't stay hidden, and Dr. Daystrom's talents are too valuable to allow him to remain away from research. M-5 units will be rebuilt (M-6 units?), let's hope without the glitches of the original, and how and where and what happens would make a good sequel.

"Bread and Circuses" Rating: 2

The Federation obviously plans to give this planet a wide berth, at least until it survives its barbaric period. (No, not the Roman culture—its terrible TV programming!)

"Assignment: Earth" Rating: 5

A midrange rating. The *Enterprise* and her crew should stay out of the 1960s. But the episode was intended as the pilot to a series, so sequels are not only possible, they were expected. Alas, 'twas not to be.

"Spock's Brain" Rating: 1

No, make that rating a zero.

"The Enterprise Incident" Rating: 9

Lots of things in this episode which could serve as fodder for sequels. (And have, in at least a couple of novels.) What became of the Romulan commander when she made it back to her home planet? What happened (if anything) between her and Spock in the meantime? Why are the cloaking devices not used by Federation ships? And so on.

"The Paradise Syndrome" Rating: 1

Miramanee is dead and so is any reason to go back to this episode.

"And the Children Shall Lead" Rating: 1

The friendly lawyer has been expelled from the space bar. And who cares what happened to the kids?

"Is There in Truth No Beauty?" Rating: 3

The Medusans are interesting and we'd like to know more about them . . . especially what they look like! And how did that partnership between Kollos and Miranda Jones work out, anyway?

"Spectre of the Gun" Rating: 3

Of interest only because of the mysterious Melkotians. But a sequel to this episode might be more at home on *The Twilight Zone*.

"Day of the Dove" Rating; 5

Kang has already shown up again in a couple of novels, and would always be a worthy adversary for Captain Kirk. And that creature wasn't destroyed—it just ran away. Perhaps to fight again another day?

"For the World Is Hollow and I Have Touched the Sky" Rating: 7

What did we learn from the Fabrini? (Wasn't McCoy supposed to be studying their medicine before *Star Trek: The Motion Picture*?) And what became of his romance with Natira? Did the colonists really reach their world and settle it? Lots to work with, here.

"The Tholian Web" Rating: 3

Again, the events of the episode cannot have a sequel, but what of the Tholians? Will they be friend or foe? Or will they ever be seen again?

"Plato's Stepchildren" Rating: 2

Another place the Federation will be better off forgetting about (and probably did). But what became of Alexander? Was his dwarfism really cured? And why isn't the psionic-power drug used in emergency situations?

"Wink of an Eye" Rating: 1

The Scalosians could show up again. Bzzz. And zzzz.

"The Empath" Rating: 4

Sooner or later, the Federation will again encounter the Vians, and have to reach an accommodation with those smug fellows. And what of Gem's people? Just how much were they affected by the emotions she brought to them? Is it now a planet full of McCoys?

"Elaan of Troyius" Rating: 2

Interplanetary feuds are hardly the *Enterprise*'s most pressing problems. Let's hope the nasty princess turned into a gracious queen.

"Whom the Gods Destroy" Rating: 3

This high a rating only because we want to know more about the exploits of Garth of Izar, who impressed and inspired Kirk so. And what happened to Garth after he was "cured"? Opportunity for both prequels and sequels, here.

"Let That Be Your Last Battlefield" Rating: 1

Lokai and Bele are probably still chasing each other around in little circles of bigotry and hate. Come to think of it, so are we.

"The Mark of Gideon" Rating: 3

We'd like to know more about the people of Gideon. Why don't they migrate? What kind of social system do they have?

And what happened when a plague was released among the population?

"That Which Survives" Rating: 1

There's not much left to tell, even though we'd very much like to know the story of Losira's race and what finally became of them.

"The Lights of Zetar" Rating: 4

The "lights" were apparently destroyed, so there's little story possibility there. But what fans want to know is *just what the heck happened between Scotty and Mira Romaine*? Popular opinion has it that they married, but when, how, who was there? And if they did marry, where is Mira now?

"Requiem for Methuselah" Rating: 7

It's possible that Flint, with his great knowledge, could have staved off his death for quite a while and still be around. And what of the work he was going to do for mankind's benefit? Surely something came of that. Most of the rating, however, is devoted to the endless fascinating possibilities for prequels to the show, relating Flint's adventures through time.

"The Way to Eden" Rating: 2

What next? Space punkers trying to find meaning in a "material galaxy"? This episode has even this much of a rating because we'd be interested in seeing more of the Earth/Federation culture the "space hippies" were protesting against, and we can't help wondering what became of Chekov's friend Irini.

"The Cloud Minders" Rating: 3

The folks on Ardana seem to have gotten things together, but what we want to know is, did Spock and Droxine ever get together again? And what, if anything, happened when they did?

"The Savage Curtain" Rating: 5

The presence of Surak in the episode whetted our appetite for more about him and Vulcan history. And it seems as if everyone forgot about the rocklike Yarnek—except Mike Barr, who featured a sequel to this episode in the first issues of the DC Comics Star Trek comic book.

"All Our Yesterdays" Rating: 5

A. C. Crispin did a wonderful job of creating the "dream sequel" to this episode, showing us there are always possibilities in even the most seeming dead end.

"Turnabout Intruder" Rating: 5

Why so high a rating? Because Janice Lester is a large part of Kirk's early years and could feature prominently in prequels. And we must remember the Federation's not-so-good track record for curing mental illness. Sick or well, she's still out there, somewhere . . . and so is that mind-transfer machine. Surely Starfleet would have tried to duplicate the process. What if they succeeded?

As we've seen, all of the Star Trek episodes are open to sequels of one kind or another; many raised more questions than they answered. Chances are that few, if any, of these such sequels will ever be done (even by fan writers), but its fun to speculate. Most of our speculation these days, however, is centered on what will be coming up in the next film. (And let's hope there will always be a "next film.")

I was particularly fascinated by Tom Lalli's article "A Speculation on *Star Trek IV*" (Best of Trek #9). Before *The Search for Spock*, everyone had a rough idea of what direction the movie would take. But now, Star Trek is at a new beginning. A thousand roads are available to the creators of *Star Trek IV*; the question is which one, or combination, to take. Mr. Lalli's analysis of the possible events of the fourth movie was excellent, but he looked at only a few of the more obvious scenarios.

Tongue firmly in cheek, I would have to name the upcoming movie *Star Trek IV: The **** Hits the Fan*. Kirk and his beloved crew are in hot water with Starfleet and with the Klingons. The *Enterprise* is destroyed. How will Carol Marcus react when she learns of Genesis' failure and David's death? What is the solution? Even Spock once admitted that there may *not* always be alternatives present.

The trouble, now, is that there are too many alternatives, causing us to have a sort of "future shock" of the twenty-third century. Whatever directions the forthcoming movie takes, fans will always say "what if?" and "why?" As long as they keep asking the questions, Star Trek will never die.

AFTER KYLE: THE FORGOTTEN HEROES OF THE ENTERPRISE

by Greg Gildersleeve

*Star Trek was an unusual show in many ways, but one of the
most striking was its practice of including a great many recurring characters in small, background roles—roles which most
television programs would fill with the first person to show up
from Central Casting. To Gene Roddenberry and the other producers of Star Trek, however, the world—particularly the ship
and crew—surrounding the stars was just as important as the
stars themselves. Thanks to this, we see comfortably familiar
faces in almost every episode. But who are they? Greg Gildersleeve
knows, and he's going to share his findings with you.*

One of the more realistic touches of the Star Trek universe is the
crew, those 420-odd other persons who made the ship come to
life through their continued presence as background characters.
Many of them appeared more than once, providing a subtle
continuity in the series.

While Captain Kirk, Mr. Spock, and Dr. McCoy are unques-
tionably the stars of Star Trek, much attention has also been paid
by fandom to the minor characters: Scotty, Sulu, Uhura, Chekov,
and Nurse Chapel. Even Yeoman Rand and Lieutenant Kyle,
who can respectfully be described as *minor* minor characters,
have been granted immortality by fandom and were considered
worthy enough to be remembered in the Star Trek movies. This
is only right, as these characters help round out the reality of Star
Trek by making it more consistent, and, yes, even more accessi-
ble by giving us more than just a few faces through which to
explore an infinite number of fantasies.

This article is dedicated to those crewmembers who made the
Enterprise even more complete, yet who were never allowed the
character development necessary for movie or fandom immortality. (Kyle, for instance, remained recognizable for three main

reasons: his blonde, rugged good looks; his distinct British accent; and his usual station as transporter chief. This is not to belittle the acting talents of John Winston, but I wonder if Kyle would have survived the series if he had brown hair and a Boston accent and was a security guard?)

One such character who didn't survive past the series was at least as important to it as was Kyle. Lieutenant Leslie appeared in at least nine episodes (compared to Kyle's eleven), usually as a security guard, sometimes as a helmsman. Bjo Trimble's *Star Trek Concordance* describes Leslie's function as utility man, which, according to my dictionary, is someone who is expected to serve in any capacity when called on. Think of it: someone who can serve in *any* capacity onboard the *Enterprise*. In various episodes we occasionally saw Uhura act as a helmsman, Chekov as science officer, and Scott as transporter operator, but Leslie could conceivably do all of those and more, on a regular basis. Going by Bertrand Russell's definition of power as the ability to achieve ends, this makes Leslie, in my opinion, one of the most powerful people aboard the *Enterprise*.

Think of the enormous training and flexibility that must be required to perform any task for which you are called. Imagine you work in a big department store, and in one day (or even one week), the manager calls on you to be a stockman, a cashier, a shoe salesman, an accountant, a sporting goods salesman, and a delivery boy. These are all full-time jobs for most people. To be able to do *all* of them must require an enormous amount of inner strength and energy. Can you imagine, then, what must be required to perform any duty (or even any number of duties) on a starship, particularly the "pride of the fleet," the USS *Enterprise*?

Yet despite the implications of his job, and the fact that Leslie always seemed to "be there" in various episodes, he had very little to say or do. Ironically, his two biggest roles came when he was under the influence of alien mind control to disobey his captain. In "This Side of Paradise," Leslie is the officer waiting in line at the transporter room who, as a result of the alien spores, tells Kirk, in effect, to take this job and shove it. And in "And the Children Shall Lead," Kirk orders Leslie to take Spock, Uhura, and Sulu off the bridge when they disobey his orders. But because of the children's interference, Leslie hears only garbled orders he cannot understand, and just stands there doing nothing but contributing to Kirk's frustration.

It is something of an injustice that Leslie (who was played by Eddie Paskey) did not so much as cameo in the Star Trek movies, and (unlike Kyle, Sulu, and Uhura) that no one has even bothered to give him a first name. That, perhaps, can be solved. In "The Naked Time," Kirk tells an officer called "Lieutenant Ryan" to take over the helm from Sulu. It is possible that, his mind being diverted by the problems at hand, Kirk accidentally called the officer by his *first* name, and the officer, being polite and perhaps shy, didn't correct him. (Kirk occasionally had problems with names. Just ask Yeoman Smith or Marla McGivers.) It is therefore likely that the officer's full name was Lieutenant Ryan Leslie, since "Ryan" was also apparently played by Paskey.

Another character I would have liked to have seen in the movies appeared in only one episode, "Obsession." Ensign Garrovick was more than a security guard; he was the son of one of Kirk's first commanders, and although both felt that Kirk should pay no special attention to Garrovick, their roles in "Obsession" suggest otherwise. Kirk comes down hard on the young ensign when he hesitates in an incident similar to the one which cost Captain Garrovick his life eleven years earlier, and for which Kirk blamed himself. Kirk "apologizes"—or comes as close to doing so as a captain can to a junior officer—when he realizes that neither his own hesitation nor Garrovick's would have made any difference. Both get to redeem themselves by destroying the cloud creature that killed Captain Garrovick.

On the surface, Kirk and Ensign Garrovick seem to have much in common. Kirk obviously admired and respected Captain Garrovick, and Ensign Garrovick seems to immediately feel the same way about Kirk. Garrovick takes to self-pity when Kirk punishes him for the hesitation, and it is Kirk's personal "apology" that redeems Garrovick in his own eyes, when the efforts of Chapel and Spock have failed to do so. Later on, Garrovick tries to knock Kirk out when he thinks the captain intends to sacrifice himself to the creature. Garrovick plans to sacrifice himself instead. This act of rashness and devotion makes Garrovick look something like a Kirk-in-training (à la Chekov), but on a more personal level; the show ends with Kirk offering to tell the ensign stories about his father.

It is unfortunate that Ensign Garrovick was never seen again. His relationship with Kirk could have expanded to the point where Garrovick could have become the son Kirk never had. (Not so farfetched; there were those who wanted Kirk's real son, the late David Marcus, to join the *Enterprise* crew.) In the movies, Lieutenant Commander Garrovick could have served as

Kirk's much-belated security chief, as well as a fine member of his inner circle.

"Balance of Terror" introduced a female character who popped up once, maybe twice later. Phaser Specialist 2/C Angela Martine was to marry Robert Tomlinson in that episode, but he was killed in the battle with the Romulan ship. One episode later (or eleven, if you go by stardates), in "Shore Leave," Angela has switched her specialty to life sciences and her last name is now Teller. She could have very quickly married someone else, but it seems unlikely since she seems to become involved with Lieutenant Rodriguez in the episode. Whatever her name, Angela was played by Barbara Baldavin, who also appeared as "Angela," a communications officer in "Turnabout Intruder." Was she commissioned and transferred to yet another department, or was "Angela," a completely different character?

Personally, I'd rather believe they are indeed the same character, perhaps a flexible utility person like Leslie. This would explain how she became an officer in the two years between "Shore Leave" and "Turnabout Intruder"; perhaps she so impressed her superiors that she was given a "crash course" at Starfleet Academy or the equivalent of officer candidate school. A battlefield promotion is also possible. People as efficient and promising as Martine-Teller and Leslie would probably now be aboard one of the newer ships, instead of the "outmoded" *Enterprise*.

Speaking of "Balance of Terror," what do you suppose ever happened to the Vulcan-hating navigator, Lieutenant Andrew Stiles? Could he now be the arrogant Captain Styles of *Star Trek III: The Search for Spock*? If Angela Martine could change her name to Angela Teller, then he could certainly change the spelling of his. Paul Comi played the lieutenant, and James B. Sikking played the captain, but there are enough similarities between the actors to pass as the same man, fifteen years removed. If so, then Stiles' experience of being rescued by Spock from the phaser coolant fumes that killed poor Tomlinson didn't teach him not to be nasty. At any rate, Stiles seems to have lived up to his ancestor, the Captain Stiles who fought in the Romulan War a hundred years earlier.

Another member of Kirk's crew who displayed ambition and not a little streak of obnoxiousness was Lieutenant Vincent DeSalle. He was a navigator in "The Squire of Gothos" and "This Side of Paradise," but was promoted to assistant chief engineer in "Catspaw." In that episode, he takes command of the *Enterprise* while Kirk and Company are elsewhere. While no doubt competent and anxious to find his missing superiors, DeSalle appeared to be overly bossy and seemed to be saying "I'm in charge and don't you forget it!" to Chekov, Uhura, and the others. He was never seen again; perhaps Scotty found DeSalle too unbearable as an assistant and transferred him to another ship. Then again, perhaps, being newly promoted and left in charge of the *Enterprise* for the first time, DeSalle was merely trying too hard to do a good job, and is now a fine, level-headed commander.

Another navigator, Lieutenant Kevin Riley, appeared twice, and if given half a chance, could have been a real hell-raiser in the series. Irish and proud enough of it to rival Chekov, Riley, under the influence of the Psi 2000 virus, proclaimed himself a descendant of Irish kings and almost caused the *Enterprise* to crash by locking himself in the engine room and shutting off the engines. To make matters worse, he tortured the crew with his off-key singing! In that episode, we learn that Riley is a close friend of Sulu (some have speculated that they were at the Academy together). Born on Tarsus IV, Riley was orphaned at age four by the murderous Kodos the Executioner, and twenty years later he himself was almost poisoned to death by Kodos' daughter in "The Conscience of the King." Riley tried to get revenge by shooting Kodos, but Kirk prevented him from doing so.

Riley's flamboyancy could have provided a contrast to the "straight" members of Star Trek's cast. Like McCoy's "twentieth-century everyman," and Chekov's "young Kirk in training" Riley's character provided a springboard for characterization and stories, as well as a chance to have fun. Now, at about age thirty-nine, Riley would be older and more sure of himself, and more apt to cause trouble without getting into it.

While McCoy and Scotty were the only regular *Enterprise* officers to hold the rank of lieutenant commander, at least five other officers of that high rank served on the ship during the series. Three of them were Security Chief Giotto ("The Devil in the Dark"), Dr. Anne Mulhall of "Return to Tomorrow" (at least she wore the braid for that rank), and Records Officer Ben Finney ("Court-Martial"). The fourth was Lieutenant Commander Kelowitz, who appeared three times, but his exact function was never explained. In "The Galileo Seven," Kelowitz was in charge of the unsuccesful landing party that searched for the missing shuttlecraft; in "This Side of Paradise," he was part of the landing party; and in "Arena," he was one of Kirk's senior officers invited to the ambush on Cestus III. Perhaps Kelowitz—who wore a blue science shirt—was a second officer, aiding Spock in the transfer from second to first officer following the death of Gary Mitchell. After a while, Kelowitz became unnecessary, since Kirk and Spock are workaholics, and he moved on to another ship.

The fifth lieutenant commander on the *Enterprise* was, of course, Gary Mitchell, Kirk's original navigator and first officer in "Where No Man Has Gone Before." This character is fascinating, not only for his psionic superpowers that made him one of the show's more interesting villains, but also because, like McCoy and Kevin Riley, Mitchell was not the basic "military type" found in Starfleet. He was looser, more casual, a bit of a womanizer, and probably not as good a friend to Kirk as he should have been (as Leslie Thompson noted in *The Best of Trek #8*). Still, Gary must have had something going for him besides his basic charm and hidden mental powers. One does not, after all, get to be second-in-command of a starship without the necessary abilities, no matter how close one is to the captain. Too, I've always felt that Kirk was a pretty shrewd judge of character, and that Mitchell could not have remained his best friend all those years if he was merely pretending, as Thompson suggested. So Mitchell appears to have been a competent officer as well as a laid-back kind of guy who was perhaps too easily swayed by his darker side, but managed to rise above it enough to be a trusted executive and friend prior to his transformation. At any rate, Mitchell would be an interesting character to include in any retroactive stories taking place before "Where No Man Has Gone Before."

Many security guards were killed during the course of the series, but Lieutenant Galloway has the dubious distinction of being the only *recurring* character to bite the dust on the show. Galloway appeared in six episodes, including "Miri," "A Taste of Armageddon," and "The Omega Glory," in which he was killed by the renegade Captain Tracey. Like Leslie, we weren't told anything about Galloway, or given any clues to his personality, except an example of his loyalty and courage; even while wounded, he valiantly tried to reach for his phaser just before Tracey blasted him out of existence. Galloway was played by David L. Ross, who was later "resurrected" as Lieutenant Johnson in "Day of the Dove."

Now that the *Enterprise* crew is visiting Vulcan, maybe they will run into Dr. M'Benga, the cultured black physician who interned in a Vulcan ward. Perhaps he could even aid Spock in his recovery from "death," much as he did in "A Private Little War." Although M'Benga was capable of handling non-Vulcan patients (he helped conduct an autopsy in "That Which Survives"), it is quite possible that he would return to the world of his medical specialty, since there seem to be few Vulcans in Starfleet. It is also conceivable that M'Benga might eventually replace the aging Dr. McCoy as the *Enterprise*'s chief surgeon— but not for many years yet.

Other crewmembers popped up on the *Enterprise* from time to time, providing a sort of "background continuity" that enhanced the realism of Star Trek. Instead of populating the ship with an endless army of faces and names, Gene Roddenberry and Company gave us occasional familiar ones, including Lieutenant DePaul, helmsman ("Arena," "A Taste of Armageddon"); Lieutenant Hansen, navigator ("Court-Martial," "The Menagerie"); Lieutenant John Farrell, navigator (Mudd's Women," "Miri," "The Enemy Within"); Mr. Lemli, engineer/security guard ("Return to Tomorrow," "The Way to Eden," "And the Children Shall Lead," "Turnabout Intruder"); Lieutenant O'Neil, transporter operator ("Return of the Archons," "The Tholian Web"); and several unnamed others.

We never learned anything about these characters, and they are easy to overlook, but to at least this one fan, their presence made the *Enterprise* seem more complete. Even though a few faces showed up in both of the last Star Trek films, the practice of naming and involving these characters in the action seems largely forgotten. Which is a shame, because they, in their own obscure but important way, serve to expand that most significant aspect of the Star Trek universe: reality. And, for us, they're fun. Spotting them was kind of an "inside" bonus for faithful viewers—"Oh, I've seen *that* guy before!"

ISHMAEL IN SPACE: LITERARY ALLUSIONS IN THE WRATH OF KHAN

by Marc Swanson

Many fans have asked us for an article discussing this subject; here it is. Perhaps the best way we can introduce it is to quote from the letter Marc sent when he submitted this article to us: "I got so reinvolved with Star Trek after reading through some of those [The Best of Trek] books, I went out and rented a VCR just to get another look at Wrath of Khan. I watched it twice through for the sheer joy of a good story, well acted and well told. While I watched, something nagged at the back of my mind. I knew there was more to this movie than slam-bang space opera, but I didn't know what. I also knew I had heard some of the dialogue before, but I couldn't remember where. Later that night as I was drifting off to sleep, it started to hit me. I got up at two in the morning to write the first draft of this article."

By portraying the future, Star Trek is helping to make it. A perfect example of this is computers:

Those who grew up on Star Trek (including myself) did not grow up surrounded by computers, but we knew about them from watching Star Trek. It its own small way, the program helped to prepare us for the thousands of computers we use daily in business, government, and even in our own homes. Star Trek showed us a world where machines stored and retrieved information with routine efficiency, and helped to prepare us for the future we have already begun to live in.

Oh sure, even in the glittering, high-tech, neutronium-plated world of the twenty-third century, there were a few holdouts. We saw living anachronisms like Samuel Cogley, the lawyer who insisted on using law*books*. But Star Trek has always gloried in the progress, both physical and spiritual, of humankind. A prime example of that progress is computers, and they turn up memorably all over the place—from Landru to the M-5 unit, from Nomad to Vejur.

However, much of the resonance and effectiveness of *Star Trek II: The Wrath of Khan* depends not upon computers, but upon books. The spirit of a handful of literary classics pervades this very *literary* film. We actually see several books in the movie—books probably about as rare in the twenty-third century as ancient scrolls are today. Those books are visual clues to the themes of *Wrath of Khan*. When we understand its literary allusions, we can also understand the film on a deeper level, because the camera does not show us these old-style books by accident. The themes and actions of *Wrath of Khan* are closely tied to the classic themes of all literature: revenge, pursuit, loss, love, friendship, sacrifice. The books behind *Wrath of Khan* call forth entire clusters of ideas and associations to our minds, and help us fit this one film, or one book, into their larger place in the field of cinema, or literature.

Even before the credits start to roll on *Wrath of Khan*, we are already in possession of one fact which points to a literary movie. As most fans are aware, *Star Trek II: The Wrath of Khan* continued the story begun in the televised episode "Space Seed." At the end of "Space Seed," Kirk offers Khan the choice of being marooned on Alpha Ceti V or reeducation by the Federation. Khan replies by asking Kirk if he has ever read Milton.

Kirk later explains Khan's query to a confused Scotty. It was a reference to John Milton's *Paradise Lost*, an epic poem dealing with the war between Heaven and Hell, God and Satan. Kirk quotes Satan's arrogant credo: "It is better to rule in Hell than serve in Heaven." Khan claims this credo for himself.

But in *Wrath of Khan*, the books alluded to have changed and the characters play out different roles. For Kirk and Spock, the book is Charles Dickens' *A Tale of Two Cities*; for Khan, it is Herman Melville's *Moby-Dick*.

Khan's transition from the proud, Byronic hero of "Space Seed" to the vengeful nemesis of *Wrath of Khan* first appears in a tidy visual metaphor. Before Khan appears onscreen, we watch Chekov and Captain Terrell exploring the cargo containers found on Alpha Ceti V. Chekov catches sight of a bookshelf and goes over to investigate. The camera gives us only a brief glimpse of the titles, but we can see *King Lear*, the Bible, and *Paradise Lost* and *Paradise Regained* standing upright on the shelf. Placed above these books are two paperbacks whose titles are very clear: another copy of *Paradise Lost* and a copy of *Moby-Dick*—

lying *on top* of Milton. The visual implication is subtle and unobtrusive, but plain: the old Khan could best be understood by reading *Paradise Lost*; to understand the new one, we need *Moby-Dick*.

Although Khan is still brilliant, still ruthless and treacherous, the years and solitude have nonetheless altered him. The Khan of "Space Seed" was an opportunist in search of power. The Khan of the film has become obsessed with revenge. In *Moby-Dick*, Captain Ahab dedicates his life, his ship, and his crew to the pursuit of the White Whale. In *Wrath of Khan*, Khan bends all his vast abilities to the pursuit of James Kirk. Ahab uses the whaling ship *Pequod* as an instrument of vengeance. Khan uses the stolen starship *Reliant*.

In *Moby-Dick* (Chapter 36), Ahab calls the crew of the *Pequod* aft to tell them of his quest. He informs them that they have not shipped on board to hunt whales, but to hunt one whale. The whole crew joins with Ahab, pledging their lives to the death of Moby Dick. But one man steps forward to speak out against this quest. Starbuck, first mate of the *Pequod*, asks Ahab why they must all join in his madness, why he must pursue Moby Dick.

A voice of reason also speaks out onboard the *Reliant*. Joachim, the helmsman, protests to Khan that they possess a starship and the freedom to use it. He wisely counsels Khan to seize advantage of the situation while he still can. Why, he asks, should they pursue this Admiral Kirk?

The old Khan may not have taken this advice, but he would have listened with respect and understanding to Joachim's calming voice, just as the old Ahab would have listened to reason. But they both give the same answer to their respective seconds-in-command: "He tasks me," they say. "He tasks me, and I shall have him."

Both men dedicate themelves, their crews, and their ships to follow the chase even into death. Ahab vows, "I'll chase him round Good Hope, and round the Horn, and round the Norway Maelstrom, and round perdition's flames before I give him up." Khan updates this vow to its twenty-third-century equivalent— "round the moons of Nibia, round the Antares maelstrom, and round perdition's flames"—but his intent remains the same as Ahab's.

Ahab reveals the source of his relentless vengeance; the White Whale bit off his leg and removed a living part of him. Khan similarly blames Kirk for the death of a "part" of himself—his wife, Marla McGivers.

When Kahn and Ahab finally join battle with their enemies, both of them are forced to fight in an alien element. For Ahab, it is the ocean; for Khan, it is space. Khan even uses the *Reliant* as if it were an oceangoing ship—Spock makes reference to his "two-dimensional" tactics. Kirk and the Whale are very much at home in their elements; they fight on familiar turf.

Khan, like Ahab, finally perishes in the battle, and the *Reliant*, like the *Pequod*, is destroyed. As Khan lies dying, seconds away from the explosion of the Genesis Device, he echoes Ahab's last words to the Whale: "From hell's heart I stab at thee; for hate's sake, I spit my last breath at thee." Unrepentant to the end, Khan dies secure in the belief that he has finally rid the universe of James T. Kirk.

But Khan has reckoned without Spock and without the other book that hovers over this story. The parallel allusions to this book are not nearly as evident or important, but one theme from it dominates Spock's role.

At the beginning of the film, Kirk carries a book under his arm. A few minutes later, Kirk reads its first words aloud to Spock: "It was the best of times, it was the worst of times" —the opening words from Charles Dickens' *A Tale of Two Cities*.

The book tells the story of Sidney Carton, a dissolute young Englishman who surmounts his own character flaws and gives up his life to save his friends. He sacrifices himself to die on the guillotine of revolutionary France in the place of another.

The parallels with Spock are obvious. He too overcomes his own Vulcan characteristics to sacrifice himself so that his friends might live. When Kirk quotes from this book at the beginning of the film, we learn that it was a birthday gift from Spock. In retrospect, we can see that this scene prepares us for the larger gift Spock will make of his own life. In literary terms, it "foreshadows" Spock's sacrifice.

Kirk drives the point further home at the end of *Wrath of Khan* when he again quotes from *A Tale of Two Cities*. He says of Spock, "It is a far, far better thing I do than I have ever done; a far, far better rest that I go to than I have ever known." These were Sidney Carton's words as he mounted the steps of the guillotine. They are also the last words from the novel, nicely rounding out Kirk's previous quotation of the first words.

Khan's quotations from *Moby-Dick* are appropriate both to his character and to the plot, even if we don't know where they came from. But when we learn that his source is an epic of madness, vengeance, and pursuit, it expands our understanding of Khan's character and his motivations. When Kirk quotes from a literary classic of self-sacrifice, our appreciation for the structure and themes of the film deepens.

Like all works of art, *Wrath of Khan* can stand by itself. But, also like other works of art, the film works on many levels at once. After Kirk reads the opening sentence from the book Spock has given him for his birthday, he looks up at the Vulcan and asks, ''Message, Spock?'' Spock replies, ''None that I am conscious of, admiral.'' The literary facets of the film work in the same way. Like Spock, we do not need to be conscious of the literary allusions and parallels in *Wrath of Khan* in order for them to do their work.

WALKING ON WATER AND OTHER THINGS JAMES KIRK CAN'T DO

by James H. Devon

James Devon's article "Beneath the Surface: The Surrealistic Star Trek" (The Best of Trek #8) was extremely popular and well liked by our readers. It was also extremely unpopular and vehemently disliked by our readers. Why this mixed reaction? We think it's because James says not only what he thinks, but what other fans think, as well . . . whether or not they know they think that way or want to think that way. Strong opinions make for strong reactions, as they say, and we're getting ready for another flood of mail—on both sides—about this article. But that only makes sense, because James himself takes both sides.

It's amazing. James T.Kirk has become a complicated phenomenon. He isn't the simple, good-against-evil Mr. Nice Guy character we all used to know and love; he's someone else. That's the way some fans would tell it, anyway. Some people have become quite vehement, claiming they've lost interest in Kirk because of a change in his character in the movies. All this despite the fact that he is undoubtedly the most "popular" character in the show. Maybe that's his problem—maybe his massive popularity has done him an injustice as far as Star Trek is concerned. Some fans are discouraged by the "flawed" Kirk they see on the movie screen, constantly bemoaning the fact that he's no longer the twenty-third-century King Arthur they imagined him to be in the series.

By the way, if James Kirk is "no Boy Scout," neither is he a King Arthur. He never was. That vicious rumor was started by some early, sweetly naive fan who evidently had no idea what medieval writing and the Arthurian legends entail. No, Kirk was no Arthur in the series and he is no Arthur now. Thank God. He was and is—at least according to the man who should be credited for creating him—a very imperfect, but idealistic human being. A man who could lust, who could be jealous, who could even let his prejudices get in the way of his decisions once in a while. A man capable of making mistakes.

Those who don't believe that might enlighten themselves by putting their hands on a copy of Gene Roddenberry's writer's guide to the series. In it, he outlined what the characters should be like. True, all of the characters developed according to what this or that writer or producer or actor did to them, but that does not fully explain what I can only call the "Mary Sue" version of Kirk. I will say what few fan writers have the guts to say these days: If it were up to the fans—and I don't just mean the lady fans out there—James T. Kirk would have nothing to offer Star Trek as a character. He'd be a wimp, a goody-two-shoes, or even worse, a King Arthur. (Thank goodness we have at least been spared a "chaste" Kirk. Then it would indeed be "King Artie, step aside!")

Jim Kirk is a man of honor, sure, but with limitations. The morals of the twenty-third century are not all that clear in Star Trek (regardless of what the K/S people, with all their convoluted skips in logic, like to maintain), but we are given no reason to expect that it is customary for a man to have quite so many women (just about one every episode) over the span of a year as does our lusty captain. I'm not knocking it, I'm just saying it isn't very "Arthurian." Of course, his loves are usually presented to us as deep, true loves (or, in some cases, old flames, as in "Shore Leave"), but even that is kind of kinky, and more than a little unbelievable on such a grand scale.

Then, of course, there are those he plays along for the sake of getting out of a fix. That's even worse. You know the story, and more than a few would-be Kirk fans find it offensive that Kirk so often finds it necessary to stoop so low. One would think a man of his brilliance and military imagination would be able to come up with a more sophisticated means of solving the problem than trying to charm, bed, or otherwise infatuate the "enemy" female in a story. Still, he does it time and time again.

But at least his behavior *does* prove that he's not entirely the white knight of the *Enterprise.* He is shrewd and tough, and if he has to play the lady along for the sake of saving his ship and crew, he'll do it. And, interestingly, he always seems to enjoy it!

The crux of it is, Jim Kirk may have nerves of steel, but his glands are quite something else. It's great that his libido is so active, but all in all it's done more harm than good as far as the *Enterprise* is concerned. He almost lost everything in "City on the Edge of Forever" because of his love for Edith. In "Elaan of Troyius" he nearly causes an intergalactic incident. (And let me pooh-pooh right here the idea that we can blame it on Elaan's magic tears. Why should Kirk always be excused for his failings? This guy is supposed to be *strong*, right? Had one of Kirk's men fallen for the old magic tear trick, Kirk would've had him court-martialed) In "Requiem for Methuselah" Mr. Spock and Dr. McCoy are just about to go crazy trying to save the crew from a deadly plague while Kirk spends his time being goo-goo-eyed over an android! (Kirk, incidentally, has trouble distinguishing androids from real ladies. Rather curious, as we all know he is a man of considerable experience. See such episodes as "Shore Leave" and "What Are Little Girls Made Of?")

So let's once and for all put an end to the myth that a macho Kirk is a sign of strength. And don't get me wrong . . . I like the Kirk who gets "tricked" by ladies with magic tears and microchips for brains. And I can even understand why the ladies in Star Trek fandom find it endearing—but don't, please don't insist upon *excusing him* for it. He flubbed, and that's that. He's human. As inferior to Mr. Spock, in certain ways, as is Dr. McCoy.

So much for the macho Kirk. In Star Trek, machismo is not necessarily a positive attribute. It's just *an* attribute, like brown hair or hazel eyes. And sometimes a hindrance as far as our beloved captain is concerned. When we get to see Kirk this way, as a man who puts love or affection or glands or whatever above his duty—however momentarily—we see a fellow who maybe isn't quite the perfect Arthur we thought he was. Arthur is a Christ figure in literature, after all, and sexual purity was something for which he strove.

Was Kirk's *Enterprise* Camelot?

I never saw a round table. That is, at no time are we able to consider that the opinion of all the characters in the series or movies are treated with equal respect. Look at the times McCoy's advice, good though it is, was rejected ("Obsession" and "Return to Tomorrow" are prime examples). In the series Kirk is, and should be, the only boss. His ship—like any military establishment—must be run by dictatorship. There are checks and balances, fortunately. We learned in "The Deadly Years" that a commander can be removed from duty. And we know that McCoy, as ship's surgeon, has perhaps the single most powerful position of authority, in that he can declare Kirk medically or mentally unfit for command. But we also learned in "Turnabout

Intruder'' that doing so isn't necessarily easy. It involves a military tribunal and a whole lot of hard proof.

Kirk tries to be fair, of course. He is fair, for the most part. That is the sign of a good commander. But there are times (again, ''Obsession,'' again, ''Return to Tomorrow'') when his judgment is clouded by good old-fashioned prejudice or ambition. In ''Obsession'' he risks all in a vendetta against the deadly cloud creature, partly because he is consumed with guilt from a supposed failure (again, macho Kirk fans—is this possible?) to stop the thing in a previous encounter when he was under the command of Captain Garrovick. He chases the creature, remember, in what is really an obsessed, blind determination, and all the time he's supposed to be elsewhere, delivering desperately needed medical supplies to another planet.

And to make things worse, Garrovick's son is now serving on his *Enterprise*. The young Garrovick, an ensign, pulls the same trick Kirk had pulled years before when he meets the blood-consuming cloud creature—he fails to fire at it immediately, which means it has time to kill a fellow crewman. (Kirk's failure was much bigger, by the way. His flub cost the life of Captain Garrovick and half the crew of his ship, the USS *Farragut*.) So now Kirk has double blinders. He's really mixed up. With extreme prejudice, he sees in the boy's failure a reflection of his own past sins. It's the only real father/son relationship Kirk has in Star Trek, and it's good writing. (The father/son relationship of *Wrath of Khan* and *The Search for Spock* was an absolute failure. Due not to Shatner or Butrick, or even their characters in the films, but to the high and mighty ''don't change my captain'' attitude of the fans.)

Well, the captain will change, my friends. Because he is a good character. All the hero worship in the world won't alter that, but it does color it, even in the eyes of Shatner himself. He seems obsessed himself, these days, with making sure that he gets full, uncontested attention on the big screen, as if, like the admiral, he feels insecure in his middle age. It is ironic that the fans, much as they love Shatner and Kirk, have been instrumental in helping to change that by responding (however unaware of what they're doing) so favorably to the movies in which there are somewhat fewer Shatner scenes and a bit more of Chekov, Uhura, Scotty, or McCoy.

So in *Wrath of Khan* and most especially in *The Search for Spock*, we have a bespectacled, somewhat rusty and confused Admiral Kirk. To those who enjoy the more realistic view of

Star Trek, it is refreshing to see Kirk make a mistake, as he undeniably did in *Wrath of Khan* when he failed to raise the *Enterprise*'s shields on approaching the hijacked *Reliant*. Please, let's not try to excuse it by saying he knew the *Reliant* to be a Starfleet vessel. He *also knew* that there was something amiss in space by that time. Precautions were in order!

But, oh, how the fans love to defend Kirk on that one. It's those hopeless thinkers who remark quite angrily that "Kirk wouldn't do that!" or "Kirk would know better!" who keep Star Trek down in kiddie land and chain Kirk to the role of superhero. *Of course* Kirk could make a mistake or forget something about the refitting of his ship (*Star Trek: The Motion Picture*) or could be lax with a rule (getting "caught with his pants down" in *The Search for Spock*). Not just because its necessary to the plot, which it is, but also because he is not Spock, either. He is human, and maybe, having been stuck much of the time on planet Earth, he's just a bit rusty. It could be he envies people like Scotty and McCoy who know what they want, and don't allow prejudices about age or the lure of ambition to run their lives. Kirk has hang-ups; why shouldn't he? And one of them is that he can't make up his mind if he wants to run Starfleet or sail the adventurous, starry skies. Until *The Search for Spock*, Kirk doesn't really know himself. He's been struggling with his desire to achieve more and more success and his almost greedy need for adventure.

In *The Search for Spock*, though, he finds out something about himself, and it is virtually his journey into manhood—at this late date! He discovers, like Dorothy in *The Wizard of Oz* and Spock in *Star Trek: The Motion Picture*, that happiness lies in his own backyard, at home. The difference for Kirk is that home is not what he thought it was. It isn't Earth, it isn't the Fleet, it isn't even the *Enterprise*. It's friendship.

As Joyce Tullock is so fond of pointing out, Kirk belongs with Spock and McCoy. He's part of them, they're part of him. Not in any altruistic, mumbo-jumbo spiritual way, but in a real, human, no-nonsense fashion. They are his friends. It's simple.

That brings to mind another of Kirk's attributes that many fans seem to resent. Occasionally, about certain things, he's not so bright. He has to learn the hard way. He has to take his time to discover that career and prestige and success are the least of it. In *The Search for Spock* he had to make a decision that literally might shatter his life. He's done similar things earlier in his career (disobeying orders in "Amok Time" so he could get

Spock to Vulcan; trying to stall moving on to his next mission in "For the World Is Hollow" when McCoy was in need of his guidance), but somehow they were not of this stature, and certainly never before was he confronted with the kind of loss he faced in *The Search for Spock*. In "For the World Is Hollow" he was perhaps ready to move on; it was a matter of obeying orders. And even in "Amok Time" he worries about the repercussions of his actions.

But in *The Search for Spock* he took a gallant stand, and we must assume at this point in the story it was primarily for McCoy. McCoy was the one who was dying, in case anyone forgets. *Katra* or no *katra*, as far as Kirk knew, Spock's body was dead and gone. But McCoy was alive and suffering and it looked like it was going to be a pretty messy business. So Kirk, now a seasoned, respected and trusted admiral of the Fleet, has reached the point where he throws it all over without hesitation, for the sake of a friend.

That is a Kirk who has grown. And that is a Kirk who, in the eyes of a lot of people, has done a very dumb thing. It's the kind of guy I can admire. But to almost anyone, he really messed up on this one. He hijacked a Starfleet ship, took her to a forbidden area in space, and blew her up. Not something that will look particularly good on his record.

I've heard from many people who don't like the James T. Kirk of the movies because they think he's overblown and arrogant. Their complaints surprise me, because Jim Kirk was *always* overblown and arrogant. It's one of his many charming flaws, and if he swaggers a bit too much for the average American science fiction fan, then maybe they should take a look around. There are a lot of swaggerers in the world. They're for real. To expect a man who can do the things Jim Kirk does to be humble is like expecting a test pilot to be afraid of heights. Kirk is gutsy, lusty, abrasive, and annoying. Those who insist this observation is just a kind of prejudice are kidding themselves, possibly because they identify with the good captain and don't care for the negative connotations of his extremely self-assured nature.

Maybe audience identification has been a lot of Kirk's problem since he found the big screen. When he was on the itsy-bitsy TV screen, we could watch and admire that glowing self-confidence and could identify with it as a sort of alter ego. His mistakes in judgment—and he did make them—weren't quite so glaring. We could always just kind of wink at them and blame them on someone or something else. Or we could even ignore them entirely. But now when Jim flashes his brass, argues with his chief medical officer, makes a mistake in military judgment, or becomes just plain pushy and manipulative (his eagerness to take over the *Enterprise* in *STTMP*) on the big screen, its a bit more than the would-be heroes in the theater audience can take. To them, Jim Kirk has been a reflection of themselves—or how they fancy themselves—and here he is, making an ass of himself in 70-millimeter. For some, it's unforgivable.

And all the time he is just being the same old lovable Jim Kirk of the series. Only, well, bigger.

If many of these complaints about the "imperfect" Kirk have reached Bill Shatner, it hasn't made him change his attitude so far. Shatner is playing the swaggering Kirk to the hilt, and he thankfully hasn't been too concerned about the good admiral's occasional lapses into imperfection. His contract allows him some script control, but the stubborn, self-centered, midlife-crisis Kirk swaggered right from Movie One into Movie Two. Only, in *The Wrath of Khan* he put on the glasses to show the underlying vulnerability of the man. And to show his vanity right there out in the open.

Lest we forget, Kirk is part of the Spock and McCoy relationship. Spock and McCoy both came to the friendship more or less unsure of themselves. But Kirk's ego taught them to like themselves, and his association with them gave them strength enough to grow to the point where—just maybe—they have even grown a bit beyond him. We have Kirk's ego to thank for that, so let's not put it down.

He was and is a man who, on the final count, forges ahead, does what he wants, and damns the regulations! Need we list the episodes in which he ignored the Prime Directive and instilled (or even forced) on an alien planet the good old tradition of the white Anglo-Saxon western world? On such occasions Kirk is hardly the open-minded man-of-the-universe. Hardly the deep, sophisticated, sensitive thinker many prefer to imagine him to be. But his behavior, in its straightforward simplicity, is refreshing. It's honest.

Now that the word "honest" has come up, it's time to explore that aspect of our non-superhero. Kirk isn't always completely honest. Not with himself, that is. We learned that in "Obsession," we learned it in *Star Trek: The Motion Picture*, we certainly learned it in "Requiem for Methuselah." Each of those stories present Kirk at a delicate time in his life, show him stumbling for a time (don't worry; Spock and McCoy will get him out of it in the end), staggering between what he knows to be true and what he wishes to be true. If he were perfectly honest with himself at all times, he'd be a bore. And he'd certainly be of no use to the feel and storyline of Star Trek. Remember, Gene Roddenberry wanted him to be *human*. Not a blunderer, certainly, though that's how those identifying fans we mentioned earlier evidently classify any mistake he might make. In their desire to worship him, they absolutely cannot forgive him an error, so they feel compelled to explain it away, or more childishly yet, blame the writer! But Kirk can be seen as a real person who has blind spots just as we all do.

Jim's blind spot, as we've noted before, primarily involves his manliness. He has trouble in two major areas: women and ego. Three, if we count his midlife crisis, but let's hope that's a passing thing. By ego, of course, I can and do mean a lot of things. In "Obsession" he felt that he had failed, and his ego was injured; happening once again upon the killer cloud had opened old wounds. In *Star Trek: The Motion Picture* he wanted command of the *Enterprise* again, when he might have served the cause better by allowing Captain Decker to hold the center seat while he himself concentrated on the overall problem of V'Ger and the immense military decisions that had to be made.

Kirk's flaws remain Kirk's flaws, too. Nowhere do we see him trying to change his nature when it comes to women and ego. These "problems," as they've been called, are not really problems in the sense of something to be corrected. Not where the character of James T. Kirk, adventurer, captain, admiral, and man of the world comes into play. They are traits, features for us to recognize, analyze, appreciate. (And to an extent, Shatner has been typecast by the macho image of Kirk. It has not helped his career. It certainly hasn't encouraged him to grow as an artist. It's ironic that because of his typecast "Kirk" image, his best performances consistently come as Kirk.)

The flawed Kirk of the movies is honestly no different from the Kirk of the series, except that he has grown into a more well-defined, believable individual. Kirk's ego and his lusty, almost cavalier attitude toward women have not changed. But his view of himself has matured. In *Wrath of Khan* he comes face to face with himself. It takes Spock's death to show him what his life has been about. And he recognizes at last, in *The Search for Spock*, his own mortality. He's seen Spock die. And now, McCoy.

In *The Search for Spock* he is very much fighting for his own life, and for a friendship that represents life.

What is he doing in *The Search for Spock*? He is being his old egotistical, swaggering, macho self. Because it works for Kirk to be that way. It's the way he keeps himself—and his friends— alive. There is nothing wrong with ego if it is well placed and used in a positive manner, as its influence on the friendship proves. Kirk's ego is very positive. He thinks he can steal the *Enterprise*. He does. He thinks he can return to Genesis and retrieve Spock's body. Well, he does. He thinks he can defeat Commander Kruge and his crew, though the odds are tremendous. He sure does that.

But Kirk pays a price in *The Search for Spock*. He makes a great sacrifice. Not his son, contrary to what Sarek tells Kirk at the end of the film. Poor David would no doubt have been killed whether Kirk had come along or not. No, the real price for saving Spock and McCoy is the *Enterprise*. And it is a fair price to pay. A good deal, in fact. A bargain. A piece of scrap metal in exchange for the lives and souls of his two best friends. (Let's not forget in our sentimentalism that *Enterprise* was about to be put in mothballs. How much better that she should die to spare the lives of her crew! How poetic! How *grand*! Would she have it any other way?)

There are those who criticize Kirk for his destruction of the ship. And they criticize the writers of the script. But to be fair, a script, when it reaches a certain point, writes itself. No, the *Enterprise* had to die. And here is a lesson for Trekkies around the world to learn, though it's surprising that they haven't learned it already: Human beings are more valuable than things. Beyond comparison.

If the Jim Kirk of the movies is a difficult character for some people to grasp, it is because he is simply more of the same Kirk we've always known. On a larger scale, Jim Kirk is seen many ways by many people, of course. And we can always expect children to see him as something of a superhero, beyond reproach. We can expect some people to see him, whether they realize it or not, as the ideal of white Anglo-Saxon Protestants, too. A sort Aryan dream boy, cleansed of the sins of prejudice and racism. There's no real harm in that, I suppose. But to those who look deeper, he has more to offer than that. He is man, a real, fallible human being who strives with the tools of his own nature to find a better way in the universe. He is complex, filled with love, filled with ambition, driven by a lust for life and sincerity of will. He has come a long way and made a lot of mistakes. He has argued with his friends and he has learned from them. He has lost them and regained them. He has loved women, begotten children, and found himself alone. He could not be a good father, because he was too good a sailor. He could not be a good husband, because he cared too much for a career that spanned not only years of his life, but space itself. It's ironic. Jim Kirk could be true only to the *Enterprise*. And he sacrificed her for his friends.

Jim Kirk is no saint, no god. He certainly can't walk on water and he has never pulled a sword from a stone. Holiness has never been his interest, purity never his ambition. And when it comes right down to it, Jim Kirk can't do a lot of things that a lot of ordinary men can do. He is too much of a renegade, almost blasphemous in the face of authority and convention. Home by the hearth and family tradition just don't suit him. They never will. But we can say this of him, and celebrate the great measure of his human success: He is a man who understands what it is to be human, to make mistakes, to be hurt by them, to learn from them. He is a hero, but he has come a long road to reach the form of heroism which is most noble. He has learned to give and give well. Most of all, he has come to know, without hesitation, the value of a friend. And he has learned all this by being the man he is, not the man of perfection, but the man of life. One of those rare men with the guts to make a decision, he has made mistakes along the way, and he has bounced back with vigor and with love.

Go ahead and swagger, Jim Kirk. You deserve it. You earned it. And most of us wouldn't have it any other way.

TREK ROUNDTABLE: LETTERS FROM OUR READERS

Cara Beckenstein
Howard Beach, N.Y.

Last year, at the advanced age of thirty-two, I discovered Star Trek. And this year I discovered the *Best of Trek* series. I knew there was such an entity as a "Trekkie," but had no idea of the extent of the obsession! Actually, I was in the bookstore looking for the paperbacks about the Star Trek movies and found yours by happy accident. Star Trek is a lot of fun for me, but I can't help seeing it in a slightly tongue-in-cheek way. Perhaps that's because I'm a "sixties person," and the show is *so* sixties. (I was too busy getting stoned in the years 1966–69 to notice television, and never saw an original Star Trek episode.) Mr. Chekov's Beatle haircut (or is it a Beatle wig?) looks too silly to be for real. A friend assures me, however, that Mr. Chekov was considered "cute" by teenaged women in those days—and probably some teenaged men, also, though that's another subject. I do like the sixties tone of Star Trek, however, because it was an era of humanitarianism. I *reach* those hairy musicians in search of Eden, and I appreciate the strongly antifascist and antiracist values that Star Trek reiterates again and again. Speaking as an incurable liberal, I now know for a fact that old hippies never die—they watch Star Trek reruns.

My tongue-in-cheek attitude comes in part as a response to the simply rotten treatment of women in the series. I thought Dr. Greenberg's psychoanalytic case study of Star Trek was extremely valuable in explaining, at least in part, why this was so, and I appreciate his taking a stand against the misogynist tone of the television episodes. Women in the twenty-third century haven't come a long way, even though they're now traversing deep space. Only the traditional jobs are available to them: There's the nurse

(Chapel), the telephone operator/receptionist/secretary (Uhura), the waitress (various yeomen), the mother (Amanda), the whore (everyone else). Even the supposedly well-educated professional types, like the historian and the anthropologist, seem more dedicated to pursuit of love and sex than to their respective academic disciplines, and any male alien with an appropriate leer can steer them right off course.

The universe is apparently populated by female aliens who prefer to wear designer underwear and not much else. Even Zarabeth, condemned to life in the Ice Age, shed her pelt to reveal a very naked navel. And, of course, women may *not* be starship captains, as that frustrated bitch Janice Lester found out. Let's face it—Star Trek thrives on a large measure of superficial T and A, supported by the underlying belief that women are monsters. The only way to tolerate this aspect of the series is to laugh at it, although every time I see a new female alien wearing hip boots and a bikini it gets harder and harder to do so.

Then there's James T. Kirk—the Luckiest Man in the Universe. I never saw someone get punched in the jaw as often as he does and walk away without a bruise. One of my favorite episodes is "The Enemy Within." I suppose I needed to see some sign of Kirk's vulnerability, and I certainly enjoyed the philosophical approach to the question of good and evil that this episode offers; McCoy, I believe, is the one who figures out that both aspects are necessary, both are good. This was a bit of insightful television writing—it still is, in fact, considering the hype and drivel TV offers these days.

I do get tired of hearing McCoy's stock phrases: "He's dead, Jim!" "I'm a doctor, not a———(fill in the blank)!" "You pointy-eared Vulcan!" and "Do something!" Also, I don't think Scotty and Chekov, with their ridiculous ethnicity, go over too well. I'm only thankful that the writers refrained from giving Uhura and Sulu any obvious, stereotypical racial characteristics. I do bemoan the fact that Nichelle Nichols was never given much of anything to do on the show. That woman had the ability to take the phrase "They're not responding, sir," and give it more emotive energy than Bette Davis. She was sorely underutilized throughout the series.

So, why do I watch at all? Well, of course, there's Mr. Spock. I have to admit that he's the reason I, like so many others, got hooked. It's difficult to explain, although I understand that reams have been written about his special appeal. I recently saw an airing of a TV special in which Leonard Nimoy discusses his favorite episodes, as well as the input he had into the development of Spock the Vulcan. I found his explanation of the Vulcan salute's evolution fascinating. Nimoy's personal involvement accounts, in large part, for the depth and complexity of Spock, and his intelligence imparts Spock with an irony and humor that might have been missing with a lesser actor.

Probably my favorite episode is "Mirror, Mirror." The transformation of characters from good to evil on the ruthless parallel *Enterprise* is fun to watch, but perhaps the most profound aspect is the implication that Spock, in his objectivity, can rise above the barbarism of his surroundings. Kirk comes across as particularly inspired in this episode. In any case, I probably like Spock because I like Leonard Nimoy. Although I do agree that in order to bring us more information about Spock's early years, another actor ought to be able to tackle the role, I still feel that Nimoy *is* Spock, and whoever attempts to put on those ears had better do his homework.

An interesting tidbit of trivia for me, as a student of astrology, is that Nimoy and Shatner were born very close together in time—within a few days of each other, and in the pioneering sign of Aries. Individuals whose Suns are in conjunction to one another often share a deeply felt common purpose and are capable of intense, mutual understanding. The concrete manifestation of this astrological principle in the relationship of Shatner/Kirk to Nimoy/Spock is heartening.

Just a few words on the articles in *The Best of Trek #9*. The spoof by Kiel Stuart proves once and for all that ridicule is the highest form of flattery. I also very much enjoyed Philip Carpenter's well-written and thoughtful rebuttal. Certainly the highlight of this issue was the psychoanalytic perspective on Star Trek and Spock by Harvey Greenberg. What good writing, what good thinking, what a wonderful approach to the series. While I don't count myself among the Freudians, I appreciated Dr. Greenberg's effort very much, and would like to read more by him.

Lastly, I'd like to comment further on the "blind spot" mentioned by Janeen DeBoard. I agree that keeping Star Trek alive necessarily requires allowing other actors to play the role so well-defined by the original cast. (I'm not convinced, however, that any of the actors we know and love are over the hill to the extent that they can't depict an ongoing adventure). But to show us the early days of Kirk, Spock, and McCoy, as well as Uhura, Scotty, Sulu, etc., the producers are obliged to cast young actors. This is progress, not revisionism! The resistance of Trekkies to the idea of new actors is very understandable. We have actual family ties, if you will, to Shatner, Kelley, Nimoy, et al, and the thought of strangers filling in their shoes may feel like infidelity. But we ought to remember that Star Trek is a fantasy, and therein lies its strength and resiliency. It can be whatever we choose. As I said earlier, Nimoy, created Spock and nobody could hope to replace him, but other actors, by studying Nimoy's performances, *can* play young Spock successfully. The imagination we as viewers employ in order to appreciate Star Trek can be called up in order to appreciate other actors' portrayals. There's no other way, ultimately, to keep Star Trek alive in the visual media. This of it from the standpoint of possibilities—endless!

Margaret Boyd
Christchurch, New Zealand

I was surprised to see in Trek Roundtable (*The Best of Trek #9*) two letters from Scottish fans saying how difficult they found it to get these books. I didn't think people living in Great Britain would have any such problem, so I am moved to tell you how it is for a New Zealand Star Trek fan.

First of all, it's expensive; it is very costly to live here. My wage of $245 (New Zealand dollars) net a week is about average for a woman. It needs a 25-cent stamp to send an internal letter, petrol is 90 cents a liter, house and car loans have interest rates from 19 to 29 percent. Losing a quarter of one's wages in taxes is also just what we're used to.

All Star Trek–related merchandise is imported, and both pricey and reasonably hard to come by. *The Best of Trek #9* cost $8.75 (NZ); its cover price is U.S. $2.95—the New Zealand dollar doesn't equate well with the Australian or U.S. dollar, or the British pound. One bookshop in the capital city operates a mail-order department, and I have a standing order with it for all Star Trek books. As this shop has cornered the market, it follows it can charge what it wants, but that's what we pay to be sure of getting them. The Star Trek novelizations cost about $9.75 each; cover price $3.50. The odd Star Trek book can be picked up from local stores, for instance David Gerrold's *World of Star Trek*, the updated version, at a mere $24.15.

But it is worse to send out for things: hassles with a bank draft, and the post office and its forms in quadruplicate—and it insists on sending the International Money Order separately from your covering letter or order form, often with hilariously disastrous results. One or the other goes missing, books have to be reordered, lost IMOs traced—I once ended up with two copies of the same book I'd paid for only once! Also, with the PO commission, the 25-cent surcharge on overseas orders, and the exchange rate that never works in our favor, the goods end up costing at least twice as much as advertised. But to finally have copies of *STTMP: The Photostory, Chekov's Enterprise*, and the *Star Trek Compendium* and to obtain missing *Star Trek Logs*— these last from England—make it all worthwhile! LP recordings that Leonard Nimoy and William Shatner had made were available from Australia. My collection grew and grew.

There is no other way of getting these things; we are so isolated here it is not possible to go traveling to these places oneself and get collectibles. So, it has to be this, or go without (unacceptable!), or send one's hapless pen pal after things.

However, as though to compensate, there is a thriving fan underground in New Zealand. Of a population numbering three million, there are six science fiction fan clubs, and two of these are Star Trek. Most have crossover membership, so everyone knows, knows of, or can find out about everyone else. Five fanzines are published regularly—of these, two are personal, nonclub efforts, and three are Star Trek–related. Of course the one I coedit is, too! There are newsletters, fan get-togethers, and conventions to keep everyone in touch with each other and what's going on.

Another area of difficulty is actually just getting to see Star Trek. Some five episodes have screened here only once. ''Whom Gods Destroy'' and ''The Gamesters of Triskelion'' I'm still waiting to see again, as they have a violence content that means TVNZ won't screen them now. (I caught the other two recently on video.) So, if you missed them in 1968–72 when Star Trek first screened here, or you weren't even born then, well, that's that. The series has just completed another repeat screening over eighteen months—with time out for cricket—on a Saturday morning, bliss! A letter campaign got its time slot changed from 5:00 p.m. on a Thursday, when it was impossible for workers to see it.

Color TV is new to me; it came here in 1972, but I got my set only last year. I was amazed to see the pretty winking lights on the *Enterprise* bridge, the paintbox-colored uniforms, the wonderful purple or orange skies, the pink and blue vegetation— to say nothing of blue eyeshadows on everyone! The advent of videos has now obviated the difficulty of getting to see new episodes; with fan get-togethers, viewing episodes is now a must and a real pleasure, especially with some rarely seen-here episodes obtained from Australian fans, complete with Australian adverts and censorship rating!

Sadly, the films reach here some months after the U.S. release date—except for *Star Trek: The Motion Picture*, which was on the next day! Usually timed to coincide with Christmas, May, or August school holiday crowds we have by then heard all about it from pen friends, *Entertainment This Week* on TV, *Starlog*, and the movie tie-in books, so it's not new to us. We had *Star Trek III: The Search for Spock* released at the movies and *STTMP* on TV within a week of each other last year. However, we didn't get the better television version of the first film. Never mind, one day we will; the person who answered all our letters said so.

Another area of disappointment is the lack of accurate, up-to-date information; although we get *ETW* on Saturdays (first in the world, via satellite), it doesn't tell us much. *Starlog* is months old by the time we get it, ditto *Starburst*, *Photoplay*, *Fantastic Films*, and all. One resorts to flicking through gossip magazines for pictures and snippets of information, or incessantly badgering one's overseas pen pals for news.

But isolated from mainstream Star Trek though we may be, we don't like the show any the less, neither do we have fewer collectibles, nor are our stories and articles any less well written or well researched, I assure you. It may be that it appeals so much because it isn't easy to do the fan thing here; it has to be worked at, and we can't simply take it for granted. And the pleasure is all the better for feeling one has really earned it!

Sarah Chambers
Oakland, Cal.

For years now, I've been convinced that I am the last of the elderly Trekkies—I was thirty years old and had a six-year-old daughter when the series began. Imagine my delight when I came upon Ann Ice's wonderful letter in the Roundtable of *BOT #6*— another dedicated Trekker my own age! I don't feel so alien anymore.

I must say that I've enjoyed all your articles, but Harvey R. Greenberg's "In Search of Spock: A Psychoanalytic Inquiry" stands out. It is serious, thoughtful, and well written. I would like to see a similar article dealing with mature, and otherwise sane, women who fantasize about capturing Spock. It seems to me that although most healthy women do not harbor rape fantasies, they do fantasize a great deal about being "overwhelmed" by or overwhelming an unattainable enigma. At least I and my friends do. The aura of mystery surrounding *pon farr* enhances the fantasy: What goes on behind the closed doors? Surely it is not handled with customary "Vulcan propriety." If it were, it would not be the opprobrium that it is for them. Perhaps an "adult" psychologist would like to tackle that one. Rape implies violence and greed as well as mental illness; *pon farr* suggests overwhelming passion, which is not necessarily sick if it's handled right.

I'm surprised that more people have not mentioned *Dwellers in the Crucible*. I thought this was an excellent book, perhaps the best of the lot, for its sensitive handling of the Vulcan concept of friendship. Of course, I finished it wishing that I had a *t'hy'la*. Most humans question whether others are worthy of their friendship. How many of us actually question whether *we* are worthy? *The Final Reflection* was another great book; so was *Pawns and Symbols*. Both presented the Klingons in a new light, and now I actually know the name of their home world (these are some of the little details that were maddeningly absent from the series). The name "Romulan" bothered me a lot; it helps to know that they call themselves the Rihannsu. The new Star Trek books pay far more attention to details than the old ones did. And I like Sulu's first name. It suits him far better than Walter.

Gary D. McGath
Hollis, N.H.

Philip Carpenter's article, " 'Approaching Evil' and 'Love in Star Trek'—a Rebuttal" was truly exceptional, worth the price of *The Best of Trek #9* by itself. I haven't read the articles that Mr. Carpenter was rebutting, so I can't comment on the accuracy of his dissection of them, but his commentary on morality in Star Trek stood by itself.

There are few things so valuable as the identification of an obvious fact that everyone seems determined to ignore. Carpenter pointed out such a fact in *Wrath of Khan*: "Spock did not sacrifice his life, because *he could not have avoided death anyway*." Even the script promotes this misinterpretation with Spock's infamous line "The needs of the many outweigh the needs of the one." I think something worse than hasty writing lies behind this line. My suspicion is that the scriptwriters, coming up with the final solution, wanted to give it the glow of sacrifice, which they believe they are expected to consider a virtue; yet they also knew that sacrifice is not logical, that Spock would not in fact practice it. So they put one foot in each world; the actions that Spock took were not sacrificial, but rather aimed at preserving what he could—the *Enterprise* and Jim Kirk—when his own life was lost; yet his words were intended to let the sloppy viewer think that Spock had committed a "virtuous" act of self-sacrfice. Fortunately, this line was nicely overturned in *The Search for Spock*.

Carpenter's analysis of "The Enemy Within" was another high point of the article. I know that the superficial interpretation of Kirk's split as a "good side" and an "evil side" was wrong, since it implied that "good" is inherently weak and indecisive, but I hadn't thought of analyzing it as one side representing reason without passion, and the other representing passion without reason.

Let me now proceed to a couple of criticisms, grounded in a firm basic agreement. First, I believe that Spock could live without Kirk, just as Kirk could live without Spock. What neither could live with is the *responsibility* for the other's death. This is what makes Spock ready to give up his life rather than abandon Kirk in the episodes mentioned; and, likewise, what makes Kirk refuse to accept the necessity of killing Spock in "Operation: Annihilate," and put his career on the line to save Spock's life in "Amok Time." I can introspectively verify this for myself, and I suspect Mr. Carpenter can do the same: If the one I love should die, I would grieve but recover; if I let her die through my own failure to act, I would very likely kill myself. In the latter case, every value I held would have to seem dispensable after such an act; and without values, there is no point to mere survival.

I also have to disagree that "since (good and evil) are absolute principles they cannot exist in some quantity or some combination." This most emphatically does not mean that I regard some evil as necessary in all of us. Rather, what I mean is that while most people default from a full commitment to valuing life, the default can be partial rather than total. The average person implicitly upholds life as a value, yet is a coward about upholding all aspects of it. Thus, some of these people will accept a "duty" to be enslaved into the military, or to support a worthless relative, or to make donations to a religion they have ceased to believe in. Every time they accept such a duty, they cripple the good in themselves; but the number who totally destroy it is small. The more basic point in Carpenter's argument remains valid, though: The extent of a person's good or evil is due to his choices, not to autonomous forces within the person.

These are minor points, which I offer in the interest of even better understanding of issues which Carpenter's article states very well to begin with.

Loretta Johnson
Bartlesville, Okla.

I was very interested in the article "Star Trek Fans—the Blind Spot." Personally, I would like to see this cast continue as long as they can and will; I definitely do not want them gradually replaced by younger actors or characters. Since before the show appeared, these characters have been developing into interesting, believable people. It would be a shame to have to start all over again, although it would be all right to introduce a couple of new characters. Eventually I think it is important that these characters die (perhaps in a new ship, and by dying, they save the galaxy). Even in that century I do not think people are immortal, and we must accept that. Once that is over with (or perhaps before), I would like to see an all new cast (same characters) fill in the blank spots (like the rest of the original mission). I would also like to see shows centering on the Vulcans, Romulans, and Klingons; shows that would look more closely at their societies (as "Amok Time" did). Perhaps someday there will be a show in which we see not only our heroes, but also the "paper pushers" and what they think of what is happening. This is what I would like to see in the future.

We'd like to note here that our mail—not surprisingly—has been running about 20 to 1 against the idea of new actors playing the same characters in further Star Trek adventures. But we're also slightly surprised at the number of fans who want to see new actors starring in adventures of the crew in their younger days—in somethng like "Star Trek: The Early Years," perhaps modeled after the prequels Dallas and other programs have presented recently. We kind of like the idea, too. In fact, what about a miniseries tracing the history of the Enterprise? Now wouldn't that be dandy? —Eds.

Robin Heathershaw
Boone, N.C.

This is my first letter to *The Best of Trek*, and I am really excited. Before I begin I would like to mention a few things about myself. I am twenty-four years old, and I'm completing a bachelor's degree in math at the University of North Carolina, at Greensboro. I grew up with Star Trek, but I became interested about ten years ago (through James Blish's *Spock Must Die!* and reruns). However, I really got hooked when *Star Trek: The Motion Picture* came out in 1979. Since then, through the films, novels, reruns, and the *Best of Trek* books, I've become a devoted Star Trek fan!

I just love the *Best of Trek* articles, especially G. B. Love's "She Walks in Beauty" (*BOT #4*), and "Kirk and Duty" by William Trigg and Dawson Hawes (*BOT #8*). I also enjoy Leslie Thompson's solutions to the infamous Star Trek mysteries. I also just loved *The Best of Trek #7* all the way through, especially the jokes and "Answer Your Beeper, You Dreamer!" by Jacqueline Gilkey. Yes, as we warp along through life hoping one day that Uhura will hear our signal and tell Scotty to beam us up, we Star Trek fans are misunderstood sometimes, aren't we?

And now the main reason for this letter: *Star Trek III: The Search for Spock*. I loved it all, and I've got a lot to say about it, too. (I also look forward to reading other fans' opinions of it.)

It knocked my socks off! It was everything Star Trek was and could have been in the 1960s. Full character development—all the old harmony returned, the crew worked together like a well-oiled wheel (or perfectly tuned "bairns"). All the magic was there, too. I love the little bits of trivia Nimoy put in. It was fun! It is a good balance between *Star Trek: The Motion Picture* and *Star Trek II: The Wrath of Khan*; between intellect and action. It was also a smooth continuation (not ending) to *Wrath of Khan*.

As a devoted fan, my heart was wrenched in two as I watched the *Enterprise* explode and die. When I realized what Kirk was planning to do, I watched the scene in shock, wanting to reach out and stop him. Chekov's fear and Scotty's disbelief were very real to me, as I'm sure they were to fans everywhere. When Kirk asked McCoy, "What have I done?" my head was reeling and one thought echoed over and over: "Why? How can we go on without the *Enterprise*?" My only consolation is that it was better that the *Enterprise* be destroyed in battle than (can I even say it?) to be dismantled and junked! No! That truly would have been a fate much worse than death. What we and the crew of the late *Enterprise* will do now depends on "whichever fleet [the crew] ends up serving in."

Finally to my main grievance: Robin Curtis as Saavik. When I first saw Saavik in *Wrath of Khan*, I felt threatened, betrayed; I thought, "Is this what's going to replace Spock?" (Remember, the "rumors" of Spock's demise were wildly flying at the film's premiere.) Then I read the novelization and saw the film again. Suddenly I realized I was wrong. Saavik acted the way she did because she was half Romulan. After learning that, I was fascinated by this new character as much as I was (and am) by Spock.

When Robin Curtis took over as Saavik, it was not Saavik I saw, but a whole new character. What made Saavik special was gone. Saavik is not another Spock, but Curtis made her appear so. Now when I see her as Saavik, I think, "Is she really Kirstie Alley's replacement? Ugh!"

For a moment recall the Romulan commanders of "Balance of Terror" and "The Enterprise Incident," the Vulcans of "Amok Time," and Spock and Sarek. There was something different, interesting, and mystical about them all (each in his or her own way). Just as T'Pau was "all Vulcan in one package," and Spock was Vulcan and human in one package, I believe Saavik was meant to be Vulcan and Romulan in one package. What a wonderful, fascinating mixture!

Alley's Saavik had this same alien mysticism about her, and a special kind of pride and intelligence, too. There was an inner conflict between the two natures in Saavik, as there was in Spock. And as Spock had learned to take the best of the two worlds he shared to make one unique individual, so must Saavik. Alley's Saavik was learning to do just that—to find a balance—and finding that balance was increasing her self-assurance.

I disagree with Joyce Tullock ("Star Trek III: A Return to the Big Story" in *BOT #3*) that Saavik in *Wrath of Khan* was so sure of herself. Recall that she was definitely unsure of herself in her reaction to the *Kobayashi Maru* test; she was bothered by the fact that she had "failed to resolve the situation." Until Admiral Kirk pointed it out to her, she had not realized that it was a test of character, that there was no way to win (well . . . almost no way). Her reaction indicates that before the test she had a pretty high level of self-confidence; afterward, however, that confidence was pretty badly shaken. She spends the rest of the film rebuilding her self-assurance.

Curtis' Saavik was overconfident. She was too sure of herself, and there was very little room growth or change. I don't think she was even close to being a "Junior League Vulcan" (with all due respect to Walter and G.B.). For one thing, she mumbled and fidgeted—Vulcans (and Romulans) *do not* fidget! Mainly, her Saavik was too shallow, too American, too Hollywoodish.

I have never seen a successful attempt at changing actors in the same role. As far as Star Trek is concerned I get very upset if people start treating it as if it were made up of any ordinary set of characters and actors. It has been proved that Star Trek is special and different, and it must be treated as such.

Jane Hickey
Edmonton, Alberta, Canada

I am a Trekker from way back; when the series first came out, I was twelve years old, in grade nine; from the very first episode I saw, I was hooked. I had always liked science fiction, and anything pertaining to the stars and universe. I think what appealed to me the most was that Star Trek had some pretty radical (for its time) ideas: women as crewmembers and even commanding ships, and minority men and women in positions of authority. Almost all the early episodes had some kind of social comment. They even had aliens as good guys (or not always as bad guys). How refreshing!

When *Star Trek: The Motion Picture* came out, I was thrilled. And despite the criticisms I have read about the movie, I enjoyed it thoroughly. It was topical and thought-provoking. While the later two movies come close to being space opera, *STTMP* did not. It lacked some of the charm of the old series, though.

When *Star Trek II: The Wrath of Khan* came along, I managed to get in on a special preview showing of it by answering a Star Trek trivia contest. I came out rather upset that my favorite character has been sacrificed, but still satisfied with its being more like the series in that there was lots of action and a wonderfully wicked villain. But it lacked the thought-provoking social comments that the early episodes of the series had.

Now, *Star Trek III: The Search for Spock* has a good balance of both. What's more thought-provoking than an underlying theme of the immortal soul, and rebirth or reincarnation? And there was plenty of action. Now that's the Star Trek I know and love.

When you take a look at all three movies, though, they all have a common theme to them. In each one there is a death and a subsequent, or concurrent, rebirth. In *STTMP*, Decker and Ilia "died" in order to be reborn, or give birth to, a totally new life joined with Vejur. In *Wrath of Khan*, Spock died, giving his life to save his friends, at the very same moment new life was being created by the Genesis Effect. And in *Star Trek III: The Search for Spock*, it was the *Enterprise* that "died" in order to give the new life (Spock) a chance. In each film, a death or sacrifice was required before new life could begin. A reaffirmation of the natural cycles in the world, and on a larger scale, the universe around us.

I was sorry to see David get killed off so quickly and easily. I think it would have been better to have developed his character a bit more; I thought it was interesting having Kirk's son around. I liked Robin Curtis as Lieutenant Saavik, but I would like to see a bit more of the Romulan "fire" in that character. It smoldered under the surface of Kirstie Alley's Saavik, and I missed it in Curtis' portrayal. Christopher Lloyd created a terrific villain. We saw a somewhat more rounded character in Kruge than the usual Klingon in his love for his ghastly pet, his relationship with the spy, Valkris, and even his frustration with having to command an unintelligent crew. And yet he was so dreadfully nasty that you were glad to see Kirk do something so out of character as to give Kruge the boot off a cliff.

It will be very interesting to see what happens to our band of heroes now. How changed will the new Spock be? Will Starfleet forgive them? Or will they be a band of outlaws, like Robin Hood and his Merry Men?

Fred Schaefer
Wolcott, Conn.

Harve Bennett has been quoted as calling the *Excelsior* a "spruce goose." Right. The *Spruce Goose* was built by Howard Hughes, with his own private funds. If it was an Edsel, it was his own loss. Starfleet would not be allowed to spend a few billion credits in taxes on a new ship that might end up a "spruce goose."

Why is Harve Bennett destroying all we hold sacred in Star Trek? He kills Mr. Spock, and then he kills David. Then he kills the beautiful lady we all love. Harve Bennett destroyed the *Enterprise*, not Jim Kirk, not the Klingons. Why? In order to tell a "good story"? Gene Coon and Dorothy Fontana told good stories without destroying the *Enterprise*.

Why does Bennett need a "catch" in each movie to get the

fans to see it? He killed Spock in *Wrath of Khan* so we could enjoy an exciting story. Fine, we all knew he was coming back. But why did he feel he had to top it in *Star Trek III: The Search for Spock*? Spock's rebirth was enough to get the crowds.

As you can tell, I am more than upset about the destruction of the *Enterprise*. I have read that fans found out about the impending doom before the movie was released and did what they could to make Bennett reconsider. Supposedly, he replied that the special effects were already filmed and that the scene was too good to waste. That's the lamest excuse I've ever heard!

Also, the *Enterprise* would never be scrapped. A more likely fate would have been to preserve her as she is. The ship would become a "floating museum," of sorts. This has been done to the *Constitution* and the *Nautilus*. A ship like the *Enterprise* would be a national (?) treasure in the Federation. She would never be scrapped.

What bugs me is that Leonard Nimoy and Gene Roddenberry and all the people involved with the production let it happen. Surely they all know what the "Big *E*" means to us. This is the end of Star Trek—Star Trek without the *Enterprise* is not Star Trek. No new ship can ever replace her. She was one of a kind. There will never be another.

I'm really worried about what we will lose in *Star Trek IV*. I don't think Harve Bennett will stop destroying what we love most about Star Trek in order to tell "good stories." Fans have not kept Star Trek alive for twenty years to have it suddenly ruined in four years' worth of motion pictures. If fans wish the "new" Star Trek to bear any resemblance to the one we have loved for all these years, they must not allow any more drastic changes in *Star Trek IV*. I hope something can be done while the fourth movie is still in production.

Fred, we understand your distress. Every fan felt it to one degree or another. But, like them or not, the events in the films produced by Harve Bennett have all taken place within the logical context of the story. Spock died because it was necessary; the Enterprise *was destroyed because it was necessary. Beyond entertainment, the primary aim of film is to engage our emotions, to make us happy, sad, glad, even angry, as you are. Considering that, don't you think that Mr. Bennett has done his job and done it well? —Eds.*

Nicole Brandon
Point Pleasant, N.J.

You're reading a letter from an apprentice Trekker. I've only been watching the show for about a year, and thanks to the people at New York's channel 11, I've only seen about three-fourths of the episodes. But what I've seen convinced me that this is simply the best television show ever put on the air, and I'm wondering why it took me twenty years to start watching it.

I was introduced to the show at college by a close friend and avid Trekker who practically pulled me by the hair into the TV lounge to watch it with her. At first, I only halfway paid attention to the episodes, taking homework into the lounge with me, but it didn't take long for me to be completely hooked. When school let out, I began watching the show on my own at home. At first, my cable company offered two ways to catch the show—Sunday through Friday nights at midnight on channel 11, and Saturday nights at 7:00 on Philadelphia's channel 17. Then, without warning, channel 17 dumped the show in favor of the moronic *Star Games*. Oh well, I thought, there's still channel 11.

Well, that same summer, that channel began a series of maneuvers that has convinced me it's staffed by NBC executives from the time of Star Trek's first run. First, they moved it to 12:30 a.m., preceded by *Twilight Zone*. Okay—that I could live with. But then all of a sudden, Star Trek was gone, and in its place was the loathsome *Space: 1999*. Somebody there obviously thought one science fiction show was just like the others.

Only the purchase of the *New Voyages* books saved me from Trek Withdrawal during July and much of August. Finally, someone returned the show to the air, and things were back on trek . . . until I graduated from college in December and returned to my at-home Trekking, only to find Star Trek pre-empted at least three of a possible six nights in favor of those ''Millionaire Maker'' hour-long commercials! This lasted until about mid-January, when the show returned six nights a week—but with nothing but first-season episodes! They'd show a few episodes, then repeat them a few weeks later! Now, I agree that most of those episodes are among the series' best, but I don't want to see them repeated so close together, especially when there are lots of second-season episodes I haven't seen yet. Plus, I miss out on seeing one of my favorite characters, Chekov. Does anyone else have this much trouble with local Star Trek outlets?

Why is everyone coming down so hard on poor Robin Curtis? Be grateful we still have a Saavik at all! She could have been quietly dropped, just like Carol Marcus.

Anyone ever consider the possibility that Vulcans evolved from Yoda's race? Both have green skin and pointed ears, and extensive knowledge of logic and mental capabilities.

Finally, I want to confess I serve double loyalties—I am a Duranie as well as a Trekker. I must say that Simon LeBon has all the makings of an excellent starship captain, and Andy Taylor has publicly confessed that Star Trek is among his favorite shows! (Hey, there's an article idea—celebrity Trekkers!)

Katherine Jones
Weiser, Ida.

I still have a hard time crediting the fact that there actually are other Star Trek fans who are writing, communicating, and celebrating diversity. When I discovered that *Best of Trek* and possibly other "fanzines" existed, I was insanely happy. (It takes so little to make a Trekker happy.) I am *not* alone. I am so tired of suggestions about my lack of sex life, maturity, sanity, intelligence as they reasons for loving Star Trek. I come by my love of Star Trek the hard way.

I suppose I could be considered a first-generation Trekker—albeit a young one. I was five years old in 1967 when Star Trek premiered. I had the good taste, even at that age, to like the program immensely. My father, a strong non-Trekker, would change the channel and have a minor riot when his oldest child then threw a temper tantrum.

I was unhappy when Star Trek was canceled, and it was a long time before reruns came to our station. I was thirteen—the same age as Miri—when Star Trek finally came to late-afternoon TV, and like that other pre-adolescent, I fell head over heels (to use a trite phrase) in love with Captain Kirk!

I had no idea that Star Trek novels even existed until I discovered *The Entropy Effect* by accident. Since then, my Star Trek literature collection has grown to an impressive (to me) fifty books. And after seeing and enjoying all three movies five times, I feel I am feeding my addiction adequately. But I have been lonely. Other Trekkers sympathetic with my feelings were sorely needed. Thank you for being there; thank you for letting me share my world of Star Trek.

Patsy Curnow
Floresville, Tex.

I have now collected all nine of the *Best of Trek* books and have decided to write and tell you what I think about them. I love them. I guess it is reassurance that there are others out there who feel the same way that I do about Star Trek.

A sticker on my car, "I'm into Horta-Culture," receives a constant and standard comment: "That isn't the way you spell horticulture." Groan!

Have you ever had someone ask you what your hobbies are? I was asked just that question not long ago. My reply? "Reading, painting, ceramics, crocheting, and writing."

The next question: "Writing? You mean . . . words . . . on paper?" in a slightly shocked voice.

"Yes," I answered bravely. "Short stories . . . twenty-to-thirty-page manuscripts, actually. I have six in print now in fanzines."

"Fanzines? What do you mean? Magazines, pamphlets, or what?"

"Well," I said hesitantly, "Star Trek fanzines. I write science fiction."

Her eyes widened and her mouth opened slightly.

So, by way of explanation, I replied, "It's just for fun. I'm just crazy about Captain Kirk, Mr. Spock, Dr. McCoy, and the rest." Knowing full well that wouldn't explain anything.

"Not . . . the skinny guy with the ears!" she said, astonished.

"By George," I thought to myself, "at least she's in the right space." They usually have me on *Galactica* or *Searcher* or even an old-fashioned British phone booth.

I have been a Trekkie/Trekker for many years. It's a subject I rarely spoke of because of just such reactions. "Beam me up who?" "Mr. Spock—isn't he that kiddie doctor?" "You mean *Star Wars*?" People, give me a break!

When I finally did come out of the closet (thanks to a cousin and dear friend of mine), I dove headfirst into my infatuation with Star Trek, and I've been swimming in it ever since.

Come on, people! I'm tired of others looking at me as if I've just beamed down from the bridge of a Klingon battlecruiser. Let's educate the populace!

I believe Star Trek's appeal lies in its "Mr. Clean" persona as shown in the characters. Old-fashioned values, such as honesty, loyalty, true friendships, learning to live with and love those different from ourselves, protecting the defenseless, etc.

I would love to have Starfleet put into space another starship and another crew for our young, up-and-coming little natives. Star Trek is shown here at 11:00 p.m. Saturday evening, and few, if any, children get to watch the show. As far as I know, I don't believe the cartoons have ever been shown here.

I particularly enjoyed Ingrid Cross' "Three Foot Pit" in *The Best of Trek #9*. She proved a three-foot pit can be a real hazard. I know—as a fanzine writer, I've fallen into a couple.

Regina Moore
Tucson, Az.

I have enjoyed your *Best of Trek* books, and recently purchased #8. I was anxious to read the reviews of *Star Trek III: The Search for Spock*, which I absolutely loved. Your own "Review and Commentary" was very insightful, but I strongly disagree with a particular point that you made in the article.

You stated that Spock would logically condemn Kirk's actions in *The Search for Spock*, because "it has been stated over and over again that Vulcans, having once declared their loyalty, would rather die than betray their oath." You go on to say that Vulcans don't expect logical behavior from humans, and that Spock "would probably expect better from James T. Kirk."

To that, I ask: How do you explain Spock's behavior in "The Menagerie"? His loyalty to Captain Pike far surpassed his loyalty to the Federation. His actions in "The Menagerie" were based on love. If Spock committed an act of mutiny in that episode, how can he condemn Kirk for his actions in *The Search for Spock*?

In "This Side of Paradise," Spock tells Leila, "I have a responsibility to that man on the bridge." He doesn't say, "I have a responsibility to the people that sign my paycheck."

What's more, in the final scene of *The Search for Spock*, Spock says to Kirk, "My father says you have been my friend. You came back for me." Kirk replies, "You would have done the same for me." We all know how true that is. But in "Review and Commentary," you imply that Spock would *not* steal the *Enterprise* and go after Kirk, if the situation were reversed, because of his loyalty to the Federation (!!!!!). I, therefore, accuse you of claiming that Spock loves the Federation more than he loves Kirk. I would be very interested in your reply to that accusation.

Hmmm. That review was written in great haste about two years ago, but we do remember our intent when writing that part—we wanted to point out the fact that Spock would have done the same thing for Kirk, no question of that, but his Vulcan stubbornness would cause him to disapprove of any actions taken to save his own life. Upon rereading the passage, we realize we could have made it clearer. Sigh . . . now you realize why writers cringe at the thought of rereading their own work . . . and can't help doing so.

That's about all for Trek Roundtable this volume, friends, as we need room for the list of Star Trek books Nicky Nicholson and Stan Campbell have compiled as a special bonus in this volume. Please keep writing; we always want to hear from you. —Eds.

THE NEGLECTED WHOLE, PART III: THE ENGINEER AND THE DOCTOR

by Elizabeth Rigel

This is the final installment of Elizabeth's series on those regular crew members which she refers to as "the neglected whole." This time around she takes a long and detailed look at both Scotty and McCoy, two characters she feels belongs together for a number of reasons. Oh? You say you didn't expect to find McCoy in this series, and why in the world would Elizabeth include him among those "neglected"? And what about Kirk and Spock? Read on. You may not agree with all that you'll read, but we can guarantee it will make you think.

(Montgomery) Scott
First Appearance: "Where No Man Has Gone Before"
Rank and post: lieutenant commander; chief engineer
Rank and post by *The Search for Spock*: captain of engineering, USS *Excelsior*

Engineer Scott is one character who has never been left hungering for action. His reputation as a "miracle worker" was earned by many long hours of experience. He has seen his beloved vessel, as well as his own heart, repeatedly scarred, but he still presents a fine example of a man satisfied with his life's work.

He was never developed much as a person; perhaps it was considered enough to have him visible and preoccupied with some technical problem. As fond as Scotty is of his "bairns," they are far from his only hobby.

Like Kirk and Sulu, Scotty is a collector of antiques. Some of his finest pieces are ancient weapons and restored armor, or other crafted metals. Unlike Kirk and Sulu, however, Scotty does not pretend to be relatively skilled with them. He prefers to admire them on display, which is wise, because Sulu might challenge him to a duel. Other antiques Scotty also enjoys are relics of his Scottish heritage, such as the woven family kilt and traditional bagpipes. As his coworkers aren't all fond of the latter, he brings them out only when he isn't expecting company, or on special occasions. It would be interesting to hear him play a duet with Spock's harp, perhaps with Uhura singing along.

Scotty has a one-track mind which excludes frolic from work, and work from leave, to better enjoy both. He has no time for nonsense when in the engine room, but when he is off duty, Scotty is quite the party animal, a veritable connoisseur of liquors and establishments which serve them. He created his own palatable beverage from McCoy's medicine stores in "The Tholian Web," and he had some success in getting the alien Kelvan invader Hanar drunk in "By Any Other Name." Unfortunately, he couldn't stay awake long enough to take advantage of it. Since Scotty doesn't have any dependence problems with alcohol, Kirk probably doesn't mind his social drinking and even joins him for an occasional nightcap.

Scotty's only problem with shore leave is that when he doesn't want it, Kirk often forces him to go anyway. The captain would never force Spock to take unwanted shore leave, yet obviously feels that Scotty, frail human that he is, cannot possibly know what is good for him. So Scotty goes on leave, and by the time he returns, Kirk is kicking himself for sending him.

For example, within hours of his arrival on the pleasure planet Argelius ("Wolf in the Fold"), Scotty was the prime suspect in several savage murders. Within the day, the entire *Enterprise* was endangered.

In "The Trouble with Tribbles," Kirk told Scotty to go mind the men in the bar with the Klingons. And naturally it was Scotty who started the fight he had been instructed to avoid. But, as he explained, he had good reason: The Klingons would not respect them if they did not defend their ship. (Kirk, of course, should be able to take care of himself.) The result is that Scotty is pleased to be punished, because he now has time to catch up on the pleasure reading that Kirk so unwisely interrupted.

Another leave Scotty did not want to take was the trip home for the funeral of his nephew, Peter Preston. To a great extent, Kirk was responsible for that death, and it is a slap in Scotty's face that Peter was not mentioned in *The Search for Spock*. It implies that Spock's death was more important that Peter's.

There is another interesting aspect to the previously-mentioned "Wolf in the Fold." McCoy stated that an accident caused by a woman brought about a temporary personality change in Scotty, with the result that he suddenly hates women. This is not necessarily logical. It is far more likely that the accident would cause an otherwise healthy man to hate only the woman responsible for the injury. It is quite possible that accident caused his subconscious to tap into a painful romantic encounter from his past, equating it with the "attack" by the same woman in the present. This affair could have ended so badly that it clouded all his personal relationships with women for a long time thereafter. Preoccupation with his work may not be the only reason Scotty has not had many lady friends.

Scotty has apparently always been work-oriented, straightforward, and somewhat naive about the ways of the opposite sex. His lost love was probably subtle, romantic, demanding, and insecure, as well as intelligent and attractive, if rather vain. He would have considered her a fine catch and thought that their love was secure. When she broke it off, he would have been stunned by her "treachery" and deeply hurt. Bitterly, he'd vow that it would never happen again.

Carolyn Palamas probably resembled his lost love, but seemed less scheming and cruel. Scotty was immediately infatuated with her, perhaps seeing in her a second chance to regain the woman he loved. Carolyn found him polite and charming, but hardly her ideal of a romantic partner. He became less involved in his work to spend more time with her; and the dignified engineer suddenly began shedding his no-nonsense exterior, showering her with unwanted affection and protection. When she abandoned him for Apollo, his possessiveness was roused to fury. Once again he was abandoned, bewildered, and bitter. This incident intensified a subconscious anger against the so-called gentle sex that remained suppressed until McCoy discovered it in "Wolf in the Fold."

Fortunately the good doctor was able to clear up the problem, and Scotty soon fell in love with the gentle Mira Romaine ("The Lights of Zetar"). Mira was realistic, shy, and equally in love with Scotty. He apparently learned his lesson, for with Mira he was less possessive, more supporting, and happier in her company. He's not so anxious this time to prove his macho fearlessness and brawn, and she does not require it of him. She would suffer any fate to protect him from the malevolent creatures that have invaded her mind. He also would risk death to save her, and his loved proved instrumental in her cure and recovery. She was equally good for him—probably one of the best things ever to happen to him.

Without question, Scotty's pride and joy is his *Enterprise*, particularly her engines, the heart of her being. Often when Kirk and Spock must leave the ship and Scotty is left in command, an emergency arises. He does not possess all of Kirk's cleverness or Spock's logic, but that makes him the most realistic when commanding. Unlike the others, he knows better than to overestimate the ship. It infuriates him that Kirk and Spock are sometimes, in perspective, downright careless or foolhardy with ''his'' ship. The feeling leads to an annoying problem: He wishes they had to clean up after themselves and gain some wisdom about how much damage can really be avoided. Yet he fears if they do learn his job, they will try to do it for him; they have their hands into his area often enough as it is.

Security (or Kirk's occasional lack of it) affects Scotty's work. Mad crewmen are not locked up, ''guests'' prove to be saboteurs, or necessary parts are stolen or damaged. But the fabled Kirk charm works on men, too: Somehow the enraged engineer is always placated, and by the end of the day things are at double efficiency. Even so, Scotty years later admitted that he ''multiplies his repair estimates by a factor of four'' in order to keep up with Kirk's demands.

Spock is even worse. His logic falters where the engines are concerned. He has picked up two attitudes from Kirk. The first is ''I don't believe in the no-win scenario''—that is, the ship can actually do everything that is required of it, and Scotty is just pulling my leg. The second is ''I know your job better than you who are trained for it; I only keep you around because I can't be everywhere at once.'' Scotty is always afraid that this time the meddlesome Vulcan will goof and blow up the ship. As Scotty said in ''The Paradise Syndrome,'' ''That Vulcan won't be satisfied until these panels are a puddle of lead!''

Scotty certainly hasn't earned such cavalier treatment. In all other matters he has shown great respect for Spock. If Spock insists that Captain Kirk is actually Janice Lester, then it must be true because Spock is a reasonable man. Scotty had faith that Spock could produce a formula (''The Naked Time'') that a row of computers would have to work on for weeks. But the engines are Scotty's domain; nothing makes less sense to him than to have Spock try to do something he could do as well, if not better.

Scotty's weak spot, if he has one, is in those engines. His rage in "Day of the Dove" and "The Children Shall Lead" demonstrate that he can be pushed over the brink. In both episodes he is deeply distressed that either Klingons or careless tinkering are trying to destroy his ship, which is bad enough, but there is also the prospect that they will simply drain her to helplessness ("We would all be lost, forever lost"). Scotty longs above all for security and stability, for established routines and well-beaten trails. He doesn't want anyone else doing his job as if he were incompetent or unnecessary. He can't bear to leave his routine and friends even for a post on the *Excelsior*, however coveted. It's not a killing fear, as Scotty is willing to part with his beautiful *Enterprise* if there is otherwise simply no hope. But while there *is* hope and life, the ship is to be well treated and protected. Clearly the careless whims of Kirk, Spock, and Starfleet are threats to that security.

It has been said that Scotty would make only a fair starship captain because his heart would not be in it. This would be true only if he honestly did not want the job. As captain, though, he would be enormously pleased to provide the prudent and considerate leadership that could prevent his engines from being damaged in the first place. Given these conditions, he would be an excellent commander.

It is primarily through happy, satisfied characters like Scotty and Sulu that one realizes how troubled Kirk and Spock really are. Sulu is a bright-eyed, swashbuckling Peter Pan, a boy who never grows up and is therefore untouched by the woes of sober adulthood. However, he is happier and more responsible than the Peter of literature, and his cheer and curiosity are his most endearing traits. Scotty is his spiritual opposite, the happy adult. Scotty loves work, devotes all his waking hours to it, and brings forth worthwhile results. But he is not crushed by work, either. He sees it as an adult's way of play, and has chosen a career that expands his natural talents and potential. To him, work that is not play is a sad and unnecessary burden.

Kirk is a negative image of Sulu and Scotty in that he has a small-boy selfishness with his toys, but very little satisfaction for his efforts. Kirk is frankly obsessed with the *Enterprise* (at least until Spock's death). He loves the power, but often stumbles under the tremendous responsibility that comes with it. He apparently believes that this is the best he deserves.

Spock, too, lacks Sulu and Scotty's contentment and sense of self-acceptance. He does gain some satisfaction from solving scientific riddles, but that is the closest he gets to happiness. He hides in work, preferring circuits and gadgetry to the unstable, uncontrollable realm of people. The *Enterprise* is both his refuge and self-imposed prison. A refuge because she has no other Vulcans, and bothersome as humans are, they obviously cannot compare to Vulcans when it comes to *real* peer pressure. But the ship has also become a prison because Spock is now afraid to leave it. Among his own people he is thought of (and thinks of himself) as a John Merrick, an "elephant man," a freak unworthy of dignity or respect because of his defective, even monstrous genes. Even his own family and betrothed wife are dissatisfied with him. So it has always been; now that the opportunity to change this pattern of thought is in his hands, he is afraid to take it. The *Enterprise* is just another battleground for him.

Scotty loves his ship in a way that feisty, grabby Kirk, and timid, refugee Spock may never understand. He loves her as a father loves his only child, not because she is a product of his life, but because of the life that is her own. Although Scotty will never abandon her while she lives, it is a mutually gentle and protective relationship. He rages against Kirk and Spock and Starfleet and the enemy because they are literally, maliciously attacking his beautiful but delicate daughter. If Scotty didn't have so much respect for the first three, he probably would have punched them all out long ago. He has no patience at all with the fourth group.

The *Enterprise* commanded such a "long look" in *Star Trek: The Motion Picture* mainly to demonstrate the different viewpoints of Kirk, Spock, Scotty, and Vejur. Scotty made his opinion quite clear by his slow cruise past her, as if to say, "Isn't she a beauty? Let me show you why I love this lady like my own kin." Shots of him here are bright, colorful, alive. And it's infectious—even a crewman flips in space with the joy of being near her.

Kirk's view is dark, animalistic, hungry, saying, "*Mine!* Only mine! Why can't I leave you? Why did I? I wish I could hold you in my hand, I'd put you under lock and key and you'd never get away from me again." His scenes are sharp and bold, but heady and disorganized, like Kirk himself.

Spock's scenes are harsh, impersonal, and infrequent. Once his refuge, the starship is now a purgatory, where his sinful nature must be purified before the religious leaders of Vulcan will accept him. He has let himself be manipulated by the opinions of other Vulcans into an "I'll show you!" struggle, which he thoroughly failed in the test of *Kolinahr*. Now, rejected and overwhelmed, he must consider the illogic of going back to a society where he has never been truly welcome, merely to "show them all"—a very emotional response to pain. He is very confused and weary, and he wants mostly to be left alone. Some of his shots are beautiful; but they only serve to emphasize what Spock is trying to ignore or hide from.

Vejur, through the probe Ilia, considers *Enterprise* a living being like itself, although physically and mentally impaired by its long illness (the infestation of carbon units). The *Enterprise* is the first "living" being Vejur has met in some time, and after its fashion, it is extremely lonely. Ilia is shown all the areas that would indeed be the heart, if not the soul, of the starship. Of course, as James Doohan noted, even Vejur has a better way to run the engines. "It is illogical that this carbon-based unit should be in charge of warp engines," the Ilia probe stated to Commander Decker, her guide. Scotty, properly miffed but enchanted by her mechanical design, tolerantly answered, "Lassie, if I were being logical right now, I'd be showing you the inside of a trash-metal compactor!" Nonetheless, Scotty and Vejur agree on the "personhood" of Lady *Enterprise*, and this proves to be an important part of determining what Vejur is and what it wants.

Surely the eighteen months Scotty spends refitting the ship is one of the happiest times of his career. It's the equivalent of escorting his teenage daughter to her first dance. The only snag is that he has to be 100 percent ready when Kirk comes back, because if he is not, Kirk will leave anyway. Kirk gets a hard lesson via the wormhole incident that he has been overly optimistic. Scotty has never and never will claim that the *Enterprise* can do more than she can. He simply works around her weaknesses, and this gives certain overeager bridge personnel the illusion that she is invincible. Indeed, she would be if everyone followed Scotty's methods.

Of course, since Scotty knows how it feels to be upstaged, he never belittles anyone else. The junior officers adore him. He never questions their efforts or muddies their boards with his hands. Their devotion allows him to better educate them in the proper way to respond to Kirk's unreasonable demands: "The such-and-so isn't working, sir. Why don't you ask Scotty about it?" (Smirk optional, but preferably well-concealed.)

Dangerous women, weird aliens, and exasperating superiors

are far from the only trials Scotty has endured in Starfleet. Probably one of his most bitter moments comes when his nephew Peter Preston is killed.

Peter died as a direct result of Khan's attack—he did not desert his post. But Kirk is equally responsible because he didn't suspect the *Reliant* enough to raise shields against her. Nor has he ever bothered to check up on Khan, not even for curiosity's sake. When Scotty watches young Peter die in sickbay, he weeps, not caring about the ruined engines or poor Admiral Kirk's troubles. He asks the universal rhetorical *"Why?"* and hears an unexpected and unwelcome answer. Khan wants revenge, he is told, and he doesn't care who stands between him and Kirk. Apparently Admiral Kirk doesn't care either.

The death of Peter was obviously an afterthought, a device to raise the tension of the postbattle scenes. Peter was proud, but not smug; spirited, but not mouthy. He loved the people and the engines his uncle did, and he would have devoted his lifetime to them. His uncle beams with pride, particularly when the youth defends him even against an admiral. He was a joy to his uncle, and could have been so to the fans—certainly more so than any of the limp personalities foisted upon them in *Wrath of Khan* and *The Search for Spock*.

Instead, we are stuck with David, the paranoid brat; Saavik (actress #1), the bewildered, whose finest quote was surely "I don't understand"; Saavik (actress #2), the babbler, who let Kruge trace her transmissions, and who thinks that *pon farr* is everyone's business; and Heisenberg, "Mr. Adventure," who confuses humor with insult. It isn't surprising, considering the rise of such mental elephants as Admiral Morrow and Captains Esteban and Styles, that Kirk is being turned out—too dangerous to the establishment. Peter was killed for the same reason. It must grieve Scotty deeply that most of those mentioned above are still alive and prospering—even Spock is back—but Scotty's ship and career are gone, and his nephew is still dead.

Scotty knew before the quest in *The Search for Spock* began that he could not possibly make eighteen months of repairs in two days. With a full house of engineers, he had predicted two weeks of work to have the *Enterprise* whole again. He has no time to make her combat-worthy, or even capable of using sleeping-gas and vacuum-pressure security measures against the Klingons. So Scotty has to let her go, and she dies in the atmosphere of the Genesis Planet. It's better than having her captured, but it is still a great loss. Somewhere in his heart he probably wishes that Spock's *katra* had been found earlier, to everyone's greater convenience. There is nothing to be done about it, but since Scotty loved the *Enterprise* as a person (and not, as Kirk did, as part of his ego), he will cherish her memory and recover. The destruction of the *Enterprise* puts him in a new and uncertain position, since he is a man of routine, but McCoy and Spock's recoveries are worth such a minor sacrifice.

So Scotty's creative juices will now turn toward the Klingon vessel. He couldn't actually learn much from it, as there are only so many ways to design a standard matter/antimatter warp drive star vessel. Indeed, he should have some free time for additional study and design work, making him happy and a more valuable officer. The only foreseeable difficulty ahead is if Scotty and Sulu, cooped up together in the same fascinating ship, get cranky and refuse to share their toys with each other. Problems, problems.

(Leonard) McCoy
First appearance: ''The Man Trap''
Rank and post: lieutenant commander; chief medical officer
Rank and post by *The Search for Spock*: commander; chief medical officer

Thanks to the efforts of writer Joyce Tullock, Leonard McCoy is certainly the most well-developed of our neglected characters. She points out his important place in the symbolic mind of ego/logic/emotion, and brings out his power to represent humanity in all its glories and weaknesses. Yet, McCoy is his own person, one who has profited most from a home in Starfleet.

He has changed little during his years aboard the *Enterprise*; most of his growing pains had passed before he joined the service. He had married, become a father, and then lost his wife and child through a painful divorce. Whether his marriage died from anger, third parties, or indifference, it was probably a marriage that never should have happened in the first place. The grief and bitterness of this divorce is presumed to be the reason McCoy entered Starfleet. After experiencing a full life cycle in a few years, a post in space was literally a chance for McCoy to start afresh. But despite his complaints, the young doctor began to like Starfleet a great deal, and there he remains today.

From a professional viewpoint, serving in deep space is a marvelous opportunity. Although space travel forces the doctor to discover and deal with many new diseases, he has made great advances in research because of them. Now and then he might even stumble across a civilization like the Fabrini which has stores of medical information priceless to modern society. And, yes, although he has lost patients to mayhem, delay, and "the unknown," his track record in this strenuous field is one of the best.

McCoy isn't much of a hobbyist. He's not a collector, except of rare or vintage beverages. (These he immediately consumes with fellow connoisseurs Kirk and Scotty.) He reads only a little, less than Kirk does. He plays few sports, although he makes a superior backseat strategist (particularly at chess, and especially if it bothers someone). Teasing Spock (or Chekov, if he's desperate) is good for both hectic days and rainy Sundays. But McCoy's favorite recreational activities are simple: a cool drink and a doze in the nearest sunshine, talking, or strolling about people-watching.

Scotty was probably his first friend on the *Enterprise*. They had no barriers of rank, profession, or culture to overcome, and they are often of like mind. If nothing else, Scotty was the most sympathetic ear when details of the haunting divorce first came up. Scotty is closer to McCoy's age and interest group, and he understands the trials of self versus commitment. He also has nieces and nephews he loves but rarely sees (Vonda McIntyre believes that he has had trouble with some of them, similar to McCoy's situation). Scotty knows more about McCoy's past than anyone, but no one will hear it from him. He is one of the few characters with the courtesy to avoid gossip and keep silent. He and McCoy also both have positions involving the well-being of ship and crew, which often puts them at odds with Higher Up. McCoy and Scotty have very little time to carry on research and development of their own, because the ambitious and slightly careless Kirk always keeps them running.

James T. Kirk was the next person with whom McCoy became well acquainted. Both men tend to be, ah, uninhibited, off ship or on. Despite the low points now and then, they also have great respect for each other's work. But even though they are only a few years apart in age, they are worlds apart in temperament. McCoy complains more, but Kirk is a nitpicker. The doctor gets along well with children; Kirk is a lousy father, even father image. Ask Charlie, or Miri, or the Triachus gang. Or David Marcus.

In fact, Kirk is little more than a boy himself. He tends to act spoiled, a condition aggravated whenever he gets what he wants, episode after episode. Although he has had some disappointments in his career, he's learned little from them. He is clever but not wise. Much of his ego is dependent on his image as a young, virile he-man, and aging terrifies him.

McCoy has accepted himself as a father, even though he's a father without his child around. Like Sulu, McCoy isn't afraid of aging. After his beginnings, nothing worse could happen to him. He worries about Kirk because Kirk hardly has enough maturity to take care of himself, and he certainly isn't mature enough to be a parent surrogate. Was McCoy that self-absorbed when he was younger? It would certainly explain his personal interest in Jim Kirk, perhaps to help Kirk avoid the mistakes he made. So if McCoy lectures him about being unprofessional, it's to protect him before Jim finds—and loses—someone important to him. Yet, by trying to shelter and shape the ambitious Kirk, he deprives him of the *need* to mature. If their friendship sometimes seems stormy, it's because McCoy has changed signals on Kirk. One moment, he's a friend and equal, and next he's a father/mentor, laying down the rules before an unwilling subject. Kirk is then prompted to respond by pulling rank, which leads to more advice, then more pulling rank, and so on. Fortunately, such spats are also easily mended over a bottle of something that Kirk never bothers to find for himself.

From a military point of view, however, many of McCoy's personal rebellions are justified. It is good for Kirk to be confident, and he can usually get himself out of trouble, but those are different things from the presumption that he is invincible. He rarely admits to mistakes (although McCoy often causes him to get his back up), and he repeats one mistake in particular: placing valuable officers in danger. Of course lives will be lost on hazardous missions, but Kirk's should not be one of them. When Kirk goes, McCoy tries to go along with him, knowing he will be needed. When McCoy cannot talk Kirk out of something, he at least offers moral support, but he has no sympathy for Kirk's belief that any suffering sent his way is unwarranted and merely the whim of cruel nature. It is hard to reason with such a person; it's harder if one takes the direct approach. McCoy is a very direct person. His famous quote ''I recommend survival'' shows where his priorities are. To him, no military or scientific need is great enough to cause loss of life. Kirk's philosophy, ''Risk is our business,'' may or not be correct, but it is the prevailing belief of Starfleet Command. A man like McCoy would not be satisfied anywhere in such an organization, but he keeps trying. As Edith Keeler said, "It's necessary."

It is a great paradox to consider James Kirk a good soldier. He is constantly on the wrong side of headquarters, because he does what he wants when he wants to. Yet Kirk is but one pawn on a board of indoctrination. Training as well as personality causes him to side against "weak" powers of diplomacy and negotiation. The result is that many alien societies find themselves being remade to fit Kirk's ideas. McCoy certainly espouses the belief that some societies "have the right to develop normally."

Probably the best example of the clash of philosophy between Kirk and McCoy is seen in "A Private Little War." The Klingon-backed villagers are decimating the unarmed hill people, among whom Kirk has friends. McCoy didn't want the hill people to be annihilated, but he doubted that equalizing the balance of power would solve anything. Arming the weaker (our) side would only stretch the skirmish into a long, hopeless war. He believed that negotiation would bring the two sides together, and the villagers would either become wise or no longer fear to break off their association with the Klingons. The planet could then become a Federation protectorate and be free of Klingon retaliation. Since anything Kirk does will violate the noninterference directive, why not do so in a way that peace will result?

Kirk, on the other hand, distrusted either the villagers or the negotiators—or both. He was convinced (whether correctly or incorrectly has never been seen) that only armed force would keep the villagers true to their word. This sort of thinking trapped the villagers in the hands of the Klingons in the first place—the notion, without proof, that the other fellow is untrustworthy. Kirk was not at all pleased by McCoy's input, although he had insisted he wanted "advice I can trust as much as Spock's." That is indeed what he got, for Spock would have said the same thing. So Kirk presents McCoy with this question: If overwhelming force, no aid, and negotiation are not being considered, what is McCoy's solution? McCoy doesn't have one. Spock would not have had one. Few indeed are the situations to which Kirk gave so much thought before bringing change down upon a people.

Given such conditions, Kirk shouldn't have been surprised that McCoy quit the service when the captain was promoted to admiral. Only friendship and duty had kept McCoy there, but his friends were now going off in new directions. Also, the many new things he had for study after his tour of duty would keep him busy for years. Certainly he did not intend to watch Kirk make a major mistake which would probably ruin his life. If Kirk no longer cared to listen to him, why bother with him anymore?

Years later, after all his friends had gone, Kirk realized that he needed to go back into space. And he recognized immediately that no matter how much he might edit, loathe, or ignore McCoy's opinions, he couldn't handle a starship without him. And McCoy noted in *Wrath of Khan* that Kirk had been sulking too long—he had better go back into space before he really did run out of time. Kirk has made this mistake so often that McCoy is almost getting used to it. (And Kirk is only fifty when he calls himself "too old." McCoy was almost that age when he *started* the *Enterprise*'s first five-year mission.)

McCoy no doubt had better luck educating Christine. She is excellent help, and his unorthodox approach to medicine is slanted toward increasing her participation, and thus her understanding and skills. She even takes his advice! What more could an employer hope for?

The one thing he never becomes involved in is her tenuous relationship with Spock. He knows from experience that there are some things, especially concerning love, that are nobody else's business. Indeed, McCoy never teases Spock about it, or even mentions it to him. Neither of them wants or needs his opinion about the matter.

Spock prefers to be single. That's understandable. He has the right to remain so, if his genes will permit it. It's just as well, because he is not mentally mature enough for a commitment with a woman, least of all Christine. All the audience sees of her is that she knows how to eavesdrop, sigh, smile sadly, and be lonely. If she acts that way in private as well, then, frankly, Spock deserves better. If, however, she is actually a supportive, understanding, worthy candidate when alone with him, and he still refuses, then *she* deserves better. McCoy never gives unsolicited advice on this point, but he has been known to give Christine special, interesting assignments to take her mind off her troubles. Apparently it works, because in *Star Trek: The Motion Picture* she has taken control of her life and become a full-fledged doctor. No doubt she hasn't been seen since because she doesn't need the *Enterprise* any more.

As far as companionship goes, McCoy obviously considers Scotty, Uhura, and Sulu the most adult officers on the ship. All of them are responsible, alert, quiet, peaceful people. They can be reasoned with, and, in turn, they can reason with him. None are known for temper, queer fits, or nuisance-making. His major regret is not having more time to spend with them.

As for the rest, McCoy was dealing with a "boatload of children" long before *Wrath of Khan*. Kirk and Chekov, of course, are well known for their keen noses for disaster, whether accidental or well-earned. McCoy teases them to keep them out of trouble, because they remind him of himself. They are both still young enough to resent it.

As for Spock . . .

All his life, Spock has been insecure. He was never good enough for his parents, his peers, or his society. Even his wife, T'Pring, did not reject him because he was a *hero* "legend" but because he was a *half-human* "legend." Though many human females would leap at the chance to be "that half-breed's wife," T'Pring did not. Vulcan had no place for him, so Spock left it. Vulcans have only two types of behavior (in addition to logic): grim and not so grim. On a human starship there is a wide variety of behavior, all of which is healthy and normal. Spock could easily be accepted on the *Enterprise*. Why then does McCoy bait Spock constantly? Isn't he good enough for him?

McCoy's brand of torment is actually kinder than Kirk's, because Kirk is an unmerciful tease, and sometimes he misses hints. McCoy notices these hints and tries to figure them out. For example, Spock calls himself a Vulcan. Yet, according to Vulcan society, he is a failure as a Vulcan. Therefore if Spock calls himself a Vulcan, he is calling himself a failure. McCoy isn't trying to cleanse Spock of his logic—there are many logical humans, like Scotty—but he does not want Spock to pretend he is something he is not, merely to please some narrow-minded Vulcan neighbor. He wants Spock to accept himself.

Of course, such self-help courses bring out McCoy's own fault. Under his benevolent goals there is a tendency to dictate changes, rather than suggest them. Thus when Spock slips up, McCoy can crow a victory and take the credit for "improving" him. It's the same mental bullying that Spock has faced on Vulcan. He *can't* change, even if he wants to, because McCoy has him backed into a corner. If he gives in, it indicates weakness. By ignoring McCoy, he provokes a renewed attack. Spock will lose face in either case, by looking like a stubborn fool or a gutless wimp.

Fortunately, there is a difference between McCoy and a fellow

Vulcan: With McCoy, Spock can fight back. Indeed, McCoy has been known to deliberately lose a quarrel for that very reason. Spock needs the opportunity to realize that he can say something critical, even insulting, to one of his persecutors and walk away unscathed. Eventually he will no longer fear the opinions of others, although he would still respect them.

Spock may be a genius, but he is still a *boy* genius. After fifteen years on his own, he still has not cut the umbilical cord, particularly from his father. McCoy, by virtue of his years of experience, is a surrogate Sarek for Spock, but one who can apply only noise, not pressure. To finally have his views heard, even to win a fight, is a wonderful lift to Spock's self-esteem. He does not need to run from this problem anymore. Yet he has a grudging respect for the cantankerous doctor, who has spent hs life *living*, while Spock has struggled to manage *existing*. He is learning that McCoy does not urge him to be more human because humans are superior, but because being a Vulcan hasn't worked. And he realizes that he too has something of value to contribute: Under his influence, McCoy has gradually become more tolerant of others.

How ironic it is that such as Kirk and Spock think that McCoy needs *their* protection. It is true that an unarmed physician will be more vulnerable to danger; however, it is hard to endanger a doctor if neither he nor the aforementioned valuable officers leave the ship. But if they go, he goes. (He will follow them into a dragon's lair.) How else will he be there to say "I told you so"? How else can he dream up his impossible cures for their carelessly spread diseases? How else can he stand in a field behind four hill people and still get shot by the villagers? Only in Starfleet.

As a doctor, McCoy is realistic about his limits. He has never pretended to be brave, but to spare others pain or misery he can find the strength to take their pain and misery upon himself. Pity and love cause him to give himself over to the hostile powers that would harm Kirk and/or Spock in "The Immunity Syndrome," "Miri," "The Empath," and "Plato's Stepchildren." He is willing to sacrifice anything of his own if it will save those he loves. And the primary role of Kirk and Spock, while he saves their lives, is to try to stop him.

Joyce Tullock did such a wonderful job describing this peculiar if affectionate setup in "The Empath" that readers are referred to her articles for that discussion.

However, it must be said that her interpretation of the events of "For the World Is Hollow and I Have Touched the Sky" leaves several major questions unanswered. In this episode, McCoy discovers that he has a terminal illness at the same time an asteroid-sized spaceship is found to be on a collision course with a densely inhabited planet. McCoy insists upon beaming over to the "world" of Yonada, where he meets and marries the beautiful head priestess. He refuses to come back to the *Enterprise*. While on Yonada he finds a way to reverse the spaceship's course. Spock does so, at the same time finding a cure for McCoy's illness. McCoy comes back to the ship. Happy ending. Now for what *really* happened.

Certainly McCoy was shocked and afraid when he realized that he was going to die. He delayed telling anyone else until he felt the time was right. Then he and the affected parties could rationally sit down and discuss the necessary adjustments. But he would do none of these things until he could digest the information himself.

All that changed when Christine found out about it. She immediately called down the captain, who, having other things to do, did not have time to discuss the matter with McCoy. No doubt he was hurt that McCoy hadn't intended to tell him right away, and he determined that his friend was already too ill to function correctly. Christine tells him to cheer up; a year is a long time. He knows it; she knows it; Kirk and Spock are the ones who don't know it.

Suddenly McCoy feels as if he's being phased out. The problem is that he isn't dead yet. Deemed too frail to leave the ship, McCoy had to force his way onto the landing party. Kirk then immediately told Spock. McCoy would have told him himself, but only at the appropriate time; as McCoy's illness has no effect on the first officer or his duties, Kirk had no right to tell him. Spock responds with smothering politeness, as if to agree with Kirk: "Let's not tire or upset him. His last days should be as comfortable as possible." Christine, Kirk, and Spock are convinced that the poor doctor has but hours to live—they had better be kind while they have the chance. This hardly takes McCoy's mind off of the situation. Indeed, it only emphasizes that he really doesn't have long to live. After an ordeal like that, it's no wonder he's irritable.

Perhaps the last straw is when Spock states that by staying on Yonada with Natira, McCoy is being illogical. Balderdash! Have Kirk and Spock forgotten that McCoy agreed to do so to get them out of an execution chamber? Natira agreed in good faith to let them go because she believed McCoy when he accepted her marriage proposal. Obviously, it never occurred to Kirk that McCoy might keep his part of the bargain. He thought the good doctor was lying to her. McCoy's statement "Is that too much to ask?" shows that he realizes that marrying a kind and loving woman like Natira is not a great price to pay for their lives. In fact, if he noses about a little, surely he can find the ship's directional controls before the planet Daran V is destroyed. . . .

Kirk interpreted McCoy's statement quite differently. He thought his friend meant, "What's wrong with being her husband? Don't I have a right to be happy?" McCoy was afraid of death, yes, but his intentions were not all selfish. Kirk simply considered McCoy's rebellion a sign of trauma and a refusal of the cruel fact of death that everyone else had accepted so reasonably. After an encounter like that, McCoy must have wondered if he was losing all that much. If Kirk wants to attribute selfish reasons to McCoy's motives, let him. The reasoning is not false; it's just not the whole truth.

McCoy's duty was to return to the *Enterprise*. He disobeyed. But he was fulfilling his long-term obligation: to find the control room when the others had failed. He needed time and the trust of the woman he would marry to do so. And he succeeded. He was also, although he did not describe it as such, pulling medical rank to find a cure for his deadly illness. He couldn't be the only person in Starfleet afflicted. He is a doctor—this disease must be slippery indeed if it could catch him. Starfleet (and Jim Kirk) would certainly overlook a little insubordination if it resulted in a cure for this killer disease. But he would not find such a cure in the Federation. But what about among the Fabrini?

The Federation is far from being the most advanced civilization seen in Star Trek. Consider that the *Enterprise* was less than fifty years old when it was considered old, worn-out. The colony ship *Yonada* has functioned smoothly for *ten thousand years*, with many more to spare. Now, surely a society that can design such a spacecraft must be vastly superior to the puny Federation. Their knowledge must seem magical in comparison to the primitive Starfleet society. Perhaps they have a cure for many things . . . including McCoy's xenopolycythemia.

Even if all these opportunities turned out to be duds, McCoy would have a home. Kirk scolds him for his decision, forgetting that not everyone is as indestructible as he is. McCoy couldn't have won the argument either by staying or by leaving, because Kirk thinks he's lost his mind along with his health. Can McCoy be blamed for seeking refuge with a beautiful woman who loves him? Natira admitted that this was her first love, but (callous as it sounds) McCoy would have died long before she could "fall out of love." The romantic aspect must have appealed to him enormously; the realization that not everyone would abandon him when he became too ill to care for himself was greatly comforting. Once Kirk and Spock understood *all* of his motives, their simpering treatment of him changed. And McCoy realized that, if he could, he would want to have his friends near him in his last year. Fortunately, McCoy found not only the control room but the library as well, in which was found a cure for him.

And what of Natira? She rightly perceived that McCoy had never intended to hurt her, and that his true motives were kind. "You came to my people with a great mission," she said, awed but thankful for his success. Then she let him go. By the time he returned to her (when the Fabrini reached their proper destination), Natira would have come to terms with her feelings of first love. They might have strengthened, in which case they could have revived the marriage. Indications are, though, that they became "just friends," and had the marriage annulled.

The good doctor, unfortunately, had but one thing to do in the first two motion pictures, and that was to lecture someone. (True, he's very good at it.) In *Star Trek: The Motion Picture*, he lectured Kirk about the foolish mistakes he was making; he pressed Spock to find his true motives for joining the mission to Vejur. In *Star Trek II: The Wrath of Khan*, he debated briefly with Spock about Genesis: Spock felt Genesis could be programmed to do great good; McCoy feared that it could do great evil. Whether good or evil, the device is activated, and Spock sees how it could be used for evil—it kills him.

Yet this tragedy gives McCoy a moment to shine. *Star Trek III: The Search for Spock* demonstrates that Spock is not overfond of death, and that he respects McCoy much more than he can admit.

Why did Spock dump his *katra* on poor, unsuspecting McCoy? He did so because the two men are so different that even if something goes wrong, everyone would know that McCoy had "company." Also, McCoy could be trusted to take care of it—or die trying (it never hurts to give someone a selfish reason to do the right thing). On top of all that, everyone else was needed to take the ship to Vulcan for the *katra* final ceremony. Failing that, they would all need their wits to take him to Vulcan illegally. Kirk, in particular, would have been unsuitable for the trust; if his political clout failed, he would need a clear head to find another way.

There can be no doubt that the events of *The Search for Spock* have made an indelible impression on McCoy. Perhaps if all had gone according to plan, there would be no difficulty. But McCoy's and Spock's minds have been mixed together for some time— how hard would it be to separate them? The priestess T'Lar had a difficult task, and no one could blame her if she could not finish all of it. . . .

Did she? Don't ask this writer . . . wait for the fourth movie.

CHEATERS AND *KATRAS*: A SHORT DISCUSSION OF DEATH

by Douglas Blake

This is an unusual article, to say the least. Originally penned before the release of The Search for Spock, *it was recalled by Douglas for complete revisions once he had seen the film. We were delighted to have him do so; it was excellent before, but in the context of events in* The Search for Spock, *could only be better. Unexpected problems caused Douglas to take over a year to complete the rewrite. (Now his greatest fear is that* Star Trek IV, *which will be released several months before this sees print, will affect the article just as much as did III.) We think the wait is well worth it, but fully expect some negative comments from our readers used to straightforward, linear articles. As we said, this article is unusual. But if you like it, please let us know, as we'd like to run other articles of a more experimental vein.*

> Man with the burning soul
> Has but an hour of breath
> To build a ship of truth
> On which his soul may sail—
> Sail on the sea of death,
> For death takes toll
> Of beauty, courage, youth,
> Of all but truth.
> —John Masefield

What, then, are we to make of this return from the dead, this newfound life which has been granted our Vulcan friend? Does his resurrection from a noble death and well-earned rest thus invalidate our treasured conceptions of heroic sacrifice and eternal friendship?

Perhaps the deed is too new upon us, too stunning in its impact and immediacy to be easily absorbed by minds which have been conditioned by life and legend to believe that that which is dead is forever dead, and that to die well is one of the goals of living. Perhaps we cannot comprehend the alien way in which our favorite alien, the alien we always *understood*, has defied, perhaps even defiled, many of our most cherished beliefs.

Spock the Vulcan, arisen.

That which is the most awful of all evils, death, is nothing to us, since when we exist there is no death, and when there is death we do not exist.

—Epicurus

Sentiments strangely Vulcanlike in their logical structure. Almost an equation: If life equals existence, and death equals nonexistence, life cannot equal death. Or to put it more convolutedly: If life equals existence and death nonexistence, then death cannot exist.

Specious logic indeed. Spock would patiently point out the fallacy. But fallacy in logic is not always a fallacy in philosophy. A fallacy in logic is especially not a fallacy in fact. We have seen that for Vulcans, at least, there are times when death does not exist. Does this, then, mean that death cannot exist?

Of course not. Vulcans, like all living humanoid creatures, do age and die. Vulcan flesh, hardy though it may be, will wither and corrupt, and death, the silent companion to all that live life as we know it, is not unknown upon Vulcan

It is the denial of death as a force upon life which marks the difference between human and Vulcan. Like Epicurus of old, the Vulcan feels that while life *is*, death cannot be, and once our bodies have died, that life which was no longer is, so why fear the death of the body when the spirit no longer exists?

Sarek told Kirk, and us, that we know nothing, nothing about the Vulcan. As much as the intricacies of Vulcan life are a mystery to us, so much more of an unfathomable dilemma is Vulcan death. Indeed, we poor humans cannot even recognize when a Vulcan, even a half-breed Vulcan intimately familiar to a human doctor, is truly dead. If our powers are so poor as to not even be able to glean a simple fact from physical evidence, how then may we expect to fathom the psychological?

Much has been written and much has been said about the intellectual capacities of the Vulcan. Much ado is made over the use of logicality as a guide for day-to-day living; even more ado has been made over the legendary (and erroneous) absence of emotion in the Vulcan makeup. But little or nothing has been said about the Vulcan's feelings or attitudes toward death. The only evidence we have been presented which suggests that Vulcans even think about death is the respect in which they hold their ancestors. Why is this so? Does the Vulcan simply consider death a natural ending to life and therefore hardly worthy of consideration as an event of importance?

We could readily accept this view. Many of us humans are more than willing to believe that the Vulcan, being emotionless and caring only for aesthetic pursuits of logic, would simply note the passing of a parent, spouse, or close friend as a matter of course, and then get on with his business, perhaps pausing a moment to express a regret for the loss of a great mind or a person of accomplishment, et cetera; as we might pause to glibly solemnize the passing of a species of bird that was rare, but unimportant to our daily lives.

This view, is, if course, incorrect. We have reams of evidence to support the fact that not only do Vulcans feel and appreciate emotion, but they do share love and feel grief at the passing of one close to them.

> And now, it seems to me, the meaning of the evolution of culture is no longer a riddle to us. It must present to us the struggle between Eros and Death, between the instincts of life and the instincts of destruction, as it works itself out in the human species. This struggle is what all life essentially consists of and so the evolution of civilization may be simply described as the struggle of the human species for existence.
>
> —Sigmund Freud

How, we may ask, could a Vulcan culture have developed if they were without emotion? Without emotion, without the ability to see beyond one's self and view beauty, pathos, honor, and all the other myriad facets of the human condition, it would be impossible to make aesthetic judgments about these facets; aesthetic judgments which, in fact, serve as the laws, customs, and building blocks of a society. Without emotion, one cannot point a finger and say, "This is good and this is bad," for the truly emotionless are without conscience or care.

Freud understood that emotion is the basis for all human action. He preferred to express it in terms of sexuality, but it may also be expressed in terms of simple emotional experience.

Experience and experiences which, once having been felt, cannot be forgotten nor ignored, and therefore constantly influencing each decision and judgment we make in our daily lives.

The Vulcan, too, experiences this Freudian gestalt. As the Vulcan has achieved a successful and prosperous civilization—a civilization built upon the ashes of an older, more belligerent, more vital, yet ultimately self-defeating civilization—we may easily dismiss the charge that the Vulcan is without emotion.

Emotion among the Vulcans is, of course, carefully controlled. Such iron control is taught from infancy, and any public breach of emotional control is thought to be the height of poor taste. And, most likely, poor breeding as well.

Freud postulates that the eternal battle between the lust for life and the fear of death has led to the development of our civilization. In simpler terms, it is the feeling which drives man to create, the desire to have something endure beyond his lifetime. Most individuals achieve this desire, however unconsciously, through the act of birthing children, for our children are the best and most visible evidence we leave behind us to prove that we once existed upon this earth. By our own very existence, we are irrefutable proof of the existence—the lives, loves, hopes, dreams, sorrows, triumphs, failures, and eventual death—of many long-ago and otherwise forgotten ancestors. The universe, and the earth itself, is unforgiving and without memory. It is only through our works impinging upon the consciousness of men coming after us by which we may be remembered.

In its grandest sense, this desire of each single individual has led, working in conjunction with the desires of other individuals, as Freud points out, to the development of civilization.

The Vulcan, however, takes a more logical view of the world. The desire to have something of himself live on after him, should it at all even exist within him, is not paramount. Having a more pragmatic view of life—and, most especially, death—the Vulcan directs his energies toward ensuring that his life is the very best that it can be during his lifetime. The Vulcan would be more concerned with the quality of his life's work than whether or not that work will be remembered; he, like Shakespeare's Marc Antony, understands that "the good that men do is oft interred with their bones."

The iron control of emotion taught the young Vulcan results in view of his world which must be curiously schizophrenic: He must appreciate beauty and difference and accomplishment and a million other things to the point of adulation, yet he must not allow this adulation to overpower his emotions. A Vulcan may become absorbed in intricate, beautiful music and may appreciate its beauty on many differing levels, but he can never—dares never—be "swept away" by the sheer joy of becoming one with the music itself. This applies to every segment of Vulcan society, as well.

Death, naturally enough, falls under the same guidelines. A Vulcan may feel sorrow, regret, pain at the passing of another, but he may not show these emotions lest he dishonor himself and the memory of the deceased. Vulcans mourn intellectually—they decry the loss to the world, the loss to civilization, to art, to statecraft, to discovery—the loss to anything but the survivors. To feel personal regret, personal loss, would be overemotional, in bad taste . . . possibly considered aberrantly self-centered.

However, we have seen dramatically that death to the Vulcan is not as death to a human. A Vulcan death need not be final; the placement of his *katra* within the Hall of Ancient Thought ensures that some part—indeed, perhaps the most *important* part—of him will survive, perhaps forever. This knowledge, this certainty that the end of physical life is not the end of one's being could account in large part for the Vulcan's calm acceptance of death . . . and life. It would probably be quite easy indeed to look at the world logically and without undue emotion when bastioned by the knowledge that the travails of life are, at best, temporary. A Vulcan whose place in the Hall of Ancient Thought is secure can look at life as a short-time preparation to an eternity of exchanging knowledge and blissful contemplation.

Or so we'd like to believe. The refusion of the *katra* into Spock's Genesis-rejuvenated body is not evidence that the soul of a Vulcan survives intact and whole. Indeed, the explanation that Sarek gives Kirk can more easily be interpreted to mean that a "copy" of Spock's knowledge and personality would be kept, and there is no indication that this essence, this *katra*, would truly be alive. The Hall of Ancient Thought could be nothing more than a depository of knowledge, a psychic Vulcan equivalent of Memory Alpha.

So, if this is true, Vulcans do know death. Spock would know death most of all, for he has served long and well among the humans and other alien species of Starfleet. Although it was not until many years after his entry into the corps that he finally began to allow himself to loosen his tight rein on his emotions and make close friends and relationships, he still must have been hard hit by the occasional swift, unexpected death of a coworker or subordinate. If nothing else, Spock's natural respect for a person who is totally proficient at his work would cause him to feel a certain measure of pain at that person's death; and as Starfleet is certainly filled with such capable persons, we may assume that more than once Spock felt that pang of regret and loss that we humans call grief.

Once having accepted Jim Kirk as his friend (and to a lesser extent, Dr. McCoy, as well), Spock, to protect his own sanity, had to begin letting his emotions show a bit and, more important, to acknowledge their affect upon him. As stated earlier, Vulcans do experience emotion, but strive to control that emotion lest it overcome a logical operative view of life, work, relationships, etc. Spock, never having fully understood such teachings from his father (who has always seemed strangely repressed, even for a Vulcan, where his son was concerned) and having always attempted to deny the existence of emotion within himself, had to therefore construct a completely new and totally individual-unto-himself style of dealing with emotion and the world.

This process, as we have seen, took many, many years, and the cost in pain and severed relationships was very high. The final result, however, should be considered well worth the effort and grief involved, for when the process was completed, Spock was able to acknowledge friendship (and, we may assume, emotion) and was able, for perhaps the first time in his life, to feel relaxed and content in his place in life.

> He does not expose himself needlessly to danger, since there are few things for which he cares sufficiently; but he is willing, in great crises, to give even his life—knowing that under certain conditions, it is not worth while to live.
>
> —Aristotle

Aristotle could have been speaking with intimate knowledge of Spock, so appropriate are his words in relation to the Vulcan and his mental conundrums. Even though Spock had, through rigorous mental effort and by dint of self-denial and, eventually, self-realization, reached a point, mentally, at which he was at peace with himself and his world, he still must have suffered from doubt and unease. Spock cared passionately for life—make that Life—but cared absolutely nothing for the trappings of life which we humans carry about with us into every relationship and endeavor. Spock would have thought you insane had you suggested that a person should risk his life for something which paid no dividends in knowledge or beauty.

In short, Spock (or any Vulcan, for that matter) would gladly risk life and limb climbing a mountain for the sheer challenge of doing so and for the beauty which one would surely see when at the peak. What would not interest him would be the reward of felt accomplishment when the mountain is conquered. To risk one's life for a fleeting emotion would be insane. But for a human, the victory often is as important as the doing, if not more so, even though most would vehemently deny this fact.

The death and startling resurrection of Spock force us to look into ourselves in an attempt to reconcile the onrush of emotion and confusion which overtakes logic with the hard and fast knowledge that Spock himself would, should, and probably does take the whole matter right in stride. As many commentators have pointed out, the death of Spock was a grand and noble thing, and to have him return in such—in dramatic terms—a casual fashion only serves to cheat us of a heroic sacrifice and cheapen the sorrow with which that ''death'' was greeted. The sorrow, the pain, was real and heartfelt, and although it is probably matched by the joy and thrill of revival which the return of Spock engendered in many, it seems, somehow, sadly wasted. We were moved and enthralled and saddened and teed off for nothing . . . or so it seems.

What, then, is the profit to ourselves from this? What manner of insights may we gain into our innermost secret souls when contemplating the death and rebirth of Spock the Vulcan? Are we to take unto ourselves a disinclination to view death as an undefeatable entity, an end which must, necessarily, come to us all and which must not be ignored in philosophical terms? Or are we to see death as a doorway to a new life, life which transcends the former realities and gives us spiritual and intellectual philosophical entrée into realms beyond those with which we are intimately, not to say instinctively, familiar? What is the message of Spock? What is the signal given by his death? What is the signpost of his resurrection?

The Democracy of Death.

It comes equally to us all, and makes us all equal when it comes. The ashes of an Oak in the Chimney are no Epitaph of that Oak to tell me how high or large that was; it tells me not what flocks it sheltered, while it stood, nor what men it hurt when it fell. The dust of great persons' graves is speechless too, it says nothing. It distinguishes nothing; as soon the dust of a wretch whom thou wouldest not, as of a Prince thou couldest not look upon, will trouble thine eyes, if the wind blows it thither; and when a whirlwind hath blown the dust of the churchyard into the church, and the man sweeps out the dust of the church into the churchyard, who will undertake to sift those dusts again, and to pronounce, This is the Patrician, this is the noble flower, and this the yeomanly, this is the Plebeian bran.

—John Donne

The Vulcan way is to think of oneself as equal to any man and every man, yet above the passions which tempt every man and any man. Spock, in his too short life and newfound resurrection, found the wherewithal to take the passions of the everyman and the aesthetic of the Vulcan and grind them into one in the crucible of his soul. We, as those who viewed Spock's battle with the forces and passions which daily plagued him and, perhaps more often than we—or he—suspected, attracted him, can readily sympathize with and empathize with this grinding process, but we can never fully understand nor even appreciate it.

It was a long, arduous process which required that the very being, the very soul, if you will, of Spock the Vulcan be disassembled and minutely examined piece by piece. Then each of those pieces had to be reassembled into a whole again, but with the addition of new pieces—Spock's humanity. The final result, as might be expected, was something quite different from that begun with, yet not so different that it was unrecognizable to us. In fact, the end result, the new reconstructed Spock persona, was probably more recognizable to us than was the old, original persona . . . for was not this "new" Spock, this gift-giving, well-wishing, quip-making Spock, the very same Spock which we had for so long desired to see? Was he not identical to that Spock which we created in our minds, a Spock of giving friendship, of unquestioned loyalty, of unhesitating willingness to die for his friends?

Certainly it was. Our perceptions of Spock as he was during the years of the series, the years of the *Enterprise*'s original voyages, were quite far removed from the reality. Liking the Vulcan, enjoying his uniqueness, his otherworldliness, his satanic good looks, and his cool, calm detachment, we decided that, since we liked him and we were likable people, then he must be likable too, and, of consequence, just like us. Reason told us—as well as Spock, numerous times indeed—that he *was not* just like us . . . he was a Vulcan, he was an alien, he controlled his emotions by choice, he lived the way he preferred and, frankly, found human ways—our ways—almost unbelievably illogical, if not outright repugnant.

However, reason, as the poet says, is not always grounds for thought. We liked Spock, we respected him, admired him, some of us even loved him. How, then, could he *not* feel the things we felt, love the things we loved? And so, because we humans cannot like, respect, admire, or love the things which we do not understand, or the things which we cannot at least slip into some pigeonhole, we allowed our perceptions of Spock to become seriously warped. The Vulcan quickly took on an aura of mystery and romantic tragedy which made him even more attractive, and so the process began to feed upon itself. In short order, we had ourselves believing that Spock was, after all, just like us anyway, kind of reticent, maybe, but a good guy and quite a hunk, for all that.

Spock's occasional emotional outbursts and the ongoing inner turmoil of his search for self-identity gave us ongoing evidence to support our beliefs, and, again, fuel to feed the flames. See, we told ourselves, gleefully nudging a mental rib, that proves it . . . Spock has feelings, just like us.

It is not at all surprising that we fans should have felt so about Spock, for the "just like us" syndrome has become quite pervasive throughout our society. Star Trek itself did quite a bit to spread the philosophy; the message delivered by most episodes was that they—aliens, Hortas, giant amoebae—are, after all, Just Like Us. This is a far cry from the series' intended statement that all beings, things, etc. are equally valuable and equally beautiful, which is a much more difficult concept to delineate, deliver, and understand. Appreciation and acceptance of difference and diversity is the way to achieve harmony with oneself and with life; shrugging a grudging acceptance that "they are just like us" signals a disdain and even fear of difference, and leaves a door yawning wide open for misunderstanding to come waltzing through.

As a group, we fans didn't—and ofttimes still don't—appreciate the diversity of the Vulcan; we were too concerned with having him be one of us, "the most human" of us all.

Spock is not just an alien, but an alien from a mature, scientifically advanced race whose principles of nonviolence and rejection of emotionalism have given them centuries of peace. Spock, the result of the first successful interbreeding of the Vulcan and human races, was fully educated and indoctrinated in the ways of the Vulcan by his father, but, upon reaching his majority, himself *chose* to continue to act and live as a Vulcan. We may assume that Spock's mother, Amanda, taught him as much as possible about what it meant to be human, and how humans thought and reacted. The lessons were probably no more real to the young Spock than were lessons concerning foreign lands and cultures to us when we were in elementary school; after all, he and his family lived on Vulcan and they (even Amanda) acted as did every Vulcan family. Why then should Spock consider the things he was told about Earth and humans even to be true, much less relevant to his own life? His father was (rather too much so, to judge by some reports) a Vulcan, his mother lived as a Vulcan, he was being educated as a Vulcan, both socially and psychologically, so what was so important about the human part of him?

This is perhaps why the young Spock was so hurt and upset by the tauntings of other youngsters. To be called names when young is bad enough, but to be called names that you know are not true, or that you believe to be not applicable to yourself, hurts all the more. Spock had been taught that while his human half might prove to be somewhat of a handicap when dealing with the control of emotions, it made no difference to what he was and could become. Amanda, and Sarek, too, in his own way, would have made sure of that. But here were other children, full-blooded Vulcans, who seemed to prove that nothing about Spock mattered *except* the fact he had human blood running in his veins.

It must have been a shattering experience. We may assume that Amanda must have attempted to prepare Spock for such childish behavior (Sarek probably considered the entire possibility not worth considering; his kind of pomposity quickly forgets the ways of childhood and expects children to act as miniature adults), but no amount of preparation could have readied Spock for the first sneered "half-breed." Name-calling would have been the first taunts he experienced, and the first to be ignored, but as he and his classmates aged, other, more sophisticated, and therefore more hurtful taunts would have surfaced. Allusions to "human genetic factors," "dilution of the species," and such would have stung terribly, whether they were meant to hurt or innocently overheard. Spock, like any human or Vulcan youngster, was in the midst of the normal teenage identity crisis, and must have had his own insecurity fueled by such comments. It was probably about this time that he began describing himself as having "a female human ancestor"—a half-truth which in the telling must have hurt just as much for the cowardice of it as for the attempt to downplay his mother's heritage.

It is nothing short of a miracle that such a dreadfully unhappy and lonely youngster as Spock ever grew up to be anything more than a competent shadow of his father. Perhaps Sarek expected him to (without really wanting him to), and maybe that is why he was so upset when Spock decided to seek his own fortune and future with Starfleet. . . . The old man may just have been afraid that Spock would fail, and that that failure would be the end of any chance Spock would ever have to be a happy, normal Vulcan. Love was always there between the two, even though unspoken, but maybe fans are wrong when they say that it was Sarek's pride and stubbornness (and Spock's, too) which caused the years-long breach between them. It may have been fear.

Whatever the cause, it eventually benefited Spock. He successfully graduated Starfleet Academy, then went on to a long and distinguished career which culminated in his appointment as captain of the *Enterprise*, and only ended (?) with his death in the battle with Khan. More important, however, was the progress Spock made in his lifelong battle between his Vulcan and human heritage. Throughout his Starfleet life, Spock formed associations and friendships which changed his outlook on life (and human beings, no doubt); these led to an eventual, but gradual, widening of the doors of emotional response. It was not until his abortive try at achieving *Kolinahr* and his insightful mind melding with Vejur that Spock finally and fully came to an acceptance of the emotionalism within himself and of the importance to such emotionalism for the fullest appreciation of life. In the ensuing years, he became more and more satisfied with his lot and happy with his friends and way of life. By the time of *Wrath of Khan*, Spock was natural and comfortable. He reminded us of his father.

Then he died.

Now he lives.

> The evil that men do lives after them,
> The good is oft interred with their bones.
> —Shakespeare

So what message does *Search for Spock* give to us? We are told it is a story about men who will do anything, sacrifice anything, for a friend. Somehow, however, we cannot help but feel that there is more. Friendship is one of the most valuable commodities which humans—and Vulcans—possess, but is friendship truly what *Search for Spock* is all about?

No. *Search for Spock* is about the need and desire of all men to defeat death. The pompous and ponderous posturings of Kirk at the end of *Wrath of Khan* come home, finally, to haunt him. The memories of Spock felt by him and members of the crew, the scathing attack of Sarek, the inner doubts that he could have done something, anything to prevent the death from occurring in the first place . . . all of these things serve to break down Kirk's carefully constructed cocoon of "acceptance." Kirk has never before in his life accepted death as either a possibility or an inevitability. To suddenly do so, in the arms of his long-lost son, was a denial of everything which he had stood for and everything he had fought for in his life and career. Kirk was more shattered than we knew. Of all of us, perhaps only McCoy knew how deeply Kirk was disturbed. At the end of *Wrath of Khan*, when everyone else is impressed by the stoicism and dignity with which Kirk is accepting the death of Spock, McCoy is the only one with the acuity to ask not if Kirk is all right, but how he *feels*. He is not put off nor fooled by Kirk's answer that he feels "young"; McCoy knows of Kirk's almost limitless propensity for building self-deluding, but outwardly rational, reactions to stress or tragedy. Kirk wasn't all right, he didn't feel young, or anything much else, for that matter. He was in the midst of his carefully constructed "reaction" to Spock's death, playing the role of the bereaved but brave friend, and all true emotion, all honest grief, was shunted aside.

Once Kirk realized that he had been fooling himself, he acted. The pose of acceptance of Spock's death—of acceptance of the very existence and importance of death—was dropped like a hot potato, and Kirk went dashing off on another of his quixotic and wonderfully daring tangents to find his friend . . . and to prove to himself, one more important time, that death *could* be defeated.

The good that Spock did was not "interred with his bones," of course, but the evil that he did lived on after him and almost destroyed Jim Kirk. In this case, Spock's "evil" was his death, which forced Kirk into the untenable and false position of pretending (to himself as well as others) that he now accepted death. Such an attitude could have resulted in Kirk's own death, for many times in his career, it was only his refusal to give in to the inevitability of death that allowed him and his crew to escape alive.

We must remind ourselves that nowhere in his conversation with Kirk did Sarek say that Spock could be brought back to life. Many fans gleefully overlook this point, instead treating themselves to the enthralling vision of a steely-jawed Kirk battling against the arrayed forces of the universe to regain his lost friend.

No. Kirk heard what Sarek was saying, and he did not, consciously or subconsciously, misinterpret it. He undertook the mission to salvage what was left of Spock, the *katra*, so that his friend could be honored and remembered. A worthy goal, and perhaps one that Kirk would have undertaken under any circumstances. But the thing which impelled him to go to any lengths was the simple fact that McCoy was suffering, perhaps would die.

Now Kirk had a chance to once again cheat death.

It was difficult to do, as always. He had to ensnare conspirators, steal his own ship, make his way to Genesis, pick up Spock's body (which he could not even be sure still existed), make his way back to Vulcan, and, as an almost incidental final topper, get off scot-free. For Kirk, this kind of thing is almost rote. No wonder he looked inexplicably happy when wishing his crew "the wind at our backs."

Imagine his chagrin when this "simple" mission resulted in surprising and, once again, deadly fashion. His son murdered. His ship destroyed by his own hand. Spock alive.

To Sarek's unspoken question "Was it worth it?" Kirk answers an emphatic, unspoken "Yes!" Once again he has gamed with death, and even though it seems that in this instance death came out ahead, Kirk is not dissatisfied. Not happy by any means, oh no, but not dissatisfied. Triumph and tragedy have always walked hand in hand with James T. Kirk. Indeed, his career virtually has been a series of major victories coupled with small defeats.

This, then, is the ultimate difference between Kirk and Spock. Spock, like all Vulcans, accepts death and defeat as part of life. Time is a fleeting thing, after all, and life must be marked by accomplishment and achievement. Defeat is part of the learning process, and to be cherished as much as, if not more than, success. To dwell upon that which cannot be is illogical. After all, regrets and bitter emotions are not suitable things to carry into the Hall of Ancient Thought.

Kirk, as you would expect, lives his life by a completely opposite viewpoint. The entire point of life is to win, to build, to explore, to find the answers to the questions before man's three-score and ten run out. Kirk often speaks of a God, but we get the feeling that he doesn't really believe in an afterlife. He's too pragmatic, too concerned with the here and now, too determined to make his mark and make it stick. Growing older depresses him, frightens him, for it means that he will have that much less time to leave that mark, and correspondingly less talent, virility, and power to make it stick. Yet the accompanying fear of failure keeps him "chained to a desk," where, if he can't go out and cheat death one more time, he can at least dodge it for a while longer.

And yet, and yet . . . Kirk and Spock are together again. There is at least one more battle to be fought, one more danger to slickly escape from. In effect, we are back where we started—the brash captain and the half-human first officer ready to take on the universe just for the sake of the Federation, friendship, and maybe a little fun.

Death need never feel cheated by these men. The great game will go on, perhaps forever. Surely Spock will see to it that his *katra* enfolds and protects Kirk's all-too-human soul. In return, Kirk will force Spock's Vulcan heart to occasionally open and reveal a little human emotion. They will continue to challenge death, and continue to win, for as long as we believe in them . . . and in ourselves.

The great end of life is not knowledge but action.
—Thomas H. Huxley

THE STAR TREK BOOK LIST

compiled by Nicky Jill Nicholson
(with additional material by Stan Campbell and Sue Keenan)

Readers have been requesting for many years now that we run a list of Star Trek books. The reason we haven't is that we felt that such a list would be outdated almost before someone could finish compiling it. But when separate manuscripts arrived from Stan Campbell and Nicky Nicholson, we realized that there are now so many Star Trek books in print that virtually no one person could keep up with them all. A list is now valuable just to help readers keep track of (and collect!) the vast numbers of books devoted to Star Trek. We make no pretense that this list is complete. We plan to run occasional updates. Your comments and additions are welcome.

Ace Books

1. *Shatner: Where No Man . . .* , by William Shatner, Sondra Marshak, and Myrna Culbreath

Ballantine and Ballantine Del Rey

Fiction

1. *Star Trek Log One*, adapted by Alan Dean Foster (All *Log* series books adapt episodes of the animated Star Trek.)
   "Beyond the Farthest Star"
   "Yesteryear"
   "One of Our Planets Is Missing"
2. *Star Trek Log Two*, Foster
   "The Survivor"
   "The Lorelei Signal"
   "The Infinite Vulcan"
3. *Star Trek Log Three*, Foster
   "Once upon a Planet"
   "Mudd's Passion"
   "The Magicks of Megas-Tu"

4. *Star Trek Log Four*, Foster
   "The Terratin Incident"
   "Time Trap"
   "More Tribbles, More Troubles"
5. *Star Trek Log Five*, Foster
   "The Ambergris Element"
   "The Pirates of Orion"
   "Jihad"
6. *Star Trek Log Six*, Foster
   "Albatross"
   "Practical Joker"
   "How Sharper Than a Serpent's Tooth"
7. *Star Trek Log Seven*, Foster
   "The Counter-Clock Incident"
8. *Star Trek Log Eight*, Foster
   "The Eye of the Beholder"
9. *Star Trek Log Nine*, Foster
   "BEM"
10. *Star Trek Log Ten*, Foster
    "Slaver Weapon"

Nonfiction
1. *The Making of Star Trek*, by Stephen E. Whitfield and Gene Roddenberry
2. *The Trouble with Tribbles*, by David Gerrold
3. *The World of Star Trek*, by David Gerrold
4. *Letters to Star Trek*, edited by Susan Sackett
5. *Star Trek Concordance*, by Bjo Trimble
6. *Trek or Treat*, by Eleanor Ehrhardt and Terry Flanagan
7. *I Am Not Spock*, by Leonard Nimoy

Reference
1. *Star Trek Blueprints*, compiled by Franz Joseph
2. *Star Fleet Technical Manual*, compiled by Franz Joseph
3. *Star Fleet Medical Reference Manual*, edited by Eilee Palestine
4. *Star Trek Introduction to Navigation Manual*

Bantam Books

Fiction
1. *Star Trek*, adapted by James Blish
   (All of the Star Trek series books adapt episodes from the original series.)

    "Balance of Terror"
    "Charlie's Law" ("Charlie X")
    "The Conscience of the King"
    "Dagger of the Mind"
    "The Man Trap" ("The Unreal McCoy")
    "Miri"
    "The Naked Time"
2. *Star Trek 2*, Blish
    "Arena"
    "The City on the Edge of Forever"
    "Court-Martial"
    "Errand of Mercy"
    "Operation: Annihilate"
    "Space Seed"
    "A Taste of Armageddon"
    "Tomorrow Is Yesterday"
3. *Star Trek 3*, Blish
    "Amok Time"
    "Assignment: Earth"
    "The Doomsday Machine"
    "Friday's Child"
    "The Last Gunfight" ("Spectre of the Gun")
    "Mirror, Mirror"
    "The Trouble with Tribbles"
4. *Star Trek, 4*, Blish
    "All Our Yesterdays"
    "The Devil in the Dark"
    "The Enterprise Incident"
    "Journey to Babel"
    "The Menagerie" ("The Cage")
    "A Piece of the Action"
5. *Star Trek 5*, Blish
    "Let That Be Your Last Battlefield"
    "Requiem for Methuselah"
    "This Side of Paradise"
    "The Tholian Web"
    "Turnabout Intruder"
    "The Way to Eden"
    "Whom Gods Destroy"
6. *Star Trek 6*, Blish
    "The Apple"
    "By Any Other Name"
    "The Cloud Minders"

"The Lights of Zetar"
"The Mark of Gideon"
"The Savage Curtain"
7. *Star Trek 7*, Blish
"The Changeling"
"The Deadly Years"
"Elaan of Troyius"
"Metamorphosis"
"The Paradise Syndrome"
"Who Mourns for Adonais"
8. *Star Trek 8*, Blish
"Catspaw"
"The Enemy Within"
"For the World Is Hollow and I Have Touched the Sky"
"Spock's Brain"
"Where No Man Has Gone Before"
"Wolf in the Fold"
9. *Star Trek 9*, Blish
"The Immunity Syndrome"
"Obsession"
"The Return of the Archons"
"Return to Tomorrow"
"That Which Survives"
"The Ultimate Computer"
10. *Star Trek 10*, Blish
"The Alternative Factor"
"The Empath"
"The Galileo Seven"
"Is There in Truth No Beauty?"
"The Omega Glory"
"A Private Little War"
11. *Star Trek 11*, Blish
"Bread and Circuses"
"Day of the Dove"
"Plato's Stepchildren"
"The Squire of Gothos"
"What Are Little Girls Made Of?"
"Wink of an Eye"
12. *Star Trek 12*, Blish
"And the Children Shall Lead" (adapted by J. A. Lawrence)
"The Corbomite Maneuver"
"The Gamesters of Triskelion"

"Patterns of Force"
"Shore Leave"

13. *Mudd's Angels*, by J. A. Lawrence
    (adapting "Mudd's Women" and "I, Mudd")
14. *Star Trek: The New Voyages*, edited by Sondra Marshak and Myrna Culbreath
15. *Star Trek: The New Voyages 2*, edited by Marshak and Culbreath
16. *Spock Must Die!* by James Blish
17. *Spock, Messiah!* by Theodore R. Cogswell and Charles A. Spano, Jr.
18. *Planet of Judgment*, by Joe Haldeman
19. *The Price of the Phoenix*, by Sondra Marshak and Myrna Culbreath
20. *The Starless World*, by Gordon Eklund
21. *Vulcan!* by Kathleen Sky
22. *The Fate of the Phoenix*, by Sondra Marshak and Myrna Culbreath
23. *Devil World*, by Gordon Eklund
24. *Trek to Madworld*, by Stephen Goldin
25. *World Without End*, by Joe Haldeman
26. *Perry's Planet*, by Jack C. Haldeman II
27. *The Galactic Whirlpool*, by David Gerrold
28. *Death's Angel*, by Kathleen Sky

Nonfiction

1. *Star Trek Lives!* by Jacqueline Lichtenberg, Sondra Marshak, and Joan Winston
2. *The Official Star Trek Cooking Manual*, edited by Mary Ann Piccard
3. *The Star Trek Puzzle Manual*, by James Razzi (also released by Scholastic Books)
4. *Startoons*, edited by Joan Winston
5. *Star Trek Maps*, by Jeff Maynard

Photonovels

1. "City on the Edge of Forever," compiled by Mandala Productions
2. "Where No Man Has Gone Before," Mandala
3. "The Trouble with Tribbles," Mandala
4. "A Taste of Armageddon," Mandala
5. "Metamorphosis," Mandala
6. "All Our Yesterdays," Mandala
7. "The Galileo Seven," Mandala

8. "A Piece of the Action," Mandala
9. "The Devil in the Dark," Mandala
10. "Day of the Dove" Mandala
11. "The Deadly Years," Mandala
12. "Amok Time," Mandala

Bible Arts

1. *Star Wars, Star Trek and the 21st Century Christians*, by Winkie Pratney

Blue Mountain Arts

1. *Come and Be with Me*, by Leonard Nimoy
2. *Thank You for Your Love*, by Leonard Nimoy
3. *These Words Are for You*, by Leonard Nimoy
4. *We Are All Children Searching for Love*, by Leonard Nimoy

Bluejay Books

1. *The World of Star Trek*, by David Gerrold (revised edition)

Celestial Arts

1. *I Am Not Spock*, by Leonard Nimoy
2. *Will I Think of You?* by Leonard Nimoy
3. *You and I*, by Leonard Nimoy

Creative Education

Star Trek, by James A. Lely

Donning

On the Good Ship Enterprise—*My Fifteen Years with Star Trek*, by Bjo Trimble

Doubleday

1. *Making of the Trek Conventions*, by Joan Winston (hardcover)

Grosset & Dunlap

The Star Trek Catalog, edited by Gerry Turnbull

House of Collectibles

The Official 1983 Price Guide to Star Trek and Star Wars Collectibles
The Official 1984 Price Guide to Star Trek and Star Wars Collectibles
The Official 1986 Price Guide to Star Trek and Star Wars Collectibles

Little Simon

Star Trek III: The Search for Spock Story Book, by Lawrence Weinberg

Nostalgia Press

The Star Trek Postcard Book, edited by Gary Gerani

Playboy Press

1. *The Making of the Star Trek Conventions*, by Joan Winston
2. *Mirror Friend, Mirror Foe*, by George Takei and Robert Asprin

Pocket Books

Fiction
1. *Star Trek: The Motion Picture*, by Gene Roddenberry
2. *The Entropy Effect*, by Vonda N. McIntyre
3. *The Klingon Gambit*, by Robert E. Vardeman
4. *The Covenant of the Crown*, by Howard Weinstein
5. *The Prometheus Design*, by Sondra Marshak and Myrna Culbreath
6. *The Abode of Life*, by Lee Correy
7. *Star Trek II: The Wrath of Khan*, by Vonda N. McIntyre
8. *Black Fire*, by Sonni Cooper
9. *Triangle*, by Sondra Marshak and Myrna Culbreath
10. *Web of the Romulans*, by M. S. Murdock
11. *Yesterday's Son*, by A. C. Crispin
12. *Mutiny on the Enterprise*, by Robert E. Vardeman
13. *The Wounded Sky*, by Diane Duane
14. *The Trellisane Confrontation*, by David Dvorkin
15. *Corona*, by Greg Bear
16. *The Final Reflection*, by John M. Ford
17. *Star Trek III: The Search for Spock*, by Vonda N. McIntyre

18. *My Enemy, My Ally*, by Diane Duane
19. *The Tears of the Singers*, by Melinda Snodgrass
20. *The Vulcan Academy Murders*, by Jean Lorrah
21. *Uhura's Song*, by Janet Kagan
22. *Shadow Lord*, by Laurence Yep
23. *Ishmael*, by Barbara Hambly
24. *Killing Time*, by Della Van Hise
25. *Dwellers in the Crucible*, by Margaret Wander Bonnano
26. *Pawns and Symbols*, by Majliss Larson
27. *Mindshadow*, by J. M. Dillard
28. *Crisis on Centaurus*, by Brad Ferguson
29. *Dreadnought!* by Diane Carey

Nonfiction
1. *Chekov's Enterprise*, by Walter Koenig
2. *The Official Star Trek Trivia Book*, by R. Needleman

Reference
1. *The Monsters of Star Trek*, by Daniel Cohen
2. *The Klingon Dictionary*, by Marc Okrand

Screenplays
1. *Six Science Fiction Plays*, edited by Roger Elwood (containing the original teleplay by Harlan Ellison for ''The City on the Edge of Forever'')

Photostories
1. *Star Trek: The Motion Picture*, adapted by Richard J. Anobile
2. *Star Trek II: The Wrath of Khan*, adapted by Richard J. Anobile

Signet (New American Library)

1. *Star Trek Quiz Book*, by Bart Andrews with Brad Dunning (retitled *The Trekkie Trivia Book*)
2. *The Best of Trek*, edited by Walter Irwin and G. B. Love
3. *The Best of Trek #2*, Irwin and Love
4. *The Best of Trek #3*, Irwin and Love
5. *The Best of Trek #4*, Irwin and Love
6. *The Best of Trek #5*, Irwin and Love
7. *The Best of Trek #6*, Irwin and Love
8. *The Best of Trek #7*, Irwin and Love

9. *The Best of Trek #8*, Irwin and Love
10. *The Best of Trek #9*, Irwin and Love
11. *The Best of Trek #10*, Irwin and Love
12. *The Best of Trek #11*, Irwin and Love
13. *The Best of Trek #12*, Irwin and Love

Tempo Books

1. *A Star Trek Catalog*, edited by Gerry Turnbull

Wallaby Books

2. *The Star Trek Compendium*, by Allan Asherman
3. *The Making of* Star Trek: The Motion Picture, by Susan Sackett and Gene Roddenberry
4. *The Making of* Star Trek II: The Wrath of Khan, by Allan Asherman (also Pocket Books)
5. *The Official Star Trek Quiz Book*, by Mitchell Maglio

Wanderer Books

1. *Star Trek II Short Stories*, by William Rotsler
2. *Star Trek III Short Stories*, by William Rotsler
3. *Star Trek II Biographies*, by William Rotsler
4. Star Trek III: The Search for Spock *Movie Trivia*, by William Rotsler (a Magic Answer Book)
5. Star Trek III: The Search for Spock *Postcard Book*
6. Star Trek: The Motion Picture—*The USS* Enterprise *Punch-Out Book*, by Tor Lokvig
7. Star Trek: The Motion Picture—*Bridge Punch-Out Book*, by Tor Lokvig
8. Star Trek: The Motion Picture *Peel-Off Graphics Book*, by Lee Cole

Warner Books

1. *Meaning in Star Trek*, by Karin Blair

(Eliminated from this list because of space restrictions were many children's books, maps, charts, magazines, posters, calendars, and records and read-along books.)

STAR TRIP III: IN SEARCH OF TAXI— A STAR TREK PARODY

by Kiel Stuart

The ship seemed strangely empty.

Wounded, it was limping home. Its captain closed his eyes, shutting out momentarily the images which flickered again and again.

Images that meant sadness and loss, death and destruction, glory and resurrection, heroism and self-sacrifice. A presence that was gone forever.

Suddenly, he leaned forward, pressing the "off" button.

Silence.

"Damn," he said at last, "that was one hell of a movie."

"Ah know," said his chief surgeon softly. "On'y one thang troubles me, Jimbo, an' Ah'm tellin' ya'll, it's a biggie."

"And what's that, McCrotch?"

The doctor's eyebrows played lacrosse on his face. "Just this: How in tarnation are we gonna top this one?"

Captain Jerk said nothing for quite some time. "Oh, we'll think of something," he shrugged.

But his eyes were worried, and he fingered a rabbit's foot in his hip pocket.

"Well," he said, glancing at his watch, "we got about another hour and a half. Wanna watch it again?"

McCrotch shrugged. "Shoot. Ah don't see why not. Got nothin' bettah to do."

Lt. Savvy and Jerk's illegitimate son, Squeaky Sparkus, stood on the observation deck. He knelt to adjust his Topsiders, then rose to face her.

"Gosh," he said brightly, "look at all those stars."

"We are in space, observant one. There are bound to be stars." Then, more softly, "He was my teacher—and my friend. His loss has changed me."

189

Squeaky blinked. "I'll say. I think I liked the old you better."

"Then you are not alone." Savvy gazed into an Infinity Mirror. It was just like the one her teacher and friend used to have in his cabin. She turned away from it. "I do not think I can remain on this ship any longer. There is too much that reminds me of what I have lost. For one thing, Captain Jerk has that film on continuous loop."

"No he doesn't," said Squeaky. "It just seems that way. But, say, I have a swell idea. Captain Mucho Dinero of the *Cooper* is going to be leaving soon to study what's happening on Genesis II. Why don't you pack a few things and c'mon along with me? Huh? We could explore it together. Won't that be fun? Pretty please?"

"I do not think so. But I will come with you nonetheless. I will give me something to do for the next forty-five minutes." Savvy strode out, Squeaky following, nipping at her heels.

In a somewhat remote sector of space, Cap'n Sleaze of the *Greasy Pirate* turned to his mate, Lieutenant Scumbucket, and snarled, "This better be good. All this rattling around in space on some unholy mission to steal some secret or other has put my digestion off. That Klingfree broad better come through with the moneybags."

Scumbucket's reply was a prolonged belch.

Klinger the Klingfree, wearing several yards of taffeta skirt and a pillbox hat and smoking a cigar, arrived on the bridge. Scumbucket turned at his entrance.

"Hey," he belched in surprise, "I thought this Klingfree was supposed to be a broad."

"So did the Klingfree army," said Klinger, chomping his stogy. "How do you think I got here in the first place?"

"So?" said Cap'n Sleaze. "Where's the money? Where's the dough?"

"On its way," said Klinger. "Heads up, everyone."

All eyes were on the viewscreen where a vast Klingfree fighter ship popped into view.

"Ooh, look," said Scumbucket and Sleaze.

The image of the Klingfree commandant flickered onto the screen.

"Wow," said Scumbucket and Sleaze.

The Klingfree commandant's deep, soulful eyes wandered back and forth vaguely. He opened his mouth to speak, closed it again, scratched his head, and finally uttered, "Gee, Alex, I forgot."

Mumbles came from the background.

"Oh, right." The Klingfree commandant's brow furrowed and relaxed. "Ahhh, hand over the stuff you were supposed to get me."

"Right away, Oh Mighty Ruler." Klinger inserted a small cassette into the MumboJumbo Transmission Unit.

'Hey, Rieger, shoot 'em now." A small, swarthy man, chained to his leader's seat, grinned wickedly as he barked instructions to the first officer.

"I can't shoot 'em now, Mean Louie," whined Alex. "I gotta wait for Lord Jim to say so." His long nose lifted a bit and he turned away.

"Shooting? Who said anything about shooting?" said Scumbucket and Sleaze.

"Shooting?" echoed Klinger. "Great! Is this how you repay a loyal subject of the Klingfree Empire?"

"I notice that ain't no Standard Issue Army Uniform ya got on, Sweet Pea," cackled Mean Louie. "C'mon, Lord Jim, we got what we needed. Shoot 'em! C'mon, before they decided to run away or somethin'."

"Well . . ." The commandant's voice faded as his eyes unfocused. "Ah . . . I suppose . . . gee, Louie, are you sure we shouldn't just, I don't know, give them a citation or something?"

"Shoot 'em, Rieger! We're wastin' time here!" Mean Louie rattled his chain.

"Hey!" protested Sleaze, Scumbucket, and Klinger, just before the Klingfree first officer reduced them to their subatomic components.

"Now ya talkin'," said Mean Louie. "C'mon, Jim, let's go see what we blew dese guys outta de water ta get." He tugged on the chain. "C'mon, c'mon." Just as they rose to leave for the Secret Stuff Room, Mean Louie turned and obliterated a tail gunner.

"Aww, c'mon, Louie, what'd you do that for?" whined Alex.

The commandant turned and blinked.

"'Cause I was itchin' to try out my new Pocket Blaster, Rieger. Why? You rather I tried it out on you?"

They all hurried to view the tape.

Aboard the *Cooper*, Lieutenant Savvy puzzled over some odd sensor readings.

"Whatcha looking at?" chirped Squeaky.

"You did tell me that there were no life forms on Genesis II," she said, "Yet these readings give every indication of life down there."

"Gosh," he said, "I wonder what that could be." He turned to Captain Dinero. "Can we go down and look, huh, can we please?"

Captain Dinero said nothing, having taken the precaution of sealing off his eardrums before the Genesis II team boarded.

"Well, I guess he'd want us to go down there, wouldn't he?" Squeaky pulled at Savvy's sleeve. "Boy-o-boy, I can't wait to see what's down there, can you? C'mon, let's go, what are we waiting for?"

"We should take a landing party. And weapons. And instruments. And a tank. And a Port-O-San."

"No, c'mon, rilly, it'll be swell. No one'll know we're gone."

Savvy sighed. "That's what I'm afraid of."

Almost home.

Soon the *Enteritis* would dock. There would be a hero's welcome.

Captain Jerk could replace the batteries in his Watchman.

"Wowee! Would you look at *that*?"

At the sound of Lulu's voice, Captain Jerk switched off the weakening Watchman and looked at Lulu. Captain though he now was, Lulu's jaw hung open. The rest of the crew followed suit. And, as he raised his eyes to the viewscreen, Jerk joined them.

El Exigente!

The newest, spiffiest Starfleece Heavy Metal Cruiser hung gleaming in space dock. It dwarfed the *Enteritis*.

"Och, Ah hear she can go at speeds exceedin' Warped Twelve," crooned Snotty. "An' thot's only th' beginnin'."

"Fantastic," murmured Jerk. "I hear she can be commanded by thought alone, through a micro-milli Feinberg Drive hookup directly to her captain's brain. Some stuff, huh?"

"And she's mine, all mine," reminded Lulu. "At least, as soon as I bail out of this old wreck."

Jerk idly cuffed him. "Remember, kid, I'm still technically an admiral."

The sound of a foghorn cut short their playful romp.

"Keptin!" Wackov's voice was tense.

"Yes?" Jerk and Lulu answered together.

"Keptin Jerk, I mean, you seely Three Mosketeers groupie. Keptin, somevon hes broken the Sani-Seal on . . ." He gulped. "On Meester Shmuck's cabin!" His knuckles clenched whitely.

Jerk's scowl was ferocious. "Wake up Security," he barked, "And have them meet me there!"

When he arrived, he discovered that someone had indeed broken in. The Sani-Seal was in shreds, the door open and flapping in the breeze.

The security goon, arriving seconds before Jerk, had already fallen asleep. Jerk toed him out of the way, and, fizzer drawn, stepped inside.

It was dark as space.

"Who—who's there?" he faltered.

A deep voice came from the darkness. "I have been, and always shall be, your friend."

Jerk's ears began to twitch. "Awright," he sneered, "now who is that? The Panicky Guy? Don't pull that crap on me, junior. I got a itchy trigger finger, and you just might force me to scratch it."

Again the deep voice from the shadows. "It is illogical to assume that you could hit anything in this extremely low light level, and doubly illogical to assume your aim has improved since your last test scores, when you failed to hit Jupiter with a fizzer bolt at point-blank range."

Jerk whitened. Only one officer knew about the Jupiter incident.

And that man was gone.

He leaped for the light switch.

McCrotch sat blinking in a lounge chair.

Jerk did a double-take. " 'Balls,' is that you? Since when did you decide to scale the summit of bad taste—even for you?"

McCrotch rose shakily, staggering over to Jerk. He grasped him by the lapels and swung him around. "Help me, Jim," he croaked.

It was That Voice.

"Take me to Mount Howaya," he whispered, then lapsed into a series of moos, tweets, whistles, and grunts, turned his neck 180 degrees, growled, "Your mother's in hell, Karras," spit up some pea soup, and collapsed.

Jerk scratched his head. "Something's funny here," he commented, and woke the goon to mop up the mess. He checked his watch. He was due in twenty minutes for a date with Admiral Tomorra at Th' Officers' Bar 'n' Grill.

Twenty minutes later, the familiar, glowing red nose of the admiral was winking at him over drinks and pigs-in-a-blanket. "So how's tricks, Jimbo?"

Jerk looked into his Piña Colada and said nothing.

"Well, glad to have the old Honker back, anyhoo. Hic. So what's on the agenda now, boy? A li'l R & R, huh?" He winked and elbowed Jerk in the ribs.

"Actually, I was thinking more along the lines of taking the *Enteritis* out again. Going back to Genesis II. Left something behind there, I think."

"Sorry boy, no can do. The *Enteritis* is being scrapped. The Front Office thinks we've milked the old girl all we can. Besides, Genesis is now a no-no. Strictly off-limits." Tomorra downed his fourth Flaming Death in a gulp.

"But—"

Tomorra tried to rise and sat down again, quickly, feathered tricorn hat askew. "Nice seeing you again, boy. Oh, and tell that Captain Zulu—"

"Lulu!"

"Whatever. Tell him not to have *El Exigente* engraved on his business card."

"What?" Jerk got up slowly.

"Thass right, boy. He ain't gettin' her. Giving it to Hunter. You know, Howard Hunter? Prissbritches?" Tomorra fell gently face-first into the hors d'oeuvres.

Jerk gaped at him.

Lulu and Wackov scurried to his side. "What did he say, admiral?"

Jerk cleared his throat. "I think we'd all better get drunk first. *Then* we can dip him in battery acid."

The Klingfrees sat around a card table. It was littered with empty beer cans, half-eaten salamis, half-eaten porcupines. Lord Jim gaped blankly into the distance. At last he said, "Ah, well, uhm, Alex and Louie, what do you think?"

Louie leaped onto the table, salivating. "Boss! Dis is de greatest thing ever! I say we take it! C'mon, let's head for dis Genesis what's its name!"

Alex shook his head. "I don't know. Maybe we should all move on to other things."

Mean Louie loosed a greasy laugh. "Hey, Rieger, you wimp, dis is a *gold mine*. I mean, we just saw a doohickey dat could revive all de old series dat ever existed! And we could own all de rights! Not to mention da fact dat our names could be in lights again . . . and we wouldn't even have to worry about ratings!'' He panted, then fell on the remains of a porcupine, growling and tearing at it.

"What the hey," said Lord Jim. "We got nothing to lose, right? Alex, set a course for Genesis II."

"Gosh, it's cold," complained Squeaky. "Maybe we should have brought parkas or something."

Icy blasts of wind howled along the surface of Genesis II. Minutes before, they had stepped from Death Valley. Before that, a rain forest.

"The climate is, indeed, erratic," said Savvy. "And I can think of a good many things we could have brought." She hefted their one fizzer. "A few more of these might have made sense. Or radiation suits. Or a tank. Or a Port-O-San."

"Aw, where's the fun in that?" He quickened his pace. "C'mon, we're almost at the capsule site."

"One thing is consistent here, though," Savvy continued. "Do you not see all those television sets littering the landscape?" She blinked hail off her eyelashes. "I wonder what that could mean?"

Squeaky said nothing.

They stepped into a clearing, and the climate was once again temperate. Somewhere in the distance rang an ice-cream-truck bell.

The Time Capsule lay completely undamaged. Brushing off the cockroaches and TV dinners, Squeaky popped it open.

"Empty!" gasped Savvy. "What could this mean?"

In his apartment, Captain Jerk surveyed the depressed gang. "Come on. This is supposed to be a party, remember? Script ideas, anyone?"

Wackov stirred his drink. Lulu ate a cheese curl. Uwhora fixed her makeup. Snotty had a soldering iron and was at work on Jerk's toaster oven.

Suddenly, the door swung open and a cloaked figure stepped in.

Jerk beamed. "That you, 'Balls'? Glad you could shake the animal tranquilizers and make it. No need for disguises, though. We're all pals here."

The figure removed his hood and glared.

Psorex. Shmuck's father.

Jerk reddened. "Uh-oh."

Uwhora rose. "Gotta go get my hair cornrowed."

"I hev to read *Var and Peace*." Wackov waved from the door.

"Ran out of solder," said Snotty, edging past.

"I'm going to Benihana's to sulk," said Lulu.

"Ahem," said Psorex, once he and Jerk were alone.

"Well, what can I do for you? said Jerk. "S'matter, didn't you get that Hallmark I sent?"

"That is not why I have come," sneered Psorex. "I must admit that your stupidity astounds me, even allowing for the fact that you are human."

"Hey, bub, ambassador or not—"

"Why did you not bring Shmuck's body to Vulgaris? You have now ruined his chances for what we like to call 'resurrection.' " Psorex flared his nostrils forcefully. "How could you be so moronic as to bungle his instructions to you?"

"What instructions?"

Psorex poked him in the eye, hastily applying the Vulgarian Cheese Meld.

"Oh," he said sheepishly.

They blinked at one another for a few moments, then, hurriedly, Jerk ran to make a batch of microwave popcorn, and they sat to watch the film again.

"Hold it," said Jerk, near the end. "Freeze frame. What's that little yellow beep box Shmuck is putting into McCrotch's skull?"

"Those are the instructions!" Psorex rose, pointing at the screen. "See? Says so right there in green letters."

"Hmmm," mused Jerk. "So that's why McCrotch has been acting all funny and saying all those dumb logical things."

"True. And you had best bring my son's body back from Genesis II, along with McCrotch, or they will both be doomed forever, and we really mean it this time."

"Okey-dokey," said Jerk. "Shouldn't be too difficult."

"Absolutely not!" roared Admiral Tomorra, when Jerk approached him later. "And if you even think of trying it, I'll have you shot." He downed a jeroboam of straight cough syrup and passed out.

"Well?" Lulu and Wackov crowded around Jerk as he strode out of Tomorra's office.

"Like I said, gang, we'd better steal it. A lot easier." He pulled them both along. "Now here's the plan. . . ."

Squeaky shaded his eyes, looking left and right.

"Down here," said Savvy. "Footprints. Leading away from the Time Capsule."

"Wow," said Squeaky. "They seem to be headed right for the Ice Age. Well, guess this was a bad idea after all. Better call Captain Dinero and go back home . . . nothing to report here . . . heh, heh . . ." He tried to go back, but Savvy blocked him.

"Remember that Captain Dinero still has sealing wax in his ears. He will not hear us. Now stand aside; we must follow those prints."

In the TV-set-littered distance, a baby's wail floated on the wind.

"Listen! What could that mean?" wondered Savvy. She set off in the direction of the cry.

"Uh-oh," blushed Squeaky, "I'm really in for it now." He watched her go, then hurried to follow.

Dr. McCrotch staggered blearily into the Playguy Club, threading his way through fistfights, video games, and tray-bearing bimbettes. At a nearby table, the being he sought had its muzzle deep into a Mai Tai. It saw him and waved a scaly, webbed paddle in greeting.

"So," said McCrotch, sitting at the table. "Here we are."

"Yes," it said, resembling nothing so much as the Creature from the Black Lagoon with a pair of Dumbo ears. "Now, stranger, let us see how close we can come to stealing from George Lucas. Hire you a ship wish to? Money got you?"

McCrotch looked briefly puzzled. "Oh. Right. Yeah, ship wish I to hire. Money plenty I got."

"Where go you wish to?"

McCrotch looked right and left around the crowded bar, then leaned close. "Genesis II take you me to."

The Creature stood. "Impossible. This kind of talking is driving me crazy. I—"

"Excuse me, sir." A baby-faced black man edged the Creature aside and grasped McCrotch's arm. "Lieutenant Hill, Security. You're going to have a nice, long rest. Won't that be fun?"

"No," said McCrotch. "To lie idle at this crucial stage would be illogical."

"Guy talks like a Vulgarian." Hill's slightly overweight partner loomed up on McCrotch's other side. "Come on, you," he said, brushing aside the doctor's feeble attempts at the Vulgarian Nerve Noogie.

Hill and Renko threw McCrotch into a large sack and carried him from the bar.

"Hoboy, Keptin, thees plan of yours sounds exciting." Wackov jumped up and down, clapping his hands.

"Yeah, at last the pace is picking up," said Lulu.

"Oh, don't worry about that," said Jerk. "We'll find a way to slow it down again. Now, everyone all set?"

They nodded.

"Okey-dokey, let's go. Now don't forget: Bowery Boys Routine Number Six. Meet you in five minutes." Jerk hurried away.

He sauntered into the Psych Ward. It was heavily guarded by the usual-issue Conan clones.

"I'm here to see the new wacko." Jerk presented his ID.

"Okay," said the guard. "Me let you in, you no stay long."

He let down the forcefield and Jerk stepped in, winking at McCrotch. "We'll have you out in a jiffy."

Lulu and Wackov were not far behind. "Ho, ho," said Guard One. "How you be, little short peanut?"

"There's a multilegged creature on your shoulder," replied Lulu. While the guard panicked, he took him out with a kendo stick. Wackov took care of the other, hitting him over the head with an unabridged version of *War and Peace*.

"Right," said Jerk. "Too bad we didn't have time for the patty-cake routine. Now let's get a move on."

"Look!" cried Savvy. "Over there on that ice floe. That must be the child we heard before." She scrambled to its side. "Odd. He is wearing Shmuck's burial shroud. I wonder where he could have gotten that?"

Squeaky shoved his hands into his pockets and tried to whistle a nonchalant tune.

"This is very odd indeed," said Savvy. "He appears to be a Vulgarian. See the ears and Secret Decoder Ring, just like the one Shmuck had?" She stared hard at Squeaky. "Did you program this into the Genesis formula?"

He shuffled a toe in the snow, not answering.

"We will get to the bottom of this later," said Savvy. "In the meantime, we must seek shelter." She picked up the child and trudged away through the snow.

Crossing his fingers behind his back, Squeaky followed.

"Whew," breathed Jerk, stretching out in the captain's chair. "Sure is swell to be back on board the old *Enteritis*."

"Sure is," chorused the others.

"Now look, gang, I know this is a real dangerous and tricky mission we're on, not to mention being illegal as all hell." Jerk paused. "So it's obvious that I can't ask you to risk your lives to save two of our oldest and dearest friends—why, just look at poor old McCrotch sitting over there trying to be logical—so I won't ask you."

"Yeah, okay, sure," said Lulu. "We'll all just hang around here and get our butts thrown in the brig. Come on, Snotty, crank over the starter."

The *El Exigente*, swift, powerful, threatening, was relatively quiet at this hour.

Hill and Renko had the bridge to themselves, and were taking advantage of the opportunity by tossing darts at a poster of "Prissbritches" Hunter.

Suddenly, a moose call sounded.

Renko switched on the viewscreen. "Oh, Lordy—They're stealing the *Enteritis*! Hunter's gonna kill us, Bobby!"

"No sweat, cowboy. This ship is brand-new Super High-Techdom, while the *Enteritis* is about to be melted down to make Cracker Jack whistles. We are *fast*. We'll nail them, you'll see."

Hunter appeared on the Bridge, livid. Speechless, he pointed a quivering finger at the fleeing *Enteritis*.

"Don't worry, sir," said Hill. "We'll catch her. This ship is *fast!*"

Jerk ignored the warning sirens as long as he could, then switched on ship-to-ship.

Hunter's voice sputtered. "You get back here this instant, Jerk, or you'll never work in this town again! I'm warning you! Rant, honk, tweet—"

Jerk switched the intercom off. "Snotty, they're gaining on us!"

Snotty only grinned.

"Snotty! That ship is capable of speeds exceeding Warped Twenty-three, and they're getting closer by the second!"

Again, Snotty grinned at Jerk. "Och, dinna worry."

El Exigente zoomed forward like an avenging angel. Then it coughed, bucked, twitched, and rolled over.

One by one, the *Enteritis* crew turned to look at the beaming chief engineer. He held up an empty bag. "Ah put sugar in their gas tank," he explained.

"Full speed ahead, you clever old dog," chortled Jerk. "We have no time to lose in saving both our old friends from doom, and we really mean it this time."

In a cave that looked very much like Superman's Fortress of Solitude, Savvy, Squeaky, and the child were shaking off ice crystals.

"Very clever," Savvy said witheringly, looking around. "Did you design this set, too?"

Squeaky shrugged.

"I have a growing suspicion as to who this young Vulgarian is," said Savvy. She put back his hood and stared. "But look at this . . . I could have sworn the boy was but seven years old when we found him. Now he is smoking Marlboros and drinking beer." She glared at Squeaky. "What explanation do you offer?" Without waiting for an answer, she took the beer and cigarettes away from the boy, searching the robes for other substances that might stunt the youth's growth. She found instead a small book. She read its title; her eyes widened.

"Look!" She sprang upright. "I was correct in my suspicions. See what he was carrying in an inside pocket?" She handed the book to Squeaky and he read its title.

"*Yes I Am Too Shmuck*," he breathed. "A volume of poetry. Gosh!"

"Explanations?" snapped Savvy.

"Aww, shucks!" Squeaky sat down hard. "Cripes, I might as well 'fess up. I used Plasmatronic Protoids in the dot-matrix tube."

"You what?" Savvy exploded. "How could you, as an ethical scientist, do this? It means that the whole world is unstable, and will soon collapse back into nothing but a pile of demographics!"

"Needed the grant money," he said.

"And that means Shmuck's metabolism is also accelerated. He is ageing before our very eyes! In my estimation, it will be mere hours before he is as he was when we knew him." She scowled and glanced at the youth, who was beginning to gnaw at the edges of his book.

"That's ninety-eight to you and me," reminded Squeaky. "Besides, think of all the *pon farrs* he has to go through."

Savvy was motionless. Then, for a brief moment, she grinned broadly.

The walkie-talkie's beep made them all jump.

"This is Captain Dinero. Took the wax out of my ears long enough to hear the Klingfree ship now screaming down on us. You're on your own, kids. But don't worry. I'm sure you'll find plenty of places to hide. Dinero out."

"Uh, oh," said Squeaky.

"You are an untrained scientist," said Savvy. "It is therefore only fitting that I send you off in an unstable wilderness to face a Klingfree invasion with our only weapon." She propelled him out of the cave with the toe of her boot, and watched until she was sure he was well on his way.

Then she went back into the cave and fell asleep.

"Hot dog," said Jerk, "Almost there, gang. We'll just pick up the, er, remains, then scoot back to Vulgaris and fix you up fine, McCrotch."

"Piece of cake," said Lulu.

"Eating sweets is illogical," said McCrotch.

Jerk muttered and opened up the throttle.

Savvy was awakened by a Klingfree boot in her ribs.

Squeaky, flanked by a pair of nasty-looking Klingfrees, waved sheepishly.

"Guess we're in for it now, huh?" he said as they were led out to face a firing squad.

"Go swallow a load of Plasmatronic Protoids," said Savvy.

"Here we are at Genesis, gang," said Jerk.

"Uh, oh," said Lulu. "Is that a Klingfree ship I see?"

"Shields up," ordered Jerk.

"Er, captain . . ." ventured Snotty.

"Yes?"

"We left in such a hurry . . . I sorrt of . . . forgot them. . . ."

Jerk closed his eyes. "Swell."

"Piece of cake, no?" muttered Wackov.

*   *   *

The Klingfree commandant scratched his head, mouth working. "Mean Louie," he called. "There's a Fodderation starship just ahead. Should I . . . ahhh . . . surrender?"

"Naw, you dork!" The communications panel burst into flame. "Shoot 'em, and den threaten dese wimps I got down here. We gotta have dat Genesis II secret!"

"Whatever you say. . . ."

In no time, both ships had managed to do equal damage to each other. "Now what, Louie?" Lord Jim waited, gaping into space.

Below on Genesis II, Mean Louie faced the frightened trio.

"Okay, youse," he said, rattling his chains. "Tell us how Genesis rejuvenates old series, and we kill you nice. Don't tell us, and we kill you mean."

"It does not work," said Savvy, jerking her head in Squeaky's direction.

"Okay, Toots. If we can't romance it outta youse, we do it da hard way." Louie began to sharpen his fangs. "Even as we speak, our fearless leader is getting dat wimpy starship captain ta surrender."

"Captain?" said Savvy. "Captain Jerk?"

"Whoever," snarled Louie, rubbing his hands. "Now, who's first?"

"I can't stand it any longer," sobbed Squeaky. "I'm a bad boy for putting Plasmatronic Protoids in the programming. I don't deserve to live!"

"Dat's right, kid," said Louie. "Here, take dis grenade. You're nothin', you're a weenie, here, lemme help ya, pull da pin like dis." Mean Louie grabbed his chain and ran.

The guards followed. Savvy dragged Shmuck along; he was occupied with pinching her bottom. They dove for cover behind an old *Bonanza* set.

The explosion started an avalanche of TV sets. Savvy took advantage of the situation to grab a walkie-talkie.

"What?" Jerk roared. "My son sat on a grenade?" He shook his fist at the Klingfree ship. "It's really war now," he said. "I mean, we surrender. You Klingfrees can come aboard in five minutes, all righty?"

"Captain," whined the crew.

"Heh, heh, heh," said Jerk, rubbing his hands. "Will we have a welcoming party for them! The *Enteritis* can't move anyway, so I'm engaging the self-destruct program. When they beam over, we'll just beam down to the planet, where it's nice and safe, and watch the fireworks. C'mon, everyone, better hurry up!''

They stood, tears in their eyes, on a trembling precipice littered with TV sets, watching the destruction of their beloved ship. Jerk felt a tap on his shoulder. ''Yeah, Lulu?'' he sobbed.

''Begging your pardon, sir, but *now* how do we get out of here?''

Jerk stopped crying at once. His face flushed. ''Er, I'm sure we'll think of something. I hope.'' He backed away hastily. ''I mean, follow me, gang.''

''Something's wrong here,'' muttered Lulu. All around them, TV sets were imploding, scenery flats collapsing, fake-front buildings flopping over.

They fought their way through the tangling vines of an old *Tarzan* set, McCrotch growing weaker and more logical by the minute.

''Whaddaya mean, dey blew up dere own ship and our whole crew?'' snarled Mean Louie, pausing to scratch some fleas.

''Ahhh, that's right,'' burbled Lord Jim. ''Everyone except me and Alex and you and the guards.''

Louie paused briefly to have conniptions.

''Gee, ahh, Louie, you think maybe we should just turn around and leave or something?'' The sound of Lord Jim's head-scratching carried over the Klingfree walkie-talkie.

''Naah!'' snarled Louie. ''Absolutely not! First we kill dis stupid Vulgarian dat's rolling around on de blacktop biting everyone's ankles, den we bring dis chick on board and torture da Genesis II secret outta her. We gotta have it so's we can take over de airwaves!''

''Not so fast!'' Jerk and company pounded into the clearing. ''The cavalry's here!''

''Gee,'' said Lord Jim, ''maybe I'd better invite them all aboard.''

Before Louie could howl a protest, transporter beams whisked away everyone except the guards, Jerk, Shmuck, and Louie.

''No, you cheese brain! Beam dem back down!''

Lord Jim materialized, looking distinctly dazed. ''What did you say, Louie?''

Louie leaped forward, gnawing at his commandant's ankle.

Across the steaming rubble of picture tubes, second-draft scripts, and press kits, Captain Jerk faced the Klingfree commandant.

His ship. His son. Gone. And the planet breaking up around them.

He grasped Louie by the scruff of the neck, pulling him free from Lord Jim's leg. "Are you the one who gave Squeaky the live grenade?"

"So what if I did, ya weenie? He deserved it anyway. Hey, ya toup's on crocked!" Louie giggled and snarled. Shards of promo packets rained down on the struggling pair. "Now put me down so's we can get on with da business of ruling de media."

"Ohhh," said Jerk. "You want me to put you down? Is that it?"

Louie nodded, slavering.

"Why certainly," said Jerk, carrying him over to the Chasm of Endless Reruns. "Here you go. Ta, ta."

"Aiieeeee," wailed Louie on a descending scale. The thud of his landing loosed a crop of papier-mâché rocks that tumbled about their shoulders.

"You killed my pet!" The Klingfree grabbed Jerk's lapels, shaking him violently. "That was a very unfriendly thing to do."

They teetered on the precipice. In the distance, Shmuck ran up a tree, barked, ran down again, had a vigorous scratch, chased a rabbit, and went to sleep.

The Klingfree thrust Jerk backward. He slid, stumbled, scratched his way up again, and pulled at the Lord Jim's leg. Suddenly, the Klingfree hung from a frail branch sticking out over the face of the precipice.

Jerk sucked in a deep breath. "You are *canceled*, hairbag!" he roared, and booted the Klingfree out to follow his beloved pet Louie.

Panting, Jerk turned to Shmuck. Crouching over the sleeping figure, he discovered the Klingfree's walkie-talkie lying nearby. He picked it up and opened it.

"Uhmm, Alex, would you, er . . . yeah, beam us up now?"

It was a credible imitation. He materialized on the Klingfree ship, fizzer in one hand, Shmuck in the other.

Alex threw his hands up. "Hey, don't shoot, we can work this out, let's be adults and talk this over," he whined. "Here, let me show you fine Starfleece people how to work the controls, just don't shoot me, huh fellahs?"

They reached Vulgaris in no time.

The red Vulgarian sun blazed down. Across the stark stone plain, beach bunnies, Greek gods, Vulgarian Elders, Dr. Who, and a parade float of Jacob's Ladders trundled by.

"Wow," said Jerk. "The vulgarian Tomato Surprise Regeneration Ritual." He glanced at McCrotch. The doctor staggered a bit and spoke.

"The whole is greater than the sum of its parts." Jerk moved to his side, then glanced at Shmuck, who stood wrapped in a beach towel, a vacant stare on his face that would have done credit to the late Klingfree commandant.

"Ohh!" said the gang. "Ahhh!"

"I only hope we're in time," said Jerk.

"Hush!" cautioned Psorex. "The mumbo-jumbo begins!"

They took their places.

"Say," Jerk whispered to Snotty, "that Vulgarian Elder—she sort of reminds me of someone—that grace, that noble bearing, that Shakespearian intonation, that brief appearance."

"Och, Ah know, coptain—it's Obi Walk-on Kenobi!"

"Gotcha."

The ritual continued. Jerk began to fidget. "Gosh," he muttered, "sure wish Dr. Who had brought some of his cute assistants along with him, like Ramona or someone. You realize I haven't even made *eyes* at a chick this whole two hours?"

"Hang on, captain," said Lulu. "Almost there."

"Captain, look!" whispered Savvy. "Here they come now."

Mouths agape, the crew of the late *Enteritis* watched as Shmuck and McCrotch groped out into the hazy red sunlight.

They paused.

They held their breaths.

McCrotch grinned, throwing his arms in the air. "Ah'm okay, everyone! Somebody gimme a mint julep an' a plate o' grits."

"Yay!" said everyone. "It worked!"

Jerk frowned. He hushed the gang up, put a gag on the once more blabberous McCrotch, and slowly approached the towel-clad Shmuck.

"Hey." He poked Shmuck in the ribs. "Remember me?"

"No," said the Vulgarian. "Should I?"

"Whaat?" ranted Jerk. "We risked our stripes, risked our lives to get you back, and you don't even remember who I am? Boy, that's gratitude for you. My son sat on a grenade, I hadda blow the *Enteritis* up, we had a big fight with the Klingfrees, I haven't had a date in hours, that damned Genesis II planet nearly swallowed us all up, and now you don't remember anything. Oh, that's just swell!'' Jerk stomped off, sitting on a nearby rock to sulk.

Shmuck blinked a little, pressing a hand to his forehead. ''Wait a minute,'' he said. ''Hold on for a brief moment in time. I think, I believe . . . why, yes, it is all coming back to me. Why, hello, admiral, Mr. Snot, Dr. McCrotch, Lieutenant Savvy, Captain Lulu, Mr. Wackov. I trust you are all feeling well?''

''Yay!'' said everyone. ''Now we know it really worked!'' They tossed their caps in the air with a mighty cheer. ''Everything's back to normal again! Shmuck's just like he was before, same age and all, McCrotch doesn't have to say 'fascinating' anymore, a terrible weapon that could doom us to reruns forever has been destroyed, and Jerk doesn't have to worry about raising a goofy son!''

''Gosh,'' grinned Jerk, coming out of his sulk to throw an arm around the Vulgarian's shoulders, ''sort of reminds you of the ending to *The Threepenny Opera*, doesn't it?''

In one voice, the gang began to sing the ''Third Threepenny Finale,'' Act Three. ''Repriev-ed!'' they warbled.

''Hark,'' said the now-restored Shmuck. ''I believe that my discerning Vulgarian ears can detect Kurt Weill and Bertolt Brecht spinning in their graves.''

''Aww,'' said Jerk, grabbing Shmuck once again, ''what does that matter now?'' He turned to the grinning, expectant crew. ''C'mon, gang,'' he bellowed happily, ''it's Miller Time!''

And they all wandered off into the Vulgarian sunset.

Alex, who had converted to Vulgarianism, watched them go. ''Wow,'' he sighed. ''Whatta bunch of swell guys!''

ABOUT THE EDITORS

Although largely unknown to readers not involved in Star Trek fandom before the publication of *The Best of Trek #1*, WALTER IRWIN and G. B. LOVE have been actively editing and publishing magazines for many years. Before they teamed up to create TREK® in 1975, Irwin worked in newspapers, advertising, and free-lance writing, while Love published *The Rocket's Blast—Comiccollector* from 1960 to 1974, as well as hundreds of other magazines, books, and collectables. Both together and separately, they are currently planning several new books and magazines, as well as continuing to publish TREK.